Bonds

Marie Anne Cope

Published Scarygirl Ltd

First published in Great Britain in 2013 by Scarygirl Ltd
Reg. No. 8336470

A CIP catalogue record for this book is available from the British Library.

Paperback ISBN: 978-0-9575359-0-9

Dedicated to Loss de Plott, because she made me do it!

ACKNOWLEDGMENTS

The idea for BONDS came when I attended a wedding, held in an old village church. At the back of the church stood an ancient stone coffin covered in engravings. It was this coffin that sparked my interest and it was during the service that my imagination took flight. If it wasn't for that wedding, BONDS would never have been born, so I thank you both.

My thanks must also go to my family and friends who have had to endure my ramblings over the years, as I brought BONDS to fruition. Thank you for believing in me.

Special thanks go to four important people. To Neil Griffiths for his unwavering help in refining BONDS; to Stephan J. Myers for his support, advice and encouragement in bringing BONDS into the open; to my soul sister, Lisa McLoughlin, whose introduction to Stephan has helped make my dream a reality; and finally to Jenny-Lee Baker whose artistry and creativity have helped bring a face to BONDS.

MAGICAL REFERENCES

Summoning

By my Goddess and by my God
I call upon the power of the four elements
Of earth, of air, of fire, of water
I call upon you to aid me and to protect me

Spell O' Binding

By my Goddess and by my God
I ask for your power to strengthen my spell
By my Goddess and by my God
I ask for your power to end this fight
Help me to rid the land of this evil presence
Through my actions, through our power
We commit him to his tomb

Spell O' Internment

You who are bound within this tomb
Will reside encased for none to see
To remain until the curse be broke
As I do will, so mote it be

Completion and Thanks

By my Goddess and by my God
My humble thanks for supporting me
I bid you take the intention behind my actions
And see it executed for all time
As I do will, so mote it be

PROLOGUE

Isabella's whimpering carried on the still night air. Anna stared at her daughter; the ice that had surrounded her heart for so long was starting to melt. As despicable a person as Isabella was, she didn't deserve this. No one deserved this.

Anna's gaze shifted to the man who held her daughter. How on earth could she save Isabella from this monster? The reality was that she couldn't.

'Why, Antony? Why did you do this to yourself?' she asked.

'You know why, Anna. No one makes a fool of me and gets away with it.' He grappled with the young woman in his arms, his hand clenched over her mouth.

'But this?' she said, gesturing towards him with her gnarled hands. 'Why did you have to go this far?' Anna stared up at him. Gone were the soft brown eyes and gentle smile; the kindness and generosity. In their place lay only evil. His eyes were like coal against his chalky white skin and his mouth was a grim line. A rare smile seemed odd on his cold face and revealed the sharpness of his teeth.

'You didn't think I'd do it, did you, old woman?' Antony's sharp fingernails caressed his captive's exposed neck as he spoke.

'Let Isabella go, Antony. I think you've made your point.'

'Made my point!' he said, shaking Isabella as if she was a rag doll. 'If it wasn't for this harlot, none of this would have to have happened.'

'Only you chose to do what you...'

'Because of her! She betrayed me. She humiliated me and, worst of all, she made me a laughing stock. In…my…own…village! Do you have any idea what that is like?'

'Let her go.'

'Or else you'll do what, old woman?' he clenched his jaw, his teeth bared. 'Do you honestly think you can stop me?'

'I didn't want it to come to this, Antony. I wanted to help you.'

'Don't patronise me, old woman. You'll never defeat me. You don't have the power.' With a flick of his wrist he snapped Isabella's neck and let her body slump to the ground.

'No!' Anna staggered over to the slain girl. Huddled over her daughter, tears running down her face, she stared up at him.

'How could you? She was your wife.'

'Pity she didn't act like it then.' He turned and started to walk away.

Anna remained hunched over Isabella, rocking the young woman back and forth, and cried. The moonlight illuminated the scene and amongst the jagged headstones she watched her son-in-law walking away. A carnal rage surged through her body and she stood up. She turned her face to the heavens and closed her eyes.

'I call upon the power of the four elements. Of earth,' she said, thrusting her hands towards the ground. The earth rumbled. Antony stopped.

'Of air' Anna whipped her hands around in a circular motion. Thunder crashed, the wind started to howl and bruised clouds scudded across the sky.

'Of fire' she said, pointing her power fingers towards the sky. A bolt of lightning shot down, connecting with her power. Anna shuddered as electricity coursed through her frail body, infusing her with the strength she was going to need.

'And of water.' She finished and clapped her hands three times. The thunder crashed overhead and the dark swirling clouds released their load.

Antony turned and stared at her, a mocking smile on his face.

'You think that will stop me, you fool?'

'By my Goddess and by my God, I call upon the power of the four elements. Of earth, of air, of fire, of water. I call upon you to aid me and to protect me.' Anna spun round on the spot, her arms heavenwards, her eyes closed; the mantra repeating on her lips.

The wind roared; the thunder boomed. A bolt of lightning struck the earth in front of Antony, throwing him to the ground. The electricity sparked and fizzed in the rapidly forming puddles. He tried to get up, but his hands and feet couldn't get traction in the mud.

Anna turned to face him and staring straight into the eyes of the man she had once loved, she pointed her arms towards him, lowered her head and started to chant the Spell O' Binding.

She struggled to hold her position, her body convulsing as the power surged through her. Her eyes never leaving his, Anna thrust her palms to the earth and the ground began to shudder. She stumbled, but held firm. A crack appeared at her feet and zigzagged its way towards Antony, growing wider as it did so.

Anna heard his laughter through the storm, but she blocked it out, the image of her slain Isabella foremost in her mind. The crack stopped at Antony's feet. She closed her eyes again and slowly raised her hands skywards.

Vines shot out of the gap and lashed themselves around his ankles. He used the traction to his advantage and hauled himself up, grabbing the sinewy stems with both hands, snapping them as though they were dried twigs. He strode towards Anna, her head still bowed as she chanted. She didn't respond as he stood in front of her and hooked his finger under her chin, tilting her head upwards. She didn't flinch as he spat in her face. She didn't shudder as he lowered his head, his cheek brushing her hair, until his mouth was next to her ear.

'You'll never stop me, Anna, remember that.' He turned to walk away and picked up the broken vines as he went. He paused for a moment and then turned back.

'Never!' he said and hurled the vines at Anna's face. She staggered backwards at the force of the impact, but she didn't break her concentration. Antony snorted in derision and turned away from her once again.

Anna regained her foothold in the mud and, drawing on all the power she had left, she thrust her palms towards him, sending a ball of light hurtling in his direction. It struck him in the lower back. Antony staggered, Anna didn't falter. She raised her hands skywards and the crevasse soon crawled with vines, which snaked across the earth and wrapped around Antony's ankles once again.

Anna yanked her hands down to her sides and the vines snapped backwards, dragging Antony off his feet. He crashed to the ground. More vines slithered from the earth. Antony rolled over, kicking his legs to try to free himself, but this time they held firm. He dug his fingers deep into the earth and tried to drag himself away, but it was futile, the mud was too thin.

He rolled over onto his back and sat up, yanking against his bindings with his hands, but they didn't budge. The vines snaked up his legs, holding him firm as more and more emerged from the ground, binding his wrists to the earth and winding around his torso. He bucked and kicked, expanding his muscles as much as he could to try to burst through, but it was impossible.

Anna opened her eyes and saw the rage on his face; the veins pulsing in his neck as he strained against his fate. He looked up and caught her gaze; the vines creeping around his neck.

'These won't hold me forever,' he shouted, the sound muted by the vines which now engulfed his head. Finally, he was still.

Anna nodded towards eight men who'd been hiding in the shadows. She had asked them to stay out of the way, for their own safety, and they hadn't objected. They moved tentatively forward now and she watched as they hauled Antony's inert form into a stone sarcophagus. The men struggled, but managed to slide the lid into place and Anna staggered forward, placing her palms flat on the lid.

'Please make sure Isabella is put with the others,' she said. The men nodded and retreated to the shadows. She turned her face to the heavens once again, closed her eyes and began to chant the Spell O' Internment.

She shuddered as a lightning bolt shot through her body. Her hands glowed and the light spread around the gaps in the sarcophagus and sealed it tight. Anna raised her arms to the heavens once more and in barely a whisper she said, 'By my Goddess and by my God, my humble thanks for supporting me. I bid you take the intention behind my actions and see it executed for all time. As I do will, so mote it be.'

She pushed her weary body away from the casket and the men crept out of hiding once again to lower it into the ground.

No one spoke to her as she left. Her walking stick was clasped in one hand, her shawl clutched around her shoulders with the other.

The wailing followed Father Tom's slow progress. The night, seemingly abhorred by what had happened, was silent. The moon, large and full, made it seem almost like day. *A wolf moon*, he thought, as he glanced into the pale orange glow.

'May God have mercy on your soul,' he said as he made the sign of the cross and moved along the line. He pulled another wooden stake out of the bag slung across his back, held it in position and hammered it in with a heavy mallet. The boy's eyes flew open momentarily, while his family watched their son die in front of them for the second time that night.

'May God have mercy on your soul,' Father Tom said for what seemed like the thousandth time. The events of the night played in his head. Never, in all his time as a priest, had he witnessed such horror. He'd heard tales, they all had, but he never thought…

His toil was interrupted as he heard the cries from the relatives turn to screams. His heart grew heavy as he watched the cart being dragged up the street, bodies being tossed in the back as if they were firewood. The families followed the progress of the cart. Father Tom stood up wearily and stretched. He was too old for this. He scanned the street and saw the number of bodies he still had to tend to. He resumed his task as his mind drifted to the job he dreaded the most. How could he be expected to do that after all the help she'd given them tonight?

Anna pushed open her front door and shuffled in. She draped her shawl over the back of a chair and poked the fire with her walking stick, causing the embers to glow. She lowered herself into her chair, leaned back and closed her eyes. The cat jumped onto her lap and nudged her for attention. She stroked him as she stared, unseeingly, at the spartan room, rendered even starker in the uncharacteristic moonlight.

'I'm sorry, Isabella,' she murmured, as tears slid down her wrinkled face. A baby cried in the depths of the house and she sighed.

'That's the last, Father,' one of the men said, as they struggled to manoeuvre the cart into place. The weight of the load made their task almost impossible, but soon they managed to empty the last of the bodies into one of the three pits they had dug.

'Just one more,' said Father Tom. He stumbled over to where Isabella's body lay, crumpled in a heap. Father Tom turned her over and stroked her pale skin. She had been so beautiful and full of life. A lump rose in his throat as he pulled a stake from his pocket. With one last look at her peaceful face he hammered it through her heart. Her eyes flew open and the hate he saw there broke his heart. Almost as quickly as they'd opened, Isabella's eyes closed again. She was finally at peace.

He lifted her gently and carried her over to one of the pits and laid her on top of the other bodies. He nodded towards the men, then turned and walked away. They lit the torches and held them against the bodies until they caught fire. Once they were certain the fire wouldn't die before its job was complete, the men turned and left, their shirts clamped over their faces in an effort to keep out the stench of burning flesh.

As the flames burned brighter, the village mourned. Father Tom lay awake in his cot, dreading what the following day would bring.

The morning dawned bright and warm. The village, battered by the events of the previous night, was still; the elements having purged it of the previous night's carnage. Water still ran from the rooftops into puddles and the dusty earth of the previous day was now slick and sludgy.

Father Tom watched the sun filter through his curtains. The sense of dread that had awoken him a few hours earlier had now settled across his chest. He heard a commotion outside, got out of his cot and went to the window. A small crowd had gathered outside his house and just as he was hoping he could pretend not to be in, one of them saw him.

'Oi, Father! Get dressed, we've got unfinished business to attend to,' shouted an anonymous voice.

He closed his eyes and willed them to go away, to let him do this alone, but they banged on his door instead.

'We'll break it down, Father,' a man shouted. Father Tom opened the window and leaned out.

'Let me get dressed,' he said to them, running his hand through his shaggy grey hair. Five minutes later he opened his front door and stepped into the street.

'Bad night, Father?' a woman asked and he nodded.

'Yeah, well, we all had a bad night. Question is what we are going to do about it?' said a heavy set man.

'I'm not sure I catch your meaning,' said Father Tom.

'You know damn well what I'm talking about,' said the man. 'The witch. How are we going to get rid of her?'

'Yeah, if it wasn't for her, none of this would have happened,' said someone else.

'Listen to you!' said an angry voice from behind them. 'If it wasn't for Anna, you'd all be dead. I don't know why she bothered.' The rabble turned to see a teenage girl standing there, fists clenched ready for battle.

'Carla's right,' Father Tom said. 'Without Anna's help, things would have been much worse.' He bowed his head. He knew he wouldn't win this.

'Rubbish!' said the thick set man. 'She's a witch and her kind attracts trouble.'

'This wasn't Anna's fault,' Father Tom said through gritted teeth. 'She went out of her way to help us last night and this is how you want to repay her?' He stared at them all, but no one met his gaze.

'Yes, she did help, Father,' said Jeremiah, the blacksmith. 'But if it wasn't for that harlot of a daughter of hers, none of this would have happened. Now, why don't you do as the law says and get rid of the witch?'

'You forget, Jeremiah, Isabella died too. Anna lost a loved one just like the rest of you,' Father Tom said, turning to the blacksmith.

'Well, Father. As I see it, you have two choices. Either you get rid of her or we will.'

CHAPTER 1

Becca could feel the weight on her chest. It was right in the centre, unmoving, like a rock. Her air supply was being restricted, ever so slowly, ever so cunningly. Then there was the noise. The resonating hum. No, breathing. No, purring. Then came the *pièce de résistance;* the slap in the face with the quilt.

'Morning, Spook,' she said, yawning and rubbing the huge grey cat behind the ears. His buzz-saw impression grew louder and he nuzzled under the covers, cuddling up to Becca's warm body, kneading her.

'Spook, that hurts!' she said, trying to push him away. Not a chance.

Becca stretched and stared around her bedroom, like she did every morning. Sunlight streamed in through the floor to ceiling windows, filtered by the voile curtains which pooled on the floor. The light brightened the plum coloured walls and cast the room in a warm glow. She stared at the over-flowing dark oak wardrobes, vowing to have a clear out at the weekend. Her gaze rested on the over-stuffed armchair in the corner and the newly acquired business suit that lay across it. Becca cringed at the thought of wearing it. It wasn't exactly her usual dress, but at least she had retained her colours; a black pant suit with a tailored plum coloured blouse. By wearing trousers she could still wear her biker boots, so at least she would be vaguely comfortable on her first day at the new site.

Dick, her boss, had told her to smarten herself up and change her sullen attitude for the new site.

'The customers will be wealthy and I am not having your "look" scaring them off, Rebecca,' he'd said last week. 'Get yourself a haircut and a proper colour, wear normal make-up and buy a suit! I don't want to see any more of this gothic trash that you insist on covering yourself in. Do what you want on your own time, but on mine...' Becca had wandered off at this point, bored with his lectures and moaning. She'd never had any complaints about the way she looked, not that she would care. She had, however, done some of what Dick had requested; he was her boss after all. She'd bought a suit. He'd have to accept the rest. She'd even decided to tone down her makeup and to arrive at work on time. She'd set the alarm clock half an hour early just to make sure.

'Shit!' Becca sat up in bed and shoved the pile of books on her nightstand out of the way so she could see the time. The old battered alarm clock read eight fifteen. The bloody alarm hadn't gone off. She was going to be late. She threw back the quilt and charged into the bathroom. Spook dashed through the cat flap in the window, out of harm's way.

No time for a shower now. Quick wash, clean teeth, spray deodorant and perfume. That will have to do. She didn't even have time to put any make-up on. *That should please Dick*, she thought, as she observed herself in the full length antique mirror. Her short jet black hair was even more spiky than usual and the heavy boots did nothing for the suit. For Becca, though, she looked very smart. Her face, devoid of the heavy black eye make-up, was fresh, clean and extremely pretty. *Oh well, here goes*, she thought.

She filled Spook's bowl to overflowing with biscuits, grabbed her keys from the counter and left the apartment. She climbed into her beat-up old Fiesta, praying it would start. The engine caught first time and Becca sent up a prayer of thanks before pulling straight out into the traffic, completely oblivious to the horns blaring as other motorists swerved out of her way.

'St Martin's church, here I come,' she said.

CHAPTER 2

Father Michael stood in the doorway of St Martin's, a tear drying on his cheek. It always saddened him when a church was finally closed. It was as if God had just given up. Of course, God had given up on this place a long time ago, but the stories had kept the visitors coming in and this had kept the roof intact. He glanced up at the roof now as he stepped inside the church for the last time. The sun's rays filtered through its bones and the pigeons were coming and going, as they had for many years. The stained glass windows remained, as did the altar, but the pews were rotten and overturned and covered in excrement.

He had been a young priest when the last visitor had left, fifty years ago. The curiosity had disappeared as the movie industry had taken off. People weren't interested in the truth; they would rather see a mockery of it on the screen. But, of course, the truth had been far worse. He'd read the records. He was fully aware of what had happened in Carlford all those years ago and, more importantly, what was buried in the churchyard. He had tried to block the developers, stressing the land had to stay consecrated for the protection of the village. Of course, no one had believed him. They'd thought his protests were only the ramblings of a senile old man. They would learn the hard way.

He shook his head as he remembered the story. At least they had agreed to move the coffins to consecrated ground; his church, St Paul's, half a mile away. He knew though, that the minute they uncovered the sarcophagus, they would never move it. There was nothing he could do about it either as the church no longer owned the land, Ramply Homes did.

Becca stopped in her tracks and stared, goose-bumps spreading across her skin. She shivered. *Christ, this place was like something out of a cheesy horror movie,* she thought.

The iron railings enclosing the churchyard, once majestic in their stance, now stood twisted and strained, exhausted by their task. Becca looked passed the knot of iron into the cemetery. The headstones, barely visible under the invading ivy, were jagged and broken; some lying flat, worn out by time. Dark gaping holes could be glimpsed amongst the criss-crossing creepers, the stones having collapsed in on their inhabitants a long time ago. Becca shuddered as she contemplated running the gauntlet. Perspiration peppered her skin as she saw the ivy catching around her ankle. She held her breath as she imagined falling into the depths of the earth. Who would hear her? How long would she be there?

She forced her gaze away from the wilderness and to St Martin's church itself. Becca felt as though the air had been squeezed out of her as she stared at the church, cold tendrils creeping up her back and reaching inside to surround her heart. She doubled over trying to catch her breath, rubbing her chest as though massaging the life back into herself.

Becca stood up and forced herself to look at the church. She had to. It rose from the bowels of the churchyard, dark and tall, the ivy reaching up the lichen covered stone, stealthily drawing the church into its forest green tomb. The stone, the colour of obsidian, emanated the horror of the secrets that it held. She could feel it, ripples on the air, and shivered again. The large stained glass windows seemed abhorrent against the darkness, their colours sparkling in the sunlight. Roof rafters jutted out into the china blue sky; ribs stripped bare by the parasites in its heart. Above the doorway,

Becca could make out the tarnished remains of a five armed symbol; its centre hollowed out and used as a porthole by its avian flock.

The sudden raucous calling made her jump and she looked up to see a murder of crows rise from the branches of a gnarled old oak tree and circle above the carcass of St Martin's. She turned her attention to the tree which, in the height of summer, stood bare and dark, its trunk blackened as though burned. Erect and noble, it guarded the earth at its base; earth that bore the same scorched barrenness.

Her curiosity roused, Becca reached out to open the warped gate. As her skin connected with the rusted iron, thunder sounded overhead and a jolt of static shot through her palm. She tried to pull away, but she couldn't. Something was holding her there. She didn't scream. She didn't panic. She didn't know why.

Father Michael jumped as thunder crashed overhead and stared up through the dilapidated roof at the now slate grey sky. *Odd*, he thought, it had been bright sunshine a few minutes before. He walked outside and saw a young woman standing at the gates of the churchyard. He shivered as he stared at her; her hands clutching the warped gates. Father Michael picked his way down the broken pathway towards her.

'Can I help you?' he asked, but the girl didn't answer him. Gently, he reached out and touched her hand. She wrenched it away as though she had been scalded and stared at him, rubbing her hand as she did so.

'Are you all right, young lady?' Still, she didn't answer him, but instead turned to stare at the churchyard. Father Michael turned to see what she was looking at. The static air was punctuated again by the cries of the crows, circling the barren oak; a tree that had not born leaves for four hundred years. It was this tree, or more precisely the land at its base, that she was staring at.

Father Michael turned round and studied her. He guessed her to be in her mid to late twenties, although her spiky hair and fresh face made her seem younger. Her face though, was pale and drawn, her knuckles white as she clung onto the iron gates. Thunder continued to crash overhead, but there had been no lightning and there was no rain. *Very strange*, Father Michael thought.

'What is it? What's the matter?' he asked.

'Who is buried beneath that tree?' Her voice was barely a whisper, hoarse and broken.

'What makes you think that someone is buried there?' A feeling of unease began to settle over Father Michael as he spoke to her.

'I can feel him,' she said and turned to stare at him. The intensity of her gaze forced him to turn away. She was making him feel uneasy and he wasn't sure why.

'No one for you to worry about, young lady. Now, what brings you here? This church is closed. If you want, I can take you to St Paul's, which isn't too far away. I'm going there now, myself.' She ignored him and pushed the gates open, crossing into the churchyard. As she did so, the sky blackened and the thunder grew louder.

Father Michael left her to it, but something was niggling him about her. It would come to him eventually, he was sure of it.

His eyes snapped open as she took her first step into the cemetery. He tried to move his head, but the ancient vines still held him tight. He listened as her steps drew closer and inhaled the stagnant air to clear the decay from his throat. He breathed out her name.

'B...E...C...C...A...' A voice carried on the wind, making her jump. She whirled round, expecting to see the priest, but there was no one around.

Becca continued to walk across the churchyard, tripping every so often on the uneven ground and upended graves. Her gaze remained fixed on the barren tree ahead of her; her conversation with Father Michael forgotten. Something was drawing her to this place and she felt powerless to stop it.

She stopped not far from the tree. The ground here was black as though recently burned; a small moss-covered stone marker was the only thing to break the harshness of the earth. She felt a slight tremor under her feet and her skin erupted in goose bumps, as though someone had brushed passed her. She shivered.

'B…E…C…C…A…' A warm breath caressed her left ear and she screamed, losing her footing. The crows, roused from their slumber, rose into the air, circling the tree, their cawing echoing through the air. Becca spun round and stumbled away from the tree and the dead ground around it. Her mind was whirling. Had she really heard her name or was her mind playing tricks on her? She jumped, stifling another scream, as she heard her name called again.

'Rebecca? Are you all right?' Dick Ramply called. He strutted through the uneven graves and grabbed her by the shoulders.

'What on earth are you doing in here? You're filthy! What happened to our little pep talk last week? I can see you've taken the minimal notice of it. Well, at least you're on time for a change, but you should be out there,' he said, gesturing towards the road beyond the broken down wall, where bulldozers and workmen were now congregated.

'You were supposed to be directing this rabble to the job of clearing the site. I get a phone call from the foreman saying there is no one here, so I come all the way down, out of a very important meeting, to find you wandering around this dump. Now come on, dust yourself down and get to work. There's a lot to do before we can even think about starting to build.'

Becca let Dick propel her out of the churchyard, her mind still on the voice she had heard. *Had it been Dick? It must have been. He never called her Becca, but what other explanation could there possibly be?*

What a day, Becca thought, as she flopped onto the huge squashy leather sofa. She stared through the French windows into the garden. The security light was on and she smiled as she watched Spook chase the moths. Daft cat, but he certainly brought a smile to her face. A flickering red light caught her eye and she groaned. She hauled herself up and shuffled over to the answer-phone and pressed play.

'*You have three new messages,*' an electronic voice beeped.

Message one: 'Rebecca! Are you there? Call me. It's urgent.'

Message two: 'It's me again. Call me, for God's sake. You know I wouldn't call you unless it was urgent.'

Message three: 'It's your mother, for the third time. I need to speak to you, urgently. Call me when you get this.'

Becca stared at the answer-phone, her finger hovering over the delete button, her mouth partially open. She hadn't spoken to her mother in over a decade, not since Rosalind's death. The brief memory of her grandmother brought a lump to Becca's throat. Pushing her mother's voice out of her mind she erased the messages and unplugged the phone. She did not want to hear her mother's voice, let alone her neurotic ramblings.

Becca wandered into the bathroom and started to run a bath. She sat on the side of the old cast iron tub and poured the lavender essence into the hot water, inhaling the nostalgic scent as the steam rose. While the bath filled, she went into the kitchen and pulled a bottle of wine from the fridge, uncorked it and took a long drink from the bottle. She closed her eyes and savoured the fruity flavour before grabbing a large glass out of the cupboard and emptying the rest of the bottle into it.

A trail of discarded clothes traced her path to the bathroom. She lit her array of church candles before sinking into the delicately fragranced water. Becca closed her eyes and let herself disappear under the surface, relishing the sting of the water on her skin. When she surfaced, Becca picked up her glass from the wicker table at the side of the bath and sipped from it. She closed her eyes again, her body relaxing as the lavender wove its spell, and allowed herself to drift off.

She was in the churchyard again, but it was night time. The moonlight illuminated the gravestones, intact and un-aged. The grass beneath her bare feet was short and the pathways between the stones well tended. The warm night air rippled through her long, white skirt and the scent of jasmine hung in the air.

'I knew you would come to me.' She shivered as his breath caressed her neck and she closed her eyes, savouring the huskiness of his voice and his cool, gentle touch on her bare shoulders.

'Oh, Antony, I have missed you so much,' she said and turned into his embrace.

'And I, you.' Becca looked into his cold, dark eyes. He leant down towards her, his lips brushing her cheek and she sighed, closed her eyes and relaxed against him. His lips caressed her neck and she groaned with pleasure. He kissed her hard, his hold on her becoming tighter and tighter, until she could barely breathe.

Becca felt his teeth pierce the delicate skin on her neck and she tried to push away from him. Panic rose through her body and her neck started to burn. She thrashed about, trying to free herself, but he held her firm. Her neck, the skin raw and inflamed, felt as though it was on fire as she clawed at him, desperate to ease the pain. His grip, though, held her fast and she could feel him drawing the life out of her. Adrenalin fired through her body and she pushed against him one last time.

'Noooooo!' Becca gulped for air as she lunged up out of the water. Her heart thundered and she gasped for breath as she coughed up lavender scented water. She felt the pain in her chest where she had swallowed the water, fighting to breathe. *Fancy falling asleep in the bath!* She berated herself, as she climbed out, her body shaking. She wrapped herself in a large fluffy white towel and rubbed her hair with another. Still panting, she regarded herself in the bathroom mirror and felt her stomach flip. Barely visible, on the left hand side of her neck, were two puncture marks.

CHAPTER 3

Becca huddled on the sofa, a cushion crushed against her body. She stared straight ahead of her, not seeing Spook's amber eyes boring into her, not seeing anything except the man in her dream.

Her mind wandered between the messages from her mother and the dream. *Were they connected?* She closed her eyes and buried her face in the cushion, shaking her head at the sheer stupidity of that thought. *How could they be connected? It was only a dream after all and she had plenty of dreams.*

'But none that leave marks,' she said and let the cushion fall to the floor, her gaze finally focusing on Spook.

'What's going on today hey, buddy?' she said and clicked her fingers. Spook jumped to attention as requested and came and curled up on her lap. Becca rubbed his ear absently as she touched the marks on her neck. They were still there. She felt her heart start to pound and her eyes filled with tears. How can a dream do this?

'How?' she said, a sob escaping her throat, unsettling Spook. She grabbed the phone beside her and punched in her mother's number, surprised she could recall it, and put the handset to her ear, waiting for the ring. She sat there, staring again, waiting, but there was no ring at the other end. In fact there was no dial tone. Damn! She'd forgotten that she'd unplugged the phone.

Becca pushed herself up from the sofa and stretched. She scratched her neck and winced, the area tender to the touch. She wandered out to the hallway and bent down to plug the phone back in. A loud bang on the door made her jump and she cracked her head on the corner of the table.

'Dammit,' she said and rubbed the top of her head to minimise the smarting. She padded to the front door, peered through the peep hole and groaned. 'What does he want this time?'

'Hi, Brandon,' Becca said smiling, tight lipped, at her bespectacled neighbour. 'What can I do for you tonight?'

'Oh, hi, Becca, I-I-I, erm, I wonder if I could borrow a cup of sugar?' Becca bit down hard on her lip to stop herself from laughing. She watched him blush to the roots of his auburn hair, sweat glistening on his brow and felt guilty for mocking him.

'Is that really why you came round?' Brandon looked up, his eyes wide and his mouth forming the 'oh' of someone caught doing something they shouldn't.

'Erm, yes, erm, no, not really, but...'

'I'm sorry, Brandon, but I really can't go out with you. I have too much on at work at the moment.'

'Oh, okay, sorry to bother you,' Brandon said. Becca turned away, ready to close the door when he grabbed hold of her arm and dragged her towards him.

'Brandon! What the...'

'Becca, what on earth have you done to your neck?'

'Nothing, why?' she said, yanking her arm from his grasp and withdrawing inside her hallway, hunching her shoulder up to shield her neck. Brandon made a move to grab her again, but she avoided his grasp.

'It looks like something has been gnawing on you, to be quite frank.'

'Yes, they have. They're midge bites, that's all. Now, if you don't mind, I'm tired.'

'Bloody big midges, Becca. More like vampire midges, ha ha,' Brandon said and doubled over as he laughed at his own joke. Becca just stared at him and then slammed the door in his face and ran for the bathroom.

Once inside, she switched the light on above the bathroom mirror and studied the marks on her neck. The puncture marks were now quite large and they were inflamed and weeping. She stared at the wounds and watched as each one pulsed as though it had its own heart beat. Becca straightened up and bared her teeth in the mirror. She measured the width of one incisor with her thumb and forefinger and then, holding this measurement steady, she positioned it over the marks on her neck.

It matched.

CHAPTER 4

Becca turned on her heel and ran from the bathroom. She grabbed the phone in the hallway and dialled her mother's number again. She paced up and down, but the phone continued to ring, not even being picked up by an answer-phone. Becca put the phone down and stood rooted to the spot. She had no idea what to do next.

She glanced from doorway to doorway, her mind undecided. The sound of shattering pottery drew her focus to the door of her studio; a door she usually kept firmly closed. Spook was attempting to slink out of the room.

'Spook, what have you done?' Becca regarded the cat, her hands on her hips. Spook looked over his shoulder, then turned his amber gaze on his owner, licked his lips and sauntered off into the kitchen.

Becca pushed open the door and saw her collection of drawing pencils strewn all over the hardwood floor. Threaded amongst them were the remnants of a mug her mother had made her, for her tenth birthday. She crouched to gather the pencils, careful to avoid the jagged edges of the pottery pieces. She'd had enough injuries for one day.

The tools of her passion retrieved, Becca sat at her draughtsman's table and arranged them in the collection of holders balanced on a shelf. Only one wouldn't fit. She rolled the pencil between her fingers until her gaze rested on the blank sheet forever present on the table, awaiting inspiration. Without much prodding, her hand went to work while her forehead furrowed in concentration and she chewed on her bottom lip.

The clock on the wall recorded her toil. Spent, she laid her pencil down and closed her eyes to soothe her dry eyeballs. When she opened them again, she stared into the face of the man who had inflicted her wounds, the man she had seen and touched, the man who had caressed her as a lover would, the man from her dream.

My god he was beautiful! she thought, her eyes devouring the details of her sketch. His hair was thick and wavy, tousled by today's definition, and was loosely pulled away from his face, she knew, by a ribbon tied at the nape of his neck. His jaw was strong and square; his lips full, pouting and, she remembered, sensuous to the touch. But it was his eyes that drew her. Forever cast into shadow by the intensity of his brows, it was those dark, empty pools that she remembered most about him. When she'd stared into those eyes she'd seen nothing but hatred; a deep rooted loathing that made her shiver, as she stared at the portrait she had drawn.

A beep snapped her away from his face and she glanced up to see her laptop battery warning light flashing. She bent to flick on the power switch and pulled the laptop on top of the sketch and opened it up. She opened her internet browser and before she realised what she was doing, she had typed in the word 'vampire' and hit the search button.

Thousands and thousands of hits appeared on her screen so Becca refined her search, typing in:

VAMPIRE+CARLFORD

She hit the search button again and found herself holding her breath, only to release it with a snort as the search engine returned with a total of zero hits. Nada.

'Idiot,' she chastised herself and closed the lid of her laptop before standing up. She stretched and turned round, catching her reflection in the window, the marks on her neck visible and very real.

'Vampires don't exist,' she said to Spook, who had wandered back in to find his mess cleared up. She picked him up, nuzzling his soft fur, the face she'd drawn clear in her mind. 'Bedtime, big guy.' Becca closed the door to her studio and carried Spook into her bedroom and under the covers with her, hugging him tightly. He stayed, for now.

She was in the churchyard again, the moonlight harsh, the night warm. She was curled in a ball on the dry ground, her body aching. Synapses fired inside her head, trying to kick-start her brain into action. She tried to push herself up, but had to stop as the dizziness threatened to return her to her dusty resting place. Her head throbbed and she could taste coppery residue in her mouth.

As her mind started to clear, Becca could make out voices. She strained to hear, but could only pick out occasional words. She opened her eyes and squinted against the glow of the moon. She could see him; his stance aggressive; his fists clenched. Becca moved her gaze a step at a time, to avoid the head spin that was still threatening, towards his adversary. She felt her heart lurch as she saw the frail old woman facing him.

Becca pushed herself to her knees and pain shot through her abdomen, causing her to crumple to the ground once more. Determined to hear what was being said, Becca gritted her teeth and forced herself onto her hands and knees. She crawled over to where Antony was standing, her clothing snagging on the uneven ground as she went. She stopped close behind him and sat back on her haunches, straining to hear what was being said, but she couldn't. Her shoulders slumped and she doubled forward as pain seared through her, bringing her to tears.

As she pushed herself up, she felt his hand clasp around her neck and she screamed. Antony dragged her forward and she clawed at his hand, her feet thrashing in mid-air. It did no good though; his grip was firm and getting tighter. Becca could hear the thundering in her ears as the blood rushed to her head. She kept her hands clamped around his wrist, but, as she fought against him, she could see black and white dots starting to cloud her vision. She felt his thumb caress her neck and she tried to move away from it, but she couldn't.

Soon she felt the pressure start to build against her neck, as he pushed his thumb into her flesh, forcing her head over to one side. She moved her hands to try and drag his thumb away, but she wasn't strong enough. She heard the bones cracking before she felt them break and then there was nothing.

Becca jolted awake, her heart hammering, covered in sweat and shivering. She jumped out of bed and fell to the floor as pain seared through her abdomen causing her to retch. She dragged herself to her feet and, doubled over to ease her stomach, she shuffled to the bathroom as fast as she could; barely making it to the sink as her stomach contracted and she vomited up what little sustenance had been in there. Becca gripped the edge of the sink for support and as she raised her head and looked in the mirror, she almost fainted. She stared in horror at her dusty form and the rivulets of blood running over her shoulder.

Dazed, she walked into the hallway. She picked up the phone and slumped to the floor, her back against the front door, her neck throbbing. She punched the numbers without looking and then listened as the phone rang and rang.

'Pick up the phone, for God's sake, Mother,' Becca said as tears spilled down her cheeks, but there was no answer. She let the phone fall to the carpet beside her, pulled herself up off the floor, shuffled back into the bathroom and turned on the shower. She stepped inside and let the hot pokers stab at her body as she stared at the rust coloured water swirling down the plug hole. As she towelled herself off, Becca inspected her body. Her thighs were decorated with purple bruises, as were her wrists, and her head ached from where he'd hit her. She wiped the steam from the bathroom mirror and studied her face and neck. Her bottom lip was puffy and had a deep gash across it, but it was the marks on her neck that drew her main focus. They were open and throbbing and itched like hell.

Wrapped in her fluffy robe and slippers, Becca shuffled into the hall and retrieved the phone. She pressed redial, but there was still no answer. Wandering into the living room, she slumped down on the sofa, drawing her knees up to her chest and rested her chin on her knees. She stared out of the French windows into the night. Maybe she should call the police, she was wounded after all.

'And say what, exactly?' she muttered to herself. How would she explain what had happened to her to the police, when she didn't even understand it herself?

CHAPTER 5

'You look like hell,' Dick said as Becca slouched into the office.

'Go to hell, Dick,' she said and slumped into her chair with a sigh. She rested her head in her hands.

'Don't speak to me like that!'

Becca scrutinised him through her fingers, saw his hands resting on his hips and shook her head.

'Look, I'm sorry. Don't give me any crap today, please. I didn't sleep last night. Is there any coffee on?'

'Of course not, that's your job. Had a beau last night, did you?'

'Something like that.' Becca shuffled over and put a fresh filter in the coffee maker and two extra heaped spoons of Columbian coffee in the pot.

'Ooh, exciting! I didn't realise you had a boyfriend! Do tell me all…'

'I haven't got a boy…'

'But you just said…what's happened to your face?'

'Just leave it, will you,' Becca said touching her lip and wincing. 'What's on the agenda today?'

'Well, if you're going to be like that, fine.' Dick said, clearly in a huff. Becca rubbed her eyes and sighed.

'Something weird happened last night, that's all and I don't want to talk about it at the moment.'

'Are you in trouble with loan sharks or dealers? Do you need some help? I know some big butch guys who can get rid of them for you.'

Becca smiled at the self-created drama and then grimaced as the cut on her lip re-opened.

'Thanks Dick, but I don't think anyone can help. Now what's on today?'

Still piqued, but somewhat mollified, Dick ran through his agenda.

'Oh, and you're going to have to smarten yourself up a bit this afternoon. We have a wealthy client coming in, who is interested in the penthouse,' Dick said, raising an eyebrow at Becca's dishevelled attire. 'Did you only buy one suit?'

'A client already?' Becca ignored his jab at her. 'We haven't even finished excavating, never mind started any building work. What's the point?'

'The point is, my dear girl, that he loved the drawings and merely wants to come and see the site. Is that a problem?' Becca shrugged. 'Well, he'll be here around two and his name is Antony something or other, so make sure you're…Rebecca, are you all right? You've gone very pale,' Dick said, concern edging his voice.

'I'm fine, I just need some air.' She poured herself a mug of strong black coffee and left the porta-cabin.

Due to the mass of excavation work needed, the porta-cabin had been set up on the pavement outside the cemetery. Becca sat on the bonnet of her car and watched as the iron monsters chewed up the earth in their quest for treasure. It was sad to see the rotted coffins being pulled out of the ground, sad to realise that the people inside them had a disturbed eternity. Becca turned away as the bottom fell out of one of the coffins and a decayed skeleton tumbled out. She heard Father Michael shouting at the workmen to take more care and she turned to see him leaning over the skeleton, as though issuing the last rites.

She pushed herself off the car and, leaving her coffee cup on the bonnet, she crossed the gateway into the churchyard. As she did so, a gust of warm air brushed past her.

'B…E…C…C…A..,' a voice whispered. She stopped to look behind her, thinking it might be Dick. There was no one there. She glanced towards Father Michael, but he was consumed with the recent incident. She stood still for a few minutes listening, then a crack of thunder made her jump. Both she and Father Michael glanced upwards to see ebony clouds racing across the sky. Spooked by the sudden change in the weather, Becca turned to head back to the office, when she heard it again.

'Come to me, B…E…C…C…A…' She spun round in the direction of the voice, but there was no one there. Without thinking, she reached up to touch the marks on her neck and was shocked to find them enlarged and pulsing. The warm air, like breath on her skin, was at odds with the continuing cracks of thunder. She looked towards Father Michael and found him staring at her. Unnerved, she turned and crossed back into the street. The sky brightened almost immediately.

Becca nearly knocked Dick to the ground as she barged past him and yanked open the door of her car.

'Don't forget. Be back for two,' Dick called after the departing car.

What the hell had just happened? Becca's mind was in overdrive as she sped to her apartment. This was getting too weird, too scary.

'Shit,' she muttered as she screeched to halt at a red light, just in time to avoid running down a couple.

'Watch where you're going, you maniac,' shouted the man and banged his palm on the bonnet of her car. He looked straight at her and Becca's heart froze as she stared into the face of her tormentor. An evil grin spread across his face.

'Come to me B…E…C…C…A..,' he said and Becca screamed. The man pushed up off her car, shaking his head.

'You shouldn't be driving, lady.' He turned to look at her as he carried on crossing the road. It wasn't him. What on earth was happening to her?

As soon as she stepped inside the apartment, she double bolted the door. Spook rubbed himself around her legs, but she pushed him away.

'Just because I'm home early doesn't mean you're getting fed,' she said as he skulked off. Becca yanked open the "drinks" cupboard in her kitchen and pulled out a half empty bottle of Jack Daniel's. Sloshing the amber liquid into a tumbler she walked into the living room, grabbed the phone and slumped onto the squashy leather sofa.

Becca took a gulp of the liquid and revelled in the burning sensation as it slid down her throat. She stared at the phone in her hand and watched as her fingers dialled the once again familiar number.

'Hello?' a female voice answered and tears slid down Becca's cheeks. It had been such a long time.

'Hello? Is there anyone there? Rebecca, is that you? Hello?' Becca cut the connection without answering and dropped the phone on the sofa, ignoring its ring less than a minute later. She gulped down the rest of the JD, wincing this time as it burned a path to her stomach. She stared at a photograph on the wall and smiled. It was of her when she was five and in it were her mother and grandmother, all of them dressed in their finest pagan regalia.

It had been a warm spring day. The blossoms on the trees were emerging and the tulips and daffodils were in full bloom. Everywhere looked glorious and everyone was happy. Daffodils had a way of making you feel happy. Every year, the villages of Carlford and Breccan got together to celebrate their pagan heritage. In the 17th century, whilst the famous witch trials of Salem were taking place, these two villages were purging themselves of their own spiritual residents. Many of the people who took part in these celebrations were descendants of those executed for their beliefs. Others simply came to look. Every year, a descendant family took it in turn to tell their story and this year Becca's grandmother was the chosen speaker. This was the first time Becca knew of her ancestry and, being five, she didn't understand a lot of what was said. One thing she did remember, though, was the tale of the demise of one of her ancestors, Anna Martindale. The story of Anna's death had terrified Becca and was the main reason she was never told more about her past, until she was much older. Becca had watched as her grandmother stood up and told her story, their story.

She shuddered now as she remembered the vivid details. Settling back on the sofa Becca closed her eyes, the whiskey having its usual effect. Her mind began to wander and images, clear as if she had been there herself, played in her mind.

CHAPTER 6

Anna's hand still held the door knob when she heard them. She prayed that there had been enough time and that Carla was safely out of sight. The small house shook as the thunder of hooves approached. The first fingers of fear spiked her body. *How many of them were coming?* She turned and leaned her back against the door. She stared at her tiny home for what she knew would be the last time, her gaze resting on the cat, curled up in front of the fire. Anna made a move towards the fire intending to put it out, as she did whenever she left the house, but she stopped. Let him enjoy the warmth while it lasted. He would have to find a new fire soon enough. She listened and heard the horses pull up near the house. She took a deep breath, opened the front door and stepped outside.

There were six of them in all, not the army she had thought she'd heard. She smiled as Father Tom dismounted and walked towards her.

'Hello, Anna,' he said, his face telling her how painful this was for him.

'It's all right, Tom. I know you did your best.' She patted his arm as she hobbled passed him, her head held high.

Jeremiah, the blacksmith, jumped down from his horse, a piece of rope in his hands, and walked towards Anna. She turned round and crossed her arms behind her to help him.

'I don't really think that's necessary, do you?' Father Tom said to no one in particular.

'Don't worry, Tom,' Anna said. 'I am ready.'

'That's Father Tom to you, you filthy witch,' Jeremiah said as he tied Anna's hands. She winced, but her head remained high.

'Come on then, witch, the whole village is waiting for you,' Jeremiah said and pushed her onto the cart behind his horse. The party turned round and, with Father Tom taking up the rear this time, they headed back towards the village.

His heart was heavy as he watched her sitting stoically on the cart, staring straight ahead of her, stray tears running down her once pretty face. They had grown up together, he and Anna, and if fate hadn't taken them away from each other then, maybe things would have turned out differently.

Father Tom's mind strayed to the children and panic filled his body. He stopped his horse. Anna turned and looked him straight in the eye and smiled. He relaxed; of course she had made sure they were all right.

'Something wrong, Father?' asked Jeremiah, as he too stopped.

'N-n-no, nothing,' said Father Tom, afraid they would ask about Carla, but they didn't. Why would they? As far as they were concerned, Carla was simply a ragamuffin who liked Anna. As for the baby, no one knew she even existed. Well, no one but him, Anna, Carla and Isabella. He and Anna had made sure it stayed that way, for the sake of Isabella and the baby.

His only worry was that Antony would return; that Anna's spell wouldn't hold him. What if he found the baby? She was the only living thing that stood between him and his freedom. Neither Anna nor Father Tom could be sure whether he knew about the baby or not. Hopefully, Anna had sent them somewhere safe.

As the party neared the village, he could smell the burning wood and he studied Anna. Her eyes were closed and she was muttering under her breath. *God help her,* he thought and turned his horse away from the village. He couldn't watch. There was nothing he could do.

Anna also smelled the burning wood and squeezed her eyes shut.

'Don't let them see your fear, don't let them see your fear,' she said over and over again under her breath. She had sensed Father Tom watching her, but she hadn't met his gaze. She couldn't. It would be too painful. She knew he had gone and she was glad. She didn't want him to watch her. She didn't want him to see the indignity of it all.

The shouts of the villagers grew louder as they drew into the main square. Anna opened her eyes and stared at the stake in front of her, surrounded by wood and straw. A replica 'burning' was taking place next to it. Anna saw the effigy, her effigy, at its core and shuddered as she stared into the flames. She felt her bowels release as the fight finally left her and she hung her head in shame. Tears slid down her cheeks as she listened to the villagers jeering and calling her names.

'Get out of the cart, witch,' said Jeremiah. Not giving her chance to respond, he grabbed her by the arm and dragged her down. She glanced around her at the people who had once been her friends. The same people she had helped over the years with the birth of their children and various ailments they had suffered. It's funny how times changed.

The hatred she saw in their faces caused her more pain than the fire ever would. She turned from them and fixed her gaze on the pyre in front of her. Jeremiah shoved her forward and she stumbled, but made sure she didn't fall. He forced her over the pile of wood at the base of the pyre and untied her hands. Before she got chance to move her stiff arms, he pulled her back up against the stake and tied her hands tightly again, the pole forcing her to stand painfully straight. A second length of rope secured her ankles and then finally, a length of rope was passed around her neck and tied firmly to the pole, forcing her to stare at the villagers.

'Burn, witch. Burn, witch.' The chanting started with the people closest to her, but soon the whole village joined in. The sound was deafening.

Anna stared at them all in turn. She searched their faces for what used to be, but she found nothing. A rotten tomato hit her in the face and the crowd started to laugh. *Oh, why couldn't this be over?* she thought as tears continued to roll down her cheeks. She just wanted it to be over.

'Any last words, witch?' Jeremiah said. Anna shook her head. She closed her eyes as he bent to light the tinder at her feet. The straw caught immediately and soon she was engulfed in flames. The crowd cheered. Anna screamed. At home, Father Tom cried.

The heat was unbearable, but she could do nothing. Her shoes had already melted away and she could feel the skin on her feet burning. Soon the pain rose to her shins. *Please let me die*, she prayed as the blistering heat spread up her body. As she screamed and writhed in agony, her gaze swept the crowd and she froze. Her mind and body were temporarily immune to their fate as she stared in horror. It couldn't be him, not after last night. The spell would keep him. She shook her head and when she looked again he was gone.

'Noooooo! He's not dead. Antony Cardover is still here.' But it was all in vain. No one could hear her. No one wanted to hear her.

The stench of burning flesh, her flesh, filled her nostrils. Her stomach clenched as the nausea overtook her and she vomited. The smoke clouded her eyes with more tears, making it impossible for her to see. A small mercy. She felt nothing now. Her pain threshold had been far exceeded and now she felt numb as her body shut itself down. Anna closed her eyes and willed the reaper to come. *Just let it be over*, she prayed. As she felt the blackness drawing in at last, Anna smiled for the last time, the jeering of the crowd fading away to nothing.

Becca snapped back to reality at the sound of the phone ringing.

'Hello?'

'Rebecca, where the hell are you?' Dick's voice screeched down the phone. 'I told you to be back for two. It is now half past and we have lost the client.'

'What do you mean?' Becca asked, still fuzzy from her daydream.

'We have lost the client. What else could it mean? Mr Antony Cardover would only deal with you. Said you were a friend of the family. Said he hadn't seen you in, like, forever. He wasn't interested in me and...' but Becca had stopped listening. The phone lay on the sofa and Becca was pacing the room.

'Antony Cardover, Antony Cardover,' she said as she paced back and forth and then she stopped, a feeling of dread settling in the pit of her stomach. That was the name of the man in her daydream. That was the name of the man in her grandmother's tale.

CHAPTER 7

'What was the name of that buyer?' Becca said as she stamped into the office, the door banging against the wall in her wake. Dick raised his eyebrows and made a point of looking at his watch.

'Close the door after you, Rebecca; you don't live in a barn, do you?'

'Dick!' She stamped her foot like a petulant child.

'Cardover. Somebody Cardover. And that's former potential buyer to you,' he said, not even trying to mask the sarcasm.

'What did he look like?' Becca ignored his attempts to rile her.

'How the hell would I know?'

'Well, didn't you see him this afternoon, for the appointment I missed, for God's sake?' Becca slammed her palms on his desk in exasperation.

'Well, no, I didn't'

'Well, who did?'

'Err, no one did. He didn't actually turn up.'

'What? You have the gall to have a go at me for missing the appointment and he didn't come anyway. You're unbelievable.' Becca slumped into a chair and massaged her temples, momentarily lost in thought.

'I think you're forgetting who works for whom around here, young lady,' Dick said, but Becca didn't respond. 'What are you so concerned about him for, anyway?' Dick continued, curiosity getting the better of him.

'How did you know he wasn't coming?' Becca said as she looked up.

'I got a phone call…'

'From him?'

'Well, if you'd let me finish…'

'Dick!'

'From an associate of his. He asked if you were there, I said no, he said the sale was off and hung up. Concise enough for you?'

Before Becca could retaliate, the office door banged open again and the foreman rushed in.

'Boss, come quick!' he said and dashed outside again. Dick and Becca almost tripped over each other in their desperation to get outside and see what had happened.

'You can't keep it. It needs to be reburied in consecrated ground. It's dangerous,' Father Michael said to the workmen as they crowded round the latest excavation.

'It's a stone box that's been in the ground for donkeys. What the hell is there to be scared about, Vicar?' one of the workmen said. 'Frightened that it holds some monster?'

'That's exactly what it contains. That is why it needs to be moved with all the others,' Father Michael said. The workmen fell silent and turned to look at him. A sense of relief flooded his veins. He had actually got through to them. Then, suddenly, a ripple of laughter went around the group, soon replaced by raucous guffawing.

'Good one, Father, you almost had us there,' one of the men said.

'But it's true…'

'Course it is, Vicar. Now, toddle off while the boss decides what he wants to do with this. After all, it's his property isn't it?' The first man gently propelled Father Michael away from the scene.

Dick and Father Michael collided at the cemetery's entrance.

'Watch it!' Dick said and carried on towards the huddle of bodies. Becca caught Father Michael as he stumbled on the crumbling step, almost losing his vertical battle.

'Are you all right, Father?'

'I'm fine, child. It's nice to see you again. Did you find what you were looking for yesterday?'

'I'm sorry, Father, I'm not with you.'

'Yesterday morning? You were here, at the gates. I spoke to you?' Father Michael regarded the same fresh young face he'd been haunted by since the previous day. She seemed so familiar, but still his ancient memory couldn't place her.

'I'm sorry, Father, but I don't know what…'

'REBECCA, GET YOUR ARSE OVER HERE. THIS ISN'T A SOCIAL GATHERING; YOU'RE SUPPOSED TO BE AT WORK.' Dick's voice boomed across the cemetery.

'I'm sorry. I have to go.'

As she crossed the gateway into the churchyard, storm clouds scudded across the sky and thunder crashed. Everyone glanced upwards at the sudden gloom. Everyone, that is, except Becca.

'B…E…C…C…A…' She heard the breathy voice as she walked towards Dick and she shivered. Again, she felt herself drawn towards the gnarled oak tree, but this time it was crowded with workmen. Becca stared straight ahead, as though hypnotised. She pushed her way through the pungent group and stopped in front of the object of their infatuation.

Without looking at it, Becca laid her hand on the cold rough surface of a stone sarcophagus. She slid her hand slowly from the top, down over the lip of the lid, until her fingers rested on the join of the lid and the base.

The absence of a gap drew her gaze to the casket. She stared at the seal and began to trace her fingers along its lines. As she moved she felt spasms resonate through her body. The brief intense pain brought tears to her eyes, but she couldn't pull her hand away. It was as though the sarcophagus was drawing her towards it, feeding on her energy.

Inside, he watched her. He felt her. He breathed her. It was almost time. Soon he would be free and she would be his. His to torture. His to torment. His to destroy. He blew towards the seal and smiled to himself.

'B…E…C…C…A…' Startled, Becca jumped away from the casket and lost her balance, falling flat on her backside. Her heart pounded in her chest as adrenalin raced round her body. Thunder cracked overhead again. This time Becca screamed.

'Oh, for God's sake, Rebecca, it's only thunder. Now, get up and tell me what you think.' Dick circled the casket again, one arm crossed across his waist, the other hand resting under his chin.

'Think about what?' Becca said as she brushed charred grass off her trousers and walked towards Dick.

'About the sarcophagus, what else? I've been talking about it for the last five minutes but, as usual, you haven't heard a word…'

Becca shut out Dick's monotone and stared at the sarcophagus in front of her, as though seeing it for the first time. She wandered around it, her hands thrust deep into her pockets, taking in the beauty and intricacy of its design.

The stone casket was huge, at least seven feet by two feet, and appeared to be made of granite. *It must weigh a tonne,* Becca thought and marvelled at how anyone could've moved it without a crane.

The side panels were intricately carved, alternately with a shield and a five armed crest. At the head and foot, a church window was etched into the granite. Becca wondered what the symbols meant. She walked around it again and stared at the unbroken seal. Etched into it were words. She carried on walking until she found what she believed was the start. Once again, her fingers traced the string of words.

'By my Goddess and by my God, I ask for your power to strengthen my spell. By my Goddess and by my God, I ask for your power to end this fight. Help me to rid the land of this evil presence. Through my actions, through our power, we commit him to his tomb. Aaargh!' Becca screamed at the electric shock that shot through her body. At the same time, the ground shook, causing everyone to stumble backwards.

'What the hell?' said Dick, his sentence left hanging as he stared at Becca. No longer on the ground, she was on top of the sarcophagus, brushing and blowing earth and other crustaceans from the lid.

'Rebecca, get down off there at once. You'll be filthy, for God's sake.' He strutted over to her and grabbed her arm, but she pulled away from him.

'There's something else written on the lid,' she said, bracing herself and leaning in close to get a better look. As soon as her palms made full contact with the stone she was hurled off it and flung across the cemetery.

'Oh my God, Rebecca! Are you all right?' Dick shouted and rushed over to the crumpled heap.

'Quick, phone an ambulance,' he said, but no one moved. 'NOW!' As one, the workmen reached into their pockets for their phones.

Dick lifted one of Becca's hands to feel for a pulse and he saw the scorch marks on the palms of her hands.

Antony Cardover removed his palms from the lid of his tomb. *That little bit of energy might just be enough,* he thought.

'I'm fine, Dick, for Christ's sake. Will you leave me alone?' Becca pushed him away. 'You're invading my space now.'

'But you were thrown a long way, and you landed so badly, and your hands..,' Dick said, deflated that his crisis had been down-graded.

'My hands are fine. Look,' Becca said and thrust damage free palms into his face. 'No burns. Maybe you were seeing things…'

'I most certainly was not,' he said. 'I…'

'Look, it doesn't matter. The ambulance men gave me the all clear, so let's forget about it and go and get a cup of coffee. Then you can tell me what your plans are for that thing, anyway,' Becca said, casting a look at the sarcophagus. She shivered and turned away, linked arms with Dick and started to head towards the office.

'What do you want to do with it, Boss?' the foreman said.

'Stick it in the crypt for now,' Dick said, with a flick of his hand.

'Stick it in the crypt. Like it doesn't weigh much, does it?' said Bill, the foreman, but Dick didn't hear him.

As Becca and Dick crossed into the street, the sky brightened.

'Thanks,' Becca said, wincing slightly as Dick handed her a cup of coffee.

'See. You're not all right, at all. Those bloody charlatans don't understand anything about medicine. I'll bloody sort them out…'

'So, what are you planning on doing with the sarcophagus then? It's certainly an extraordinary looking thing,' Becca said, sipping her coffee, hoping he'd take the bait.

'Well..,' he said and snapped his phone shut, his face turning all dreamy and wistful. He rushed over and perched on the desk next to her.

'What I thought was, that we could get it cleaned up and use it as the centre piece in the penthouse.'

'It'll look a bit odd, given how modern the apartments will be, won't it?'

'That's just it. I thought we could make the penthouse something different, something special. I thought we could get the designers to do something "gothic", using the sarcophagus as the focal point. What do you think?'

'Do you honestly think people will spend hundreds of thousands on an apartment with a dead body in it?'

'Typical. Always criticising my ideas. I thought with you being a Goth, you might appreciate what I was aiming to do.' Dick stalked off and slumped behind his desk.

'I'm not a Goth. But even if I was, it doesn't mean I would want a coffin, with a real body inside, in my home,' Becca said and shuddered. 'Besides, you have no idea who's inside or what they might have done. You saw Father Michael. He was getting really het up about moving it. Maybe they were a mass murderer or something…'

'Even better. A nasty story adds a bit of spice, don't you think?'

'Dick, that's appalling,' Becca said, astounded at the depths he would stoop to make a sale.

'I knew you wouldn't understand. I'm going to do it anyway because I recognise what will appeal and what … where do you think you're going?'

'I'm beat and I have a class to get to. I'll see you tomorrow.' Becca got up and left before Dick could do any more pontificating.

As she left the office, she glanced towards the cemetery, feeling herself inexplicably drawn towards it once again. In the gathering dusk, she stood at the rusting railings and stared through them towards the crumbling church. She squinted into the gloom, convinced someone was watching her. She could feel the pressure of someone's stare, but she couldn't see anything. She shook her head and chastised herself before walking to her car.

'Soon, Becca, soon you will be mine…' The hairs on the back of her neck stood on end as she heard the whispered words, but she fought the urge to turn round. Instead, she jumped into her car and skidded away from the site.

CHAPTER 8

Becca slammed the door behind her and double bolted it. She rested her head against the coolness of the wood and closed her eyes. What a weird couple of days. Her heart finally under control, she opened her eyes and stared straight into two huge orange pools.

'Am I glad to see you,' Becca said and dropped to the floor, enveloping Spook in a huge bear hug. She nuzzled her face into his thick grey fur and listened as the familiar resonating sound increased tempo and speed. Becca smiled and cuddled him even tighter. He knew exactly how to cheer her up.

Deciding his time as a good Samaritan was over, Spook flexed his paws and sank his claws into Becca's arm.

'Oww, you little sod!' she yelped and released him. He ran into the kitchen and sat by his food bowl, a "butter wouldn't melt" look plastered across his face.

'Typical,' said Becca. 'Cupboard love, that's all it is with you.' She rubbed the cat behind his ears and filled his bowl with biscuits. Grabbing a bottle of water out of the fridge, she wandered into her bedroom to get changed. The suit was discarded, with other remnants, on the battered armchair and Becca pulled on a pair of tight jeans, a fitted T shirt and her Converse.

'Right, I'm off. I'll see you later,' she said, wandering into the kitchen to grab her keys. She observed Spook munching away. 'In case you're bothered, I'll get something at college.'

The door slammed shut behind her, but Spook didn't flinch.

CHAPTER 9

Inside his tomb, Antony grew restless. His mind was plagued with memories. Memories he had hoped would fade with time, but they hadn't. It was as if it had all happened yesterday.

He'd been taken with her the first time he'd seen her. The day she'd walked into his father's workshop had been one he'd never forget. How could he – it had been the most embarrassing, yet the most exhilarating day of his life.

His father, Julius, had been ill for some time and had been treated by Anna Martindale, a known witch, but one who really did help people. Antony had been picking up most of the work while his father was ill. Carpentry had not been something that had come easy to him, nor had it been something he had wanted to dedicate his life to, but he had loved his father and the small business of Cardover & Son had been his father's life. So, being a dutiful son, Antony had started to learn the tools of the trade.

Julius' illness had meant that more and more of Antony's time had to be spent fulfilling orders so that the business could stay afloat and food could be put on the table. Gradually, Antony's skills had improved under the watchful eye of his father and he'd even started to think about it as a long term profession. After all, he'd no other skills.

The day he'd met Isabella had been a particularly busy day for Antony, so much so that he hadn't even glanced up when the bell above the workshop door had sounded.

'Is Julius in the back, Antony?' Anna had asked.

'Yes, Mrs Martindale, he's having a bad day today,' he'd replied without looking up.

'Wait here, Isabella, and for goodness sake behave yourself.'

Unused to Anna having anyone with her, Antony had stopped what he had been doing and had turned to find out who the visitor was, who had been chastised.

He had been struck dumb at the sight of her. She had been stunning. With her long dark curly hair and creamy skin, she had been like a goddess to him. Her chocolate brown eyes had been full of mischief as she had watched him and smiled, her tongue dancing over her full lips. It had all been too much for him and he had been mortified by his body's reaction to her. Isabella had run out of the workshop laughing, but she had turned in the doorway and had blown him a kiss.

He should have stopped then. It had been obvious that she would be nothing but trouble, but it had been too late. He had been smitten. Thoughts of her had consumed his every waking hour, so much so that his interest in the business waned. He had spent all his time pursuing Isabella, but to no avail. She had continually refused to court him. She had flirted, teased and played games with him, but had then dropped him saying he was too immature and inexperienced for her.

Julius' death had brought a halt to Antony's romantic notions, as he had no other choice but to support himself. The shift in his attitude had yielded two-fold benefits. The carpentry business had grown steadily under his applied attitude and soon word had spread of Antony's gift for making anything from wood. People had come from miles around to see the pieces he had kept on display in his workshop and to commission him to build something for them. It had appeared everyone wanted an original Cardover, even Isabella.

Everyone had warned him about Isabella, even Anna, her own mother. They'd told him how selfish she was, how little she cared about anyone except herself and they'd warned him that one day she would rip his world apart, but he'd refused to listen. Isabella Martindale had finally agreed to be his wife and he couldn't have been happier.

The wedding should have been an alert to the life he'd been about to condemn himself to. Isabella, in true style, had flirted with every man present without a care. Antony had watched her rub herself up against them, touch their faces, kiss their cheeks, while he had sat and drunk mug after mug of ale, his temper building. Finally, when one of the guests had grabbed Isabella and had pulled her into an inappropriate embrace, Antony had snapped. He'd thrown his ale to the ground and had dragged his new wife from the arms of another man before pummelling the unfortunate victim into the ground, almost killing him. Isabella had giggled the whole time, clearly ecstatic that men had been fighting over her.

Despite this abhorrent behaviour, Isabella had apologised to Antony and had wheedled her way, very easily, back into his good books. His infatuation with her had prevented him from staying angry at her. Instead, he'd turned it around in his mind and made it so that it had been the men who had been harassing his wife and he had simply been defending her honour.

Even though she'd been his, it had been like owning a wild untamed stallion. She'd done exactly what she'd wanted without a thought or a care for anyone else, especially him. Antony had tolerated her selfish behaviour because he'd known she was his. They had been man and wife, "til death do us part". But, one day, Isabella had crossed a line and there had been no going back.

Antony had been working long hours to finish making the necessary pieces for a large order and rarely had any spare time. When he had stopped, he had slept. He had warned Isabella about this and had assured her that it would only be for a couple of months. He had also told her that the money he made from the order would allow him to take some time off after and he would spend that time with her. Isabella hadn't seemed that bothered, the money he'd make taking the sting away.

True to form though, after a couple of weeks, she had completely forgotten what he'd told her and had started complaining. The complaints had ranged from boredom to how much he worked, but they had always centred around one thing – he had been neglecting her and if he wasn't careful, he would lose her. Antony had tried to spend more time with her, but he had needed the money to keep a roof over their heads and food on the table. Isabella had seemed to accept this eventually and had left him alone to get on with his work. Antony had been relieved and had vowed to lavish her with time and affection once the job had been completed.

What Antony hadn't been aware of was how Isabella had been coping with her boredom. Never short of admirers, she'd decided to teach Antony a lesson for neglecting her. She had begun to conduct various affairs with other men in the village. Although nothing had ever been overtly flaunted, she had known that he would find out eventually, which had been the plan. It had always been about her. What Isabella had wanted, Isabella had managed to get.

Anger rippled through his body as he remembered the time he had discovered her betrayal. He flexed his muscles within his tomb and the last of his decaying bindings snapped.

It had been a Thursday night, quite late, and he had recently secured an order to furnish the Duke's estate, an order that would keep the money coming in for well over a year. Exhausted, but happy, he had decided to go to the Inn for a drink before going home and breaking the good news to

Isabella. As he'd walked through the door of the Inn, he'd noticed several groups in there. Most people had fallen silent when he'd walked in, but one group had been quite drunk and had been laughing and jeering.

He'd ignored them and had settled down to enjoy several mugs of ale and some conversation with the Innkeeper. The men had been quite vocal though and Antony had eventually tuned into what they had been saying. He'd shaken his head in disgust as he'd listened to them describing their latest conquest and had been about to strike up a conversation with the Innkeeper again, when he'd heard Isabella's name. He'd tuned in again, thinking he'd been mistaken, but the descriptions had been too accurate. He'd glanced towards the Innkeeper, only to find him nervously wiping the counters and furtively glancing at the drunken group.

Antony had spun round to face the group, upending his stool in the process. The drunken men had glanced up and, on seeing Antony, had frozen mid sentence. Within seconds they had thrown their tankards to the floor and had headed for the door, knocking over tables and chairs as they went. Antony had lunged after them, but he'd tripped over the obstacles they'd thrown in his path. By the time he'd made it outside, they'd gone. He'd stomped back into the Inn, only to find everyone staring at him.

'What the hell is your problem?' he'd said, but no one had answered. 'Well?'

'I don't think we're the ones with the problem,' one man had said, his voice wavering.

'What's that supposed to mean?' Antony had said and had slammed his fist on the bar.

'Why don't you calm down, Antony?' the Innkeeper had said.

'I am calm. I just want to know what's going on.'

The Inn had been silent. No one had wanted to be the one to tell him.

'It's your wife,' an old man had said, from a table near the door. 'She's been running around behind your back.'

'What exactly do you mean by that?'

'She's been "lying" with other men,' the first man had said. 'Men from this village,' he had added, seeming proud that he'd revealed the infidelity.

'She's done what? I don't believe you. She wouldn't.'

'I'm sorry, Antony, but it's true,' the Innkeeper had said.

Before he could say anything else, Antony had grasped the Innkeeper by the throat and had dragged him across the bar until their noses had been touching.

'Who?' Antony had said, loud enough for everyone to hear. He followed the Innkeeper's gaze to the table where the rowdy group had been sitting.

He had been the laughing stock of the village after that. He had also never seen Isabella again, until that last night. Anna had kept her well hidden from him.

'BITCH!' he bellowed into the confines of his tomb and slammed his fists into the lid of the sarcophagus. The force cracked the seal and four hundred years worth of fetid air seeped into the crypt of St Martin's church.

CHAPTER 10

As the seal broke, Becca froze mid sentence.

'B…E…C…C…A…' She shivered as she heard the now familiar whisper.

'Ms Martin? Are you okay?' said one of the students, but she didn't hear him. She was transfixed by the figure standing at the back of the room.

'Antony,' she whispered and, as though hypnotised, she started to walk towards him, her hand outstretched.

'Come to me, Becca,' he said and she smiled as she looked at him. His tall, dark frame seemed to fill the back of the room as the images began to change in her peripheral vision; the students and desks melting into nothingness. Becca felt a gentle breeze ruffle her hair, could see the outlines of trees to her left and right, and heard an owl hoot in the distance. She shivered and rubbed her bare arms against the chill.

'Come, Becca, soon you will no longer feel the cold,' Antony said and opened his arms to her. Becca started to run towards him, the thought of his embrace filling her with happiness.

She was almost with him when someone jumped out of the shadows in front of her, grabbed her by the shoulders and started shaking her. Becca tried to push them away, but they were too strong.

'Antony!' she shouted, but he had disappeared.

'Antony, where are you? Where are you?' she repeated over and over, tears running down her cheeks.

'Ms Martin?' she heard a voice. 'Wake up, Ms Martin,' the voice urged. The shaking had stopped now, but she could feel someone gently patting her face.

'For God's sake, get off,' she said and shoved the hand out of the way. 'What the hell do you think you're doing, Ben?' she said as she stared up at the young man sitting astride her. Ben blushed and stood up before helping her to her feet.

'You went all funny, Ms Martin, like you were in a trance,' Ben said. 'It was like you were sleep walking, but you were awake. I just wanted to stop you before you fell, but you started hitting me and…'

'Who's Antony?' another student interrupted.

'What?' Becca asked, puzzled.

'Why were you crying, Miss? Is he your boyfriend?' someone else interjected.

'He was here,' Becca said.

'No one was here, Ms Martin,' Ben said.

'He was here, at the back of the room. You must have seen him!'

'There was no one here,' Ben said again and tried to guide her to a chair, but Becca shook him off.

'That's all for tonight,' she said and left, leaving a class of perplexed students behind.

'But he was there,' Becca muttered as she sped along the main road towards home. She skidded to a halt outside her apartment and barely remembered to lock the car in her haste to get inside. She burst through the front door, letting it bang against the wall, sending Spook hurtling through his cat flap. Becca raced into her studio and grabbed her sketch pad. She dropped to the floor and hastily drew the man she had seen less than half an hour ago. Jumping up, she took the new sketch to the draughtsman's table and, pulling the other drawing from underneath her laptop, she laid them side by side. The pictures were identical. The man she'd seen that evening, at the back of her class, was the same man who had been plaguing her dreams.

Antony smiled to himself from within his tomb. Little by little he was getting to her. Soon, she would be his. Forever. He pushed against the lid of the sarcophagus and the stone grated against its base. The sound echoed through the empty skeleton of the church.

Hearing a noise, a lone workman, on his way home for the night, stopped and headed back to the church. He stood at the top of the steps to the crypt and stared down into the inky blackness.

'Is there anybody down there?' he called. There was no answer, but he decided to go down to make sure it wasn't some kids messing about. He got halfway down the steps when he smelt it. The stench of decay and decomposition. He gagged at the offensive smell and immediately returned to the fresh air of the night.

Antony tried to slide the lid away, but he wasn't strong enough yet. Another visit to Becca was needed. He closed his eyes, cleared his mind and whispered her name.

'B…E…C…C…A…' Becca snapped out of her reverie at the sound of his voice. She inspected her brightly lit studio, but saw no one. There were no shadows, but the gaping windows led to the dark abyss. Becca jumped up and lowered the blinds without looking out of the window. She didn't want to see. Turning her back she scanned the dishevelled room. Discarded canvasses were stacked against the walls, some complete, some not. A virgin canvass awaited her on the easel, but she had no interest.

Becca dragged the chair away from the table and looked underneath. Nothing. She shoved the chair back and it banged against the bench and scattered pencils and brushes all over the floor; un-noticed. Grabbing one of the pictures off the table, she picked her way across the hardwood floor, switched off the light and closed the door behind her. She laid the picture on the table in the hall and then closed and locked the front door.

Exhausted, her mind whirling, Becca needed to talk to someone, but who? Only one person would listen to her without laughing. She dialled her mother's number, her hand shaking; her heart pounding. What would she say if she answered? It had been ten years since they'd spoken and…

'Hello?' Becca opened her mouth to reply, but nothing came out.

'Hello? Rebecca, is that you? I need to talk to you…hello?' Becca disconnected without saying a word as tears spilled down her cheeks. She couldn't do it. Too much time had passed. She was alone now.

She wandered into the kitchen and grabbed the bottle of Jack Daniel's from the cupboard. Not bothering with a glass, she made her way into the living room and curled up on the sofa. Becca took a huge gulp from the bottle and watched Spook squeeze his ample form through the cat flap in the French doors.

'Come here, baby,' she crooned and patted her lap. The grey cat immediately jumped up and settled himself, purring loudly. Becca took another swig and stared out of the windows, watching the trees moving in the wind. As the security light clicked off, Becca screamed and Spook scattered.

'Leave me alone!' she shouted and hurled the bottle at the window, where Antony was standing. The bottle fell short and smashed all over the wooden floor. Becca looked again at the window, but he was gone.

In his tomb, Antony laughed out loud.

CHAPTER 11

'Good morning, Ramply....'

'I'm not coming in today, Dick,' Becca interrupted.

'Oh God, what's happened now? A little tiff with the boyfriend, is it?'

'Shut the hell up. You've got no idea.'

'Well, as your employer, do you not think it appropriate that you tell me why you will be absent from work?'

'I can't.'

'Well, I suggest you get your arse to work pronto, that is, if you still want a job.'

'Dick, please, I can't come in. There's stuff going on that I need to sort. I'll make it up to you, I promise,' Becca said and put the phone down. She sighed and leaned against the deep cushions on the sofa, her bed the previous night. Her gaze rested on the shattered glass and sticky mess that decorated her living room floor. She shifted her gaze to the window, but of course, there was no one there.

She dragged herself off the sofa and towards her bedroom to get dressed. She had to find out what was going on.

Father Michael sat at his desk, replying to correspondence, when he heard the gentle tap at the door.

'Come in,' he said, without looking up. Quickly lost in his letters again, he didn't hear anyone come in.

'Father?' the young woman almost whispered, but Father Michael didn't seem to hear.

'Father?' she said a little more loudly.

'What? Oh, I'm sorry, I get distracted so easily.'

'I'm sorry, Father, I didn't mean to disturb you, it's just that..,' her voice trailed off as huge sobs shook her tiny frame.

'Now, now, child, come and sit down,' Father Michael said, as he guided her into a comfy armchair. 'Would you like some tea?' She nodded and sniffed, fumbling in her pockets for something.

'Here.' He handed her a box of tissues and then disappeared for a minute to organise refreshments. Once he had located his housekeeper and made the request, he returned to the distraught young woman in his office.

He closed the door behind him and went and sat down opposite his visitor. She certainly appeared calmer than she had a few minutes before.

'Now, child, do you want to tell me what's troubling you and what brought you here today?' Father Michael's voice was soft. The young woman, however, remained silent. She stared at her knees, the toes of her shoes scuffling with each other, her fingers massaging her left earlobe.

'Well, how about we start with your name then?'

'Becca…Martin,' she said.

'Well, I'm pleased to be finally introduced to you Becca Martin. My name's Father Michael and I…'

'Who's in the stone casket?' Becca interrupted.

'Why do you ask?' Father Michael said, a little guarded.

'Is it Antony Cardover?' she continued, ignoring his question.

'How do you know about Ant…?'

'It is, isn't it?'

'Well…'

'Yes or no?'

56

'Yes, but how do you know about him?'

Becca remained silent, lost in her thoughts. He studied her face. It looked so familiar, and he could almost hear his brain churning in the hope of placing her.

'Why is he in a stone casket, was he rich or something?'

'No, he wasn't rich.'

'Then why a stone coffin and not an ordinary one? And why is the ground burned and the tree bare? What was he?'

'Well, well, so many questions..,' Father Michael paused, not knowing what to say to her. There was a knock at the door, giving him a welcome moment to collect his thoughts.

'Aaahhh, tea, just what the doctor ordered. Thank you, Mrs Munroe, that will be all.' The housekeeper nodded and glanced at Becca with a frown as she left.

'Milk and sugar?'

'Just milk, thanks,' Becca said and picked up a shortbread biscuit off the plate. Father Michael watched as she turned it over and over between her fingers, but made no attempt to eat it.

'Well?' Becca prompted after Father Michael didn't respond.

'Are you familiar with the history of the town, Becca?'

'A bit, I guess, why?'

'So guarded for one so young. It's not a secret. I'm merely surprised you don't know.'

'Didn't really pay attention in history class.'

'This isn't something they would teach you in history. It's not something the town is proud of. It's more likely to be something your parents would have told you as their parents would have told them.'

'Oh, well, that explains that then.' Father Michael waited for her to elaborate, but she didn't. She went back to playing with the biscuit.

'Wait here a moment,' he said and disappeared into a room behind his office. He balanced precariously on a stool as he reached to the highest shelf and grappled with a huge tome above his head. At last, his fingers got a grip and he pulled.

'Do you need a hand, Father?' Father Michael jumped and lost his balance. In his efforts to stop himself falling he let go of the book and it hit the floor, hard, making the whole room shake.

'Good heavens, child, you almost gave me a heart attack,' Father Michael said as he placed his feet firmly on the floor, but Becca wasn't listening. She was flicking through the pages of the book, as though searching for something.

'This is him! This is Antony,' she stated, pointing at a drawing she had settled on. Father Michael shuffled over and peered over her shoulder.

'Yes, it is.' He stared at the picture on the page and, more specifically, at the other person in it. A young woman almost identical to the one in front of him. That's why Becca had seemed familiar.

'Anna?' Becca asked.

'No, not Anna. It's Isabella, Antony's wife,' Father Michael said and turned over the page to reveal the full scene.

'That's Anna,' he said, pointing at an old woman at the edge of the picture.

'Oh my God,' said Becca, her voice high. 'I've seen this. I've been there. I've been her.' She thrust a finger at the picture of Isabella, burst into tears, and ran from the room. Father Michael grabbed the book and went after her. Becca was sitting in a chair, her knees pulled in tight to her chest, rocking back and forth.

'What do you mean, you've seen it, child? You can't have, it happened over four hundred years ago.'

'In a dream,' she said as he opened his mouth. 'A dream that left me with these.' She showed him the yellowing bruises on her wrists and her almost healed lip. 'And these.' She pulled down the scarf she had tied around her neck, to reveal the puncture marks. 'Only these are from a previous dream, but they were made worse in this dream. I also have bruises on my thighs, from where he…' Becca let her voice trail off and lowered her head.

'What?' Father Michael said.

'I knew you wouldn't believe me,' she shouted and jumped up out of her chair. 'No, I didn't know you wouldn't believe me. I actually thought you would, of all people. After seeing the way you behaved when they unearthed that casket, I thought you would believe me.' Tears filled her eyes again and she turned on her heel and headed for the door.

'Becca, wait,' Father Michael said and struggled to reach her, but just managed to grab her arm before she left the room. She turned towards him and he could see the disappointment in her eyes.

'I didn't say I didn't believe you, I…'

'Yes, you did.'

'No, I didn't, now come and sit down and tell me the full story.'

Becca relaxed a little and followed him back into the room and sat down.

'What's the point in telling you? What are you going to be able to do to help me?'

'I don't know, child, but it always helps to tell someone when something is troubling you. Tell me what's happened, right from the start, and we'll see if we can figure it out.'

So she did, all of it, finishing with her throwing a bottle of Jack Daniel's at Antony's image the previous night.

'You must be connected to them, in some way. The picture of Isabella and everything you've told me seem to indicate this is the case. Have you any knowledge of your family history?'

'Only about Anna and the story of her being burned at the stake. I heard the story as a child, from my grandmother. She's dead now. The story was about our family's ancestry, but that's all I'm aware of.'

'Well, if you are related to Anna, you are definitely related to Isabella.'

'Why?'

'Because Isabella was Anna's daughter. I don't see how though, because Isabella was Anna's only child and she was killed.'

'Did Isabella have a child?'

'No. You must be connected to Anna in a different way. According to history, Anna had a sister, Elizabeth. Maybe it is her you are actually related to. Will anyone in your family know the details?'

'I don't have anyone else, not now my grandmother is dead.' Becca felt a twinge of guilt for saying this, but she had been alone for the past ten years.

'That's a shame because you could really do with finding out.'

'Why can't you tell me?'

'I don't know the full story; no one does. It was a closely guarded secret. A secret that Anna shared with no one, as far as the books go. All I can tell you is what is in here.' Father Michael pointed at the book laid out in front of him. 'Antony Cardover was a very dangerous man after it happened and God knows what he may be…'

'After what happened?' Becca interrupted.

Father Michael sighed and examined the book. 'Antony killed a lot of people and then he killed Isabella. The whys and wherefores are not detailed in the book, only the events of that night. I believe Isabella betrayed him and this is why he did it.'

'Then why wasn't he captured and hung or whatever they used to do to murderers back then?'

'It wasn't that easy.'

'What do you mean?'

'Let's just say, Antony was a lot faster and a lot stronger than anyone else.'

'So, they had weapons didn't they? Why not bring him down that way?'

'He couldn't be killed by conventional methods, or at all for that matter.'

'Why, was he some sort of superhero gone bad,' Becca snorted with laughter, but Father Michael's expression remained serious.

'Becca, I think it would be better if you talked to your mother about all this. I think there is a strong connection between you and Antony, and she will be the one to know what that is.'

'I told you, I don't have any family.'

'I'm afraid I don't believe you, child. You have looked away from me both times you said you had no family.'

'Why can't you just tell me what he was?'

'You wouldn't believe me if I did, child.'

'Try me; I'm a lot more open minded about things nowadays.'

Father Michael sighed and looked Becca straight in the eye. 'Antony Cardover was some form of vampire.'

Becca sat and stared at him, her mouth open, the dreams she'd had rerunning in her mind. Without thinking about it, she reached up and touched the puncture marks on her neck.

CHAPTER 12

'A vampire?'

'I know, ridiculous isn't it, but that is what he is.'

'No, not ridiculous. Well, yes it is pretty far out, but it makes perfect sense given my dreams and these,' Becca rubbed the marks on her neck and flinched as pain shot through her.

'Is that why he was buried in the stone sarcophagus then, because he was a vampire?'

'Yes, they needed something strong enough to contain him, so...'

'How did he get out then?'

'He isn't out, not yet anyway...let me finish, child,' Father Michael held up his hand to silence another of Becca's interruptions. 'The land in which he was buried had to remain consecrated to keep him from roaming again. The spell that Anna placed on the casket would keep him there as long as he stayed buried in holy soil. The destruction of the church and the removal of the graves have disturbed the balance. Once the altar is removed, he will be free.'

'But I've seen him in the classroom and at home,' Becca said.

'You've seen his spiritual form, not his corporeal one. He can't do you any real harm until he is corporeal again.'

'What do you mean; he can't do me any real harm? What do you call this?' Becca snapped, brandishing her wounds.

'He can't kill you.'

'Great. Now I feel much better. He can torture me, but he can't kill me.'

Father Michael said nothing; she had a right to be angry.

'So, all we have to do is move the casket to consecrated ground again. To your church. Then everything will return to normal,' Becca said, a little spark lighting her eyes. Father Michael considered her and shook his head.

'I'm afraid it's not that simple.'

'Why not? You said…'

'Yes, but you've seen him, which means his spirit is free. The spell has been broken, so moving him to a different churchyard is not enough to keep him entombed. The spell needs to be recast.'

'Well, how do we do that?' Becca asked

'That, my dear, I don't know. I have no knowledge of what the spell was and even if I did, I don't know of any witches to do it.'

'Well, who would?'

'Maybe your mother?' Father Michael said. Becca turned away from him, her cheeks burning at yet another reference to the family she had told him she didn't have. After a few minutes she got up.

'Thanks, Father,' she said and left. Father Michael watched her through the window as she climbed into her battered old Fiesta. *Such a shame*, he thought, *to have to carry such a burden.*

'May God be with you, child,' he said and returned to his correspondence.

Disappointed and disturbed, that's how she felt, and scared. There was no other way to sum it up. As she drove aimlessly around, Father Michael's words bounced around inside her head. She had found out so very little, yet what she had found out had shaken her to the core. Knowing what Antony was had only made her predicament worse and the fact he would be free once the altar had been removed, scared her to death.

Her aimless driving had led her to the site. How apt. Her timing couldn't have been any more perfect. In the late afternoon, the sunshine beating down on her through her open window, Becca watched as the workmen carried the altar outside, in smashed pieces, and hurled it into a skip. Once the last piece was in, the skip was lifted onto the back of a lorry and driven towards the exit of the cemetery. As the lorry crossed the boundary, the ground shuddered. Becca shivered, fear running its hand up her spine. It was done. The last vestige of the church was gone. There was nothing left to keep him there. Becca closed her eyes and leant against her seat. She knew what she had to do.

CHAPTER 13

She sat on the sofa, the phone in her hand, unable to make the call. It was weird that it hadn't been a problem the previous night, granted Becca hadn't actually spoken, but now the walls were back up and the animosity she felt towards her mother was all too clear. It had been a long time, but her mother's words still hurt, as though they'd been said only yesterday.

'If you can't accept who you are, then you're no daughter of mine,' Ginnie Martin had said.

'What? Just because I don't believe in all this bullshit witch crap you keep spouting on about, you disown me?' Becca had said, hurt by the vehemence in her mother's voice.

'Don't use language like that in front of me, young lady,' Ginnie had snapped. 'It is a sacrilege that you do not accept your ancestry. What you are and what you should be has been pre-ordained for centuries.'

'Oh, give me a break. So, I'm supposed to just accept the fact that you say I'm a witch and go and tell all my friends about it? Oh, that will make me so much more popular than I am already. Good one, Mum.'

'It's not about telling anyone, Becca. It's about accepting it for you. It's about learning to channel and use your given powers to help others and better…'

'So, how come you don't do it, huh, Mum? You're so obviously a huge fan. How come you get to sit it out?'

'I wasn't blessed with the gift. I was born to the wrong generation. Your grandmother has it and you have it, but I don't.'

'So, instead, you want to live your desire to be a misfit through me. Well, it isn't going to happen, Mum. Not ever.'

'Rebecca Martin, if you don't take this responsibility seriously then you are no longer welcome in this house,' Ginnie had said, her voice deathly calm.

'Fine,' Becca had said and she'd run upstairs, packed her bags and had left.

She hadn't spoken to her mother since. She stared at the phone in her hand and punched in the number. It just rang and rang and rang.

'To hell with this.' She threw the phone down, grabbed her jacket and left for her art class.

'Free at last,' Antony said as he pushed the lid of the sarcophagus aside. He stood, but his weak body, not yet fully restored, caused him to hunch over like a frail old man. He examined his hands in the darkness and saw that the bones were still only loosely threaded with tissue and flesh. He needed to feed. He needed that heartbeat to restore him, to make him whole again.

'Hello? Is there anyone down there?' a voice echoed through the crypt and Antony saw a shadow block the fading light at the top of the stairs. He lay back down in the sarcophagus and scraped his skeletonised fingers along its side. The noise had the desired effect.

'Tom? Is that you?' the man said and Antony heard his footsteps as he descended the stairs. 'What are you doing down here? Do you need a hand?' The footsteps stopped and Antony heard a click and then the cellar was swept by a beam of light.

'Tom? What the hell?' The beam rested on the open sarcophagus.

'Come on,' Antony muttered. The footsteps grew louder as the man approached and Antony could smell his bad breath before he saw him. The man leaned over the sarcophagus and shone the beam straight into Antony's face, casting the rest of his body into shadow.

'Jesus Christ! Tom have you…aaargh!' Antony gripped the man by the throat and dragged him into the sarcophagus. The torch was knocked from the man's hand, hit the floor and went out. The man put up a good fight, much to Antony's pleasure, making the blood pump round even faster. He sank his teeth into the man's neck and gulped down the adrenalin filled blood. He heard the heartbeat pounding in his ears and as it slowed, he slowed his feasting. The second the heartbeat stopped, he hurled the man out of the sarcophagus and pulled the lid into place. He could feel the tissues building themselves. Soon he would be whole.

Becca had been exhausted when she got home and had gone straight to bed. Now, plagued by images of the past she tossed and turned, her bedclothes long since confined to the floor.

She jolted awake and sat bolt upright, a raging thirst gripping her throat. She ran into the kitchen and yanked open the fridge door. Instead of reaching for a bottle of water, she grabbed a steak off the top shelf and plunged her teeth into it. As she tore at the raw meat, the blood dripped down her chin onto her pyjamas. Spook sat and watched, his ears back, his hackles raised.

The steak gone, Becca searched for more meat. There was none. Her thirst far from sated, she frantically scanned the kitchen for a cure. Her gaze rested on Spook. She lunged for him, but her thick socked feet lost their grip on the tiled floor and Becca lost her balance. She fell and hit her head on the work top. She felt the warm blood begin to run down the side of her head as she hit the floor. Becca lay there, inert and unconscious. Blood smeared her mouth and a fresh flow oozed from her head wound onto the kitchen floor.

Spook sat and watched, the plastic window of his cat flap safely between him and his owner.

CHAPTER 14

'Jesus Christ,' Becca groaned and raised her hand to the side of her head.

'Ouch,' she yelped as she pressed a little too hard. When she inspected her hand, dried blood patterned her fingertips.

'What the hell?' she said and pulled herself up to a sitting position. Her world spun rather rapidly at the movement and she put her head on her knees to try to stop it. When the dizziness abated, she slowly raised her head and looked around.

She was on the kitchen floor, a small dried pool of blood next to her. She turned her head, to be rewarded with a searing pain, and saw the fridge door was wide open. *Great*, she thought, *everything in it will be spoiled.* As she scanned the rest of the room, each movement of her eyes yielding further pain, she saw an empty packet of meat on the edge of the worktop. Then her gaze rested on Spook, who sat a good distance away and stared at her, his huge orange eyes mere slits of colour.

'Hey, Baby, come and give Mummy a cuddle,' Becca said to him, but Spook only growled at her.

'Spook! What was that for?' She pushed herself towards him, but he hissed at her and ran out through his cat flap.

Becca slumped against the cupboard and closed her eyes. *What the hell had happened last night?* She remembered coming home from her class and going straight to bed, but that was it. She had no idea why she had ended up on the kitchen floor, or why Spook was behaving so strangely.

She turned round and reached up to grasp the worktop behind her and then slowly hauled herself to her feet. She wobbled slightly, but steadied herself and then shuffled over and closed the fridge door. She'd investigate potential spoiling later. She looked at the empty steak packet on the counter and pangs of hunger started inside her. She stared at the droplets of blood glistening in the discarded carton and started to salivate.

'Jesus,' she jumped as the phone jolted her out of her trance. She grabbed the packet and threw it in the bin as she shuffled passed to get the phone.

'Hello?' she croaked as she flopped onto the sofa, to be greeted with a jolting pain in her temple. The sticky mess of Jack Daniel's and glass bade her good morning.

'Have you been drinking?' Dick's voice squealed down the phone. 'I don't care, just get to work, Rebecca, I need you,' he said, his voice wound tight.

'Dick, I…'

'Someone died. The place is swarming with uniformed men and I can't do it alone,' Dick said, almost hysterical.

'OK, I just need a bath then I'll…'

'Now, Rebecca!' With that, the line went dead.

Becca sighed and pushed herself up. She caught sight of Spook outside, watching her, but when she started walking towards the window, he ran off.

'Stupid cat,' she said and headed for the bathroom to survey the damage. She grabbed some cotton wool out of the cupboard above the sink and soaked it in some warm water. She dabbed at the bloody area, wincing every so often. Blood swirled down the sink and Becca was relieved to see that the wound seemed to be healing. Now, for the blood around her mouth. *How had that got there?* It certainly hadn't run down from her head wound. Her mind briefly flitted to the empty steak packet as she scrubbed at her face with soap and water, but she dismissed the thoughts quickly. *Never.* She swallowed some paracetamol, threw on some clothes and left.

CHAPTER 15

Jakes stood on the pavement outside St Martin's church, memories flooding his mind, as the hubbub of crime scene activity went on around him. He hadn't been here in over forty years, not since he was a small boy and his mother had brought him. It had been derelict way back then, but nothing like the desolation he saw now.

He remembered how his mother had loved to tell him the tale of what had happened here four hundred years ago and he remembered the thrill of excitement that he'd felt every time she'd done so. Jakes shuddered, a shiver running up his spine, as he thought of the past.

'Sir? They're waiting for you in the cellar,' a uniformed officer said, bringing him out of his reverie. Jakes nodded to the officer and stepped over the threshold into the cemetery.

As she pulled up at the site, it was a flurry of activity. Police cars had created a first line of defence, their blue lights flashing away in the morning sunshine. Beyond them, Becca could see yards of blue and white tape being wound around the site, as though it was a birthday present. Close by, officers were talking to site personnel; a sheeted corridor the only path to the church.

Becca got out of her car and steadied herself on the door as her world did a quick spin. *Jesus*, she thought, as black and white dots appeared before her eyes, *what happened last night?* She closed her eyes and leant her forehead against the car, the coolness alleviating the nausea which threatened.

After a few deep breaths, Becca opened her eyes and focused on the flurry of activity before her. *Where was Dick?* She pushed herself away from the car she'd been using as a crutch and headed towards the plastic tunnel. *Maybe one of the officers will know where he is*, she thought.

As she crossed the boundary into the churchyard, the sky darkened and thunder clapped. Everyone looked up. Everyone, that is, except Becca. It was as if she hadn't even noticed. Her gaze was fixed on the church and she headed there, ignoring everything else that was going on around her.

As she passed the gnarled oak tree, the ground shuddered and Becca stumbled, falling to her knees. *What the hell?* She tried to stand up, but her world span around her once again. She closed her eyes and leant forward, resting her hands on the ground. But no sooner had she made contact, when she screamed and wrenched them away. Becca stared down at her palms and saw what appeared to be scorch marks.

She sat back on her haunches and rubbed her palms on her jeans, yelping in pain. Becca tugged at her shirt to try to ease the sudden clamminess that she felt. Her head hurt even more now and she leant forward again, careful not to touch the ground, and retched. Her neck had started to throb and she reached up to touch the wounds. They were swollen and sore again. Becca straightened up and looked around for Dick. Everyone was busy and not paying her the slightest bit of attention. Everyone, that is, except one man, who seemed to be watching her.

He must have been in his early fifties, his ruddy complexion ageing him prematurely. He had dark collar length hair, which was messy and obviously didn't command much of his attention. He reminded her of Colombo, with his trench coat and piercing stare, except he was taller and seemed to have blue eyes. But he was stocky all the same. He was starting to creep her out, so she shifted her gaze.

'Dick?' she called.

'Rebecca!' came back a high-pitched squeal, which grated through her head. Dick appeared beside her and dragged her to her feet before hugging her, a little too tightly.

'Where have you been? I've been waiting ages for you! Oh my God, Rebecca, it's awful! His neck, it's…oh, God, what are we going to do? This is going to delay everything and, oh my God, Rebecca, it was so awful.'

'Dick, calm down, will you, I can't keep up.' Becca grabbed his arms and shook him. Dick stopped babbling and looked at her, his eyes wide, panic evident. 'Now, take a deep breath and tell me what's happened.'

'I found him this morning. It gave me the shock of my life. I just thought I'd go and check out my prize exhibit and what happened? I tripped over a dead body. You should see the state of his neck, Rebecca. It looks like an animal has been chewing on him. Are you all right?' Dick grabbed Becca's arm, as her knees sagged, and lowered her to the ground.

Becca reached up to turn her shirt collar up to shield the marks from Dick. She dropped her hands back into her lap and looked down at them.

'You look like shit. You have been drinking, haven't you?' Dick said, but Becca didn't answer him. She was too busy staring at her wound free palms.

'Robinson?' called DI Jakes. 'Do me a favour and go and have a chat with that young lady, will you, before she disappears?'

'Yes, Sir. Any particular reason?' DS Robinson said.

'I'm not sure yet, but she's been acting odd ever since she arrived. Can you breathalyse her as well?'

Jakes didn't hear Robinson's reply; his mind was on the young lady in question. He'd watched as she'd jumped away from the earth, as though burned, and then he'd witnessed her tentatively touch her neck, the same side of her neck as the wounds on the victim in the crypt.

CHAPTER 16

Inside the sarcophagus Antony smiled and withdrew his hands from the side of his tomb. Her hands had touched the earth from where he'd been disinterred. He had felt her; really felt her, for the first time. His body shuddered as her energy coursed through his veins. Her time was near. Soon she would be his, always his, as Isabella never had been.

His anger at Isabella's betrayal had consumed him. He had thought of nothing else but finding her and her many lovers and destroying them, as they had destroyed him. Only then could he rest. Only then could he continue with his life and maybe, just maybe, trust someone enough again.

Antony had scoured the village for the men who'd humiliated him, but he'd found no one. Their homes had been devoid of them, their families distraught. No matter how much pressure he'd inflicted on them, their whereabouts had remained a mystery. He had spent a week searching for them, a pointless week. His anger had steadily increased as the days wore on. The futility of his search and their ability to disappear had made him so mad that when he'd decided to turn his attention to his wife, he had been beyond reasoning.

He hadn't waited for an answer because he hadn't even knocked. He'd simply lifted his huge foot and, with all his hatred fuelled strength, kicked the once solid door. It had splintered and fallen to the floor and Antony had marched into the house.

'Where is the slut?' He'd strode across the tiny living room and had thrown open one door after another.

'She isn't here, Antony,' Anna had said, her voice calm. She had continued to mix her ingredients as Antony tore her home apart.

'Where are you hiding her, Anna?' he'd said through gritted teeth, his eyes glaring under a furrowed brow.

'I'm not hiding her anywhere.' Anna had faced him. His body had been shaking and he had slammed his fist onto the wooden table, dislodging the mixing bowl and sending it crashing to the floor.

'Liar!' He'd advanced on Anna, grabbed her by the throat and had pinned her up against the wall. 'Where is that lying, scheming, selfish slut of a daughter of yours?' His measured words had left spittle on Anna's face, but she'd remained calm and she'd held eye contact with him.

'I don't know where she is, Antony. She came here asking to stay and I said no. After that, she left and that is all I know.' Antony had stared into her watery blue eyes and had known that she'd been telling the truth. Anna had no more condoned Isabella's behaviour than he had.

He'd released her and then had inspected the carnage. A prick of guilt had jabbed at his conscience, but he'd pushed it away. She was, after all, the bitch's mother. Without another word, he'd left.

Antony had spent the next few weeks in a drunken stupor, picking fights with anyone who had dared to even look at him. He'd been convinced that everyone had known about Isabella's betrayal and that the entire village had been laughing at him behind his back. The tankards of ale had only served to fuel this paranoia and it had driven him almost insane.

One evening, whilst he'd sat festering at home, fantasising about squeezing the life out of Isabella and her lovers, a message had been thrown through his window, tied around a rock. He'd never seen the messenger, but the message had filled him with hope.

Without a moment's thought he'd stolen a neighbour's horse and had set out into the forest to find the man who supposedly could help him find Isabella. A warlock named Ebenezer Lightwoller.

The warlock's shack hadn't been hard to find. Antony had been passed it hundreds of times, but had never realised that anybody had actually lived there. All the windows had been boarded up and the roof had been full of holes, but from the tumbledown chimney wisps of smoke had been rising, signalling occupation.

Antony had tethered the horse to a nearby tree and had approached the dwelling. The door had been opened to him before he'd had chance to knock.

'Why, do come in,' a well-spoken voice had welcomed and Antony had obeyed without a second thought. The door had been closed quickly behind him and Antony had found himself in a cramped gloomy room. The only source of light had come from a weak fire burning in the hearth.

Antony hadn't been able to see his host, but he'd heard him shuffling around the room.

'Sit,' the voice had said and Antony had fallen backwards onto a chair, as it had been shoved into the back of his legs.

'Did you send me the message?' Antony had asked, getting straight to the reason for his visit.

'Why, yes, I believe I did.'

'Who are you?'

'Why, I believe you know the answer to that, Mr Cardover, as I did sign my note.'

'Why do you want to help me?'

'Why, I do believe you need help finding some people and I do believe that I can help you do just that. Would you care for a drink, Mr Cardover?'

'No, I don't want a drink. I want to know why YOU want to help ME.'

'Why, if you don't want my help you can always leave,' the voice had said and Antony had heard shuffling towards the door. In the light cast by the open door, Antony had finally seen his host. Ebenezer Lightwoller had been a very old man, his long grey beard and hair almost touching his waist. He'd had a hunched back and skin that had been almost translucent, but his eyes had been sharp and had appeared younger than the body they had formed part of.

'You were in the Inn that night. You know exactly what happened,' Antony had said, remembering the old man who had been the only one brave enough to tell Antony what Isabella had done.

'Why, yes I was,' Ebenezer had said and he'd closed the door and had come and sat across the table from Antony. He'd poured him a drink from a pitcher that had been sitting in the middle of the table.

'Drink,' Ebenezer had said.

'What is it?'

'Why, something that will help you in your quest.'

Antony had raised the cup to his mouth and had sniffed, but hadn't been able to make out the strange smell. He had been about to put it down again when, against his own will, his hand had raised the cup back to his mouth and he had drunk the contents. The liquid had been thick and warm with a slightly familiar taste to it.

'What…'

'Why, what would you give to be able to find your wife and her lovers, Mr Cardover?' the old man had interrupted.

'What do you mean?' Antony had said as pains had started stabbing at his insides. Ebenezer, meanwhile, had refilled Antony's cup and, again, Antony had drunk it.

'Why, I simply mean, how much do you want to find these people and what are you prepared to give in return?'

The pains had got worse and had been weaving their way through his body, throbbing and stabbing as they went.

'I've brought some money,' Antony had said, struggling to catch his breath. 'I can get some more if it isn't enough.' He'd reached into his pocket and had dropped the purse full of coins in front of the old man.

'Why, it's not your money I want, Mr Cardover. I want to understand how badly you want revenge and what you would sacrifice to have the chance to punish her?'

'I-I don't understand,' Antony had said, sweat heavy on his brow.

'Why, would you give your own life for the chance to make her suffer for what she has done to you?'

'Of course I would,' Antony had said and clutched his chest as he felt his heart being squeezed. 'What have you...?'

'Why, that's all I needed to know. Don't worry; it won't hurt much longer.'

Antony had stared in disbelief as the old man had closed his eyes, turned his face heavenward and raised his hands. He had begun chanting in a language that Antony had never heard and as his chanting had intensified, Antony's pains had grown less and the warlock had started to get younger. His grey hair had changed to ebony, his spine had straightened, his body had filled out and his skin had become thicker and unlined.

'What in God's name have you done? How did...?' But Antony hadn't been able to finish.

'Isabella will return, Mr Cardover. She will be in need of her mother's care soon, so she will return. You must bide your time until then, as you will not find her. The men you seek will also return to their families, but you must wait. Disappear for a while. They must believe that you have left the village for good. Only then will the ones you seek return. You will recognise them when you return, you will feel it. Goodbye, Mr Cardover.'

Ebenezer had marched to the door and opened it and had indicated that it had been time for Antony to leave.

'But what's just happened? The chanting, you, the pains. You owe me an explanation,' Antony had said, his anger suddenly stronger than it had ever been.

'I don't owe you anything, Mr Cardover, but I will give you some advice. Although you will need no invitation to visit the men who cuckolded you, your family will be another matter.'

'What...' Ebenezer had held up his hand to silence Antony.

'You will need to convince them to let you in, as this is not something they will willingly do, for they will know what you have become, be sure of that. One final word of advice, Mr Cardover; make sure you destroy Isabella and all her descendants. Only then will you find peace again.'

'What do you mean "find peace again"?'

'You will see, Mr Cardover, you will see.' Ebenezer had closed the door in Antony's face. Incensed and outraged at what had just happened, Antony had kicked down the door to the shack.

'You can't slam the door in my face like...' but the shack had been empty, completely empty. There had been no table, no chairs and no sign of a recent fire in the hearth.

Antony clenched his fists as he remembered that day. He'd soon realised what the warlock had meant about not being at peace.

He'd done as the warlock had said. He hadn't gone back to the village, he hadn't said goodbye to anyone, he'd simply never returned. Instead, he'd carried on through the forest, in no particular direction, aimlessly riding. The pains had started about four hours in. *Stomach cramps*, he'd thought, but a hundred times worse. He hadn't been able to continue riding, the pains had been tearing through his body, and so he'd dismounted and collapsed against a tree for support. He had been sweating quite badly and he had been able to hear a pounding noise in his ears, which got louder and louder as the thirst grew. A thirst he had never experienced before. It hadn't been a thirst for water or any other beverage; it had been for something else and it had made him delirious.

He'd soon learnt, when a rabbit had scurried passed him and all his senses had jumped to attention. It hadn't been only his senses that had made him realise what the warlock had done, it had been the physical changes that he had felt as well. When he had sensed the animal, he had felt his facial features start to shift. As he'd lifted his hands to touch his face, he'd seen the elongated nails, sharpened into points and his face had felt distorted into lumps and bumps, with his eyebrows more protruding than normal. But it had been his teeth that had given it away - the extra teeth that had appeared in his upper jaw, the fangs that had jabbed into his lower lip. That's when he had realised the monster he had been turned into.

It had been then that the rage had taken over; that the realisation of how stupid and how naïve he'd been had finally sunk in. He had been more than angry; he'd been out of his mind. He'd torn up bushes and plants, he'd ripped limbs from trees and then he'd turned and regarded his horse. The pounding in his head and the thirst had been driving him to distraction. He'd lost control and he had lunged at the horse and had sunk his fangs into its exposed neck. The horse had bucked and whinnied, but Antony had held firm. The pounding had lessoned; the thirst had been quenched.

Sated, Antony had thrown the horse to the ground. It was then he'd realised his second mistake of the day.

CHAPTER 17

'We're good to go, if that's all right, Frank?' the coroner said, tapping Jakes on the arm.

'What…oh, right, yes,' Jakes said and moved out of the way to let them pass, his mind already absorbed elsewhere again.

*There was something strange about the girl…Rebecca…*he thought, consulting his notebook for her name. He'd watched her from the minute she had entered the churchyard and her behaviour had been particularly odd.

Her collapsing and being sick had been the behaviour of someone who'd already seen the body, in his experience, not someone who'd yet to see it. Then, there was her skin. She had been covered in perspiration, as though she had a fever. Finally, there was her neck. He hadn't been able to see what she had been touching, but the fact was, she'd been touching the same side of her neck as the victim's wounds.

There must be a connection somewhere, some kind of cult maybe? He hoped Robinson was doing his job properly for a change. It was odd that two people who worked at the site both appeared to have afflictions in the same place. Maybe Ramply knew something about it; he was the boss after all. Jakes made a mental note to speak to Ramply about the marks.

Jakes, now alone in the crypt, rested his gaze on the closed sarcophagus in front of him. He walked towards it and gently placed his hands on it. It was cold and rough to the touch. He walked around the sarcophagus several times, his left index finger pressed to his lips, and then he stopped and bent down for a closer look. He wiped some of the dirt and debris away with his finger and pulled a torch out of his pocket and shone it on the join of the lid and the base.

Jakes could make out some words that had been cut clean in half by the slight gap. *Had this tomb once been sealed to make these words complete?* He grabbed his notebook out of his pocket and tore several pages out. He then pulled a pencil from behind his ear, a storage place he'd learned from his father. He placed the paper against the writing and then coloured over it with his pencil until the lettering appeared on the page. Ever so carefully he placed the next piece of paper in position and took the rubbing, then he placed another and this carried on until he'd been all around the sarcophagus. Once he'd finished, Jakes folded the pages and thrust them in the pocket of his raincoat.

He then walked around the casket a few more times, his finger to his lips. He had seen this before, he was sure of it, but his brain couldn't quite place it. He took his notebook out again and sketched the depictions of the shield, the five armed crest and the church window, which were carved into the sides of the sarcophagus. He would look it up when he got home. He returned his notebook to his pocket and walked right up to the sarcophagus. Placing his hands under the slight lip of the lid, he got as firm a grip as he could and he tried to lift the lid. It wouldn't shift at all, not even a millimetre. Jakes had always prided himself on being strong, out of shape maybe, but still strong; however, no matter which angle he tried it from, he couldn't make it move.

'Do you need some help, Sir?' said DS Robinson as he walked down the stairs into the crypt, a look of concern decorating his angular features.

'Ah, Robinson, good timing. Come and get on the other side of this,' Jakes said.

Robinson hurried across the room, stood on the opposite side of the casket to Jakes, and braced his hands under the lid.

'After three,' said Jakes. 'One…two…three, lift.' Both men strained to lift the lid, but to no avail. It simply wasn't going to budge.

'What was all that in aid of?' Robinson asked as he rubbed the tips of his fingers with his thumbs.

'I don't know. I wanted to see if we could move it. Just trying to understand what the victim was doing down here.'

'What, do you think Dracula crawled out of his coffin and killed him?' Robinson said and burst out laughing. 'Honestly, Sir, they'll pension you off if they hear you talking like that.'

'Well, you saw the marks on his neck, didn't you?' Jakes said and shrugged as he climbed the stairs out of the crypt.

'You're not actually suggesting that some mythological creature killed that guy, are you? Anything could have made those marks,' Robinson said, taking the stairs two at a time after him.

'Like what?' Jakes stopped and faced his partner.

'Well, I don't know,' Robinson said, looking at his feet for the answer.

'Well, I'm not ruling anything out at this stage. Did you question the girl?' Jakes said, before any further well meaning comments emanated from Robinson's uncontrollable mouth.

'Yes, I did.'

'What did she have to say?'

'Nothing really, just that she was home until Ramply rang her to come to the site.'

'So, she was home all evening and all night, was she?'

'I think so.'

'What do you mean, "I think so"? I thought you'd questioned her.'

'I have,' said Robinson, his shoulders pulled back and his chin pulled in; his usual defensive posture.

'Well, obviously not well enough. If you want something doing…is Ramply still here?'

'He's in the office. What do you want me to do?'

'Go and watch the post mortem and advise me of cause of death as soon as, while I go and do the job you were supposed to have done.'

'I thought Dracula did it..,' said Robinson, in a clumsy attempt to lighten the mood. Jakes looked at him, raised his eyebrows, and stalked off in the direction of Dick Ramply's office.

CHAPTER 18

Jakes knocked on the door to the porta-cabin.

'Mr Ramply? It's DI Jakes. I'd like a word, if I may?'

'Enter,' came a feeble voice from inside and Jakes opened the door and stepped into the office.

'Are you all right, Mr Ramply?' Jakes studied the man in front of him. Dick Ramply was lying on top of his desk with a damp cloth over his eyes.

'Oh, yes, I'm fine Detective Inspector. It's just the shock of it all, it's given me a terrible headache,' said Dick as he removed the eye mask and pulled himself up to a sitting position. Jakes rolled his gaze to the ceiling. *Bloody drama queen.*

'What can I do for you, Detective Inspector?' Dick's voice was weak.

'What do you make of the marks on the victim's neck? Have you ever seen anything like them before?'

'Well, no, actually I haven't,' said Dick, suddenly animated.

'So, you haven't noticed the same marks on Rebecca's neck?'

'No, why? Has she got some too?'

'So, you've no idea what they could be or where they could be from?'

'I've already said, no. They do look like vampire bites, though, like in the old movies, don't they?' said Dick, but Jakes didn't answer him.

'Well, thanks for your time, Mr Ramply; we'll keep you posted on developments. Could you tell me where Rebecca lives please, as I need to ask her a few questions?'

'Your colleague has already questioned her. What else do you need to ask her?'

'Mr Ramply, if you could just let me have her address.'

'Yes, yes, all right,' Dick said, picking up his Blackberry and searching.

'Rebecca Martin, Rebecca Martin..,' he muttered. 'Ah, here it is.' Dick read out the address and Jakes scribbled it down.

'Thanks again, Mr Ramply,' he said and left.

CHAPTER 19

Jakes climbed into his silver Ford Mondeo and glanced at the address Ramply had given him. It wasn't far away, in the nice part of town; the newly reclaimed and developed part. The traffic was light and Jakes' mind drifted to his first sight of Rebecca Martin. He still couldn't work out what it was, but she was definitely under the influence of something. Maybe now he'd find out.

He pulled into the car park of the apartment block, next to a battered old Ford Fiesta. He climbed out of his car and looked around him at the well-tended grounds, his gaze alighting on a huge grey cat, which was sitting looking at him from the shade of a willow tree. He liked cats and they liked him, but as he crouched down and tried to attract the cat, it simply stalked away and disappeared into the building, presumably through a cat flap.

Jakes shrugged and stood up. Maybe his charm was wearing off. He walked to the front door and scanned the list of buzzers for the one marked "Martin" and pushed it. He waited and soon heard the familiar crackle as the handset was picked up.

'Hello?' a female voice croaked.

'Rebecca Martin?' Jakes said.

'Yes.'

'It's Detective Inspector Jakes. I was at the site; you might remember seeing me?' There was silence from Becca's end of the phone so Jakes continued.

'I need to ask you a few questions. May I come in?'

'That other detective asked me questions,' Becca said, her voice flat.

'I know, but I need to clarify a few points with you, if I may?'

The line went dead and he was about to press the buzzer again when the door clicked open. As he entered, a front door opened to his right, roughly where the cat had disappeared into the building. Rebecca Martin stood, dressed in flannel pyjamas and big furry slippers, her hair spiked to within an inch of its life and her skin, so pale he could almost see straight through it.

'Are you all right?' he asked, genuine concern in his voice.

'I guess,' Becca said. 'I think I've just got a touch of food poisoning or something.' Becca showed him into the living room and his gaze fixed on the sticky mess and broken glass near to the patio doors.

'What happened here?' he pointed and Becca glanced at the debris she had yet to clean up.

'Nothing,' she said. 'Would you like a drink?' She turned her emerald eyes on Jakes and he was rocked by the emptiness he saw there.

'Black coffee, three sugars,' he said and sat down on the leather sofa as she left the room. In her absence he glanced around and was impressed by the simplicity and warmth of the room, decorated in complimentary shades of coffee and cream. He settled back and studied a photograph on the wall. In it, two equally happy and smiling women, whom he presumed to be her mother and grandmother, flanked a happy, smiling young Rebecca. All were dressed up as witches.

As he stared at the picture he felt something rub around his legs and glanced down to see the grey cat depositing fur on his trousers. He smiled and rubbed the cat behind the ears and was rewarded with a purr. He heard footsteps and looked up.

'What a beautiful cat,' he said. 'What's his name?'

'Spook,' Becca said, but as she drew close to him, Jakes felt the cat stiffen. Once she had passed, Spook darted out of the cat flap in the patio doors.

'Wow, has he been misbehaving or something?'

'What? Oh, no..,' Becca said glancing towards the patio doors. 'He's been behaving oddly all day, ever since I woke up on the kitchen floor and found...' Becca drifted off.

'What were you doing on the kitchen floor?'

'Nothing. What can I do for you, Inspector?' she said, playing with a dressing on her neck.

'What have you done to your neck?'

'Oh, just some insect bites. I always react badly to them.' Becca looked at him and he thought he saw fear flit across her eyes.

'Inspector?' Becca prompted, snapping him back to the present.

'Sorry, Ms Martin...'

'Becca, I'd rather you called me, Becca.'

'Okay, Becca. I wanted to establish exactly where you were last night.'

'I told the other guy I was here,'

'What? All night?'

'Well, yeah, most of it, after I got home from college.'

'College? What do you do at college?'

'I teach. Art.'

'What time did you get home?'

'Oh, I don't know. Probably about nine thirty. That's what time I usually get home.' Becca nodded in confirmation.

'What did you do for the rest of the evening?' Jakes scribbled in his notebook. The room had gone silent and he looked up to see tears running down Becca's cheeks.

'Hey, don't cry,' he said, fishing a handkerchief out of his pocket and handing it to her. 'Tell me what happened when you got home.'

'That's just it,' she said, a sob escaping her throat. 'I don't remember all of it.'

'Well, tell me what you remember and we'll take it from there.'

'I told you, I don't remember, didn't I?' Becca's clenched fists thumped the sofa as she stared at him.

'Okay, okay, just calm down, Becca.'

'I am calm,' Becca said, rubbing at the dressing on her neck.

'I think you should take the dressing off and let the air get to it.'

'I don't care what you think,' Becca said through gritted teeth. She jumped up off the sofa and started pacing back and forth.

Jakes watched her unexpected agitated behaviour. Her gaze flitted this way and that, never resting on anything for more than a few seconds. Her fists clenched and unclenched in a steady rhythm, like a metronome. *She's got to be on something,* Jakes thought, not for the first time.

'Tell me what's happened,' he said as he tried to keep his voice as neutral as possible so as not to irritate her.

'What makes you think anything has happened?' She rounded on him and the look in her eyes made him pull back. The once bright emerald green were now dead onyx pools and Jakes felt the hairs rise on the back of his neck as she stared at him.

'D-d-do you mind if I look around?' he said, all of a sudden wanting to be anywhere other than under that gaze.

'Knock yourself out,' Becca said and turned to stare out of the patio windows. He studied her for a minute. He watched her crouch down, her hands clenched like claws, and hiss through the window. As Jakes shifted his gaze to see what she was hissing at, he saw Spook on the other side of the glass, hunched down; ears back flat against his head.

'I thought you wanted to poke around, Inspector?' she said as she stood up and turned to face him, her black eyes boring into him.

'I-I-I'm just going,' he said and left the room.

Jakes wandered into the hallway and, as all the doors were closed, he picked the first one on his left. The kitchen. He walked in and studied his surroundings. The floor was white smooth tiles, a large American style fridge freezer in brushed aluminium faced him and white units ran the length of the kitchen either side, topped with grey, white and black speckled worktops. To the right of the door, a round glass table stood with four chrome chairs, enjoying a beautiful view of the gardens through double glazed patio doors. Next to the patio doors was a cupboard, which took up the space behind the units on the right. He didn't see any appliances and correctly assumed them to be built in to the units. The chrome rubbish bin stood in the corner near the door and Jakes flipped open the lid to see an empty steak packet lying on the top.

He let the lid close and he scoured the work surfaces. His gaze rested on the counter top to his right, where he saw what appeared to be blood on the edge. He bent to get a closer look and fumbled in his coat pocket for one of the swab kits he carried there, just in case. Taking care, he wiped the cotton wool swab over the dried blood and then inserted it into the safety of its casing. He marked the tube with the date, time and place and then let his gaze drop to the floor, where he found a small puddle of what also appeared to be dried blood. Unsure as to whether it had the same origin as the sample he had already taken, he took another swab.

Jakes walked further into the kitchen and scrutinised the other work surface. He bent down lower so he could get a better look and thought he saw faint finger marks in blood on the edge. He also saw little droplets of blood, which could have come from the meat container he had seen in the rubbish. He swabbed both areas.

He walked out of the kitchen and was about to open the next door when he heard a voice behind him.

'That's my art room,' Becca said. 'But you can go in if you like. The bathroom's over there,' she said and indicated the door opposite, 'and the other door is my bedroom. Would you like another coffee?'

'Err, yes, that would be lovely, thanks,' Jakes said. He tried to look in her eyes, but she kept them cast downwards, so he crossed the hall to the bathroom door. He walked in the room and was amazed by what he saw. It was almost like he'd walked into a dungeon, but a cosy one. The room was completely tiled, including the ceiling, with granite coloured tiles. A small window and a vent decorated the far wall. He switched the light on and the ceiling illuminated with a dozen tiny down lighters. In the centre of the room was a huge freestanding bath and there were candles mounted on floating shelves on the walls. A double heated towel rail adorned one wall. Jakes didn't think he'd ever seen such a beautiful room.

'Coffee's ready,' Becca called and Jakes snapped back to what he'd come in here for. He turned towards the sink on his right and scanned the bowl, but saw no signs of blood. He reached beneath the sink and picked up the rubbish bin. He lifted the lid and saw several balls of cotton wool, all with a pinkish red tinge to them. He extracted one and dropped it into a plastic evidence bag, which he sealed and marked before stuffing it in his pocket with the swabs.

Jakes replaced the bin and went to re-join Becca in the living room.

CHAPTER 20

Jakes took the cup of coffee out of Becca's shaking hands and studied her pale face. Her eyes briefly met his and he saw that the emerald green had returned; tarnished though with something he didn't recognise.

'Tell me what happened last night, Becca.'

'I-I-I've already told you, Inspector. I don't remember.'

'I think you do.' Jakes studied her as he sipped his coffee. Becca was looking down at her lap, the handkerchief he'd given her twisted tightly around her fingers, her knuckles white.

'Take your time,' Jakes said and when Becca looked up at him, he saw real fear in her eyes.

'I-I don't really know how to explain..,' she drifted off again and twisted her feet inwards to face each other, like an uncertain child. Jakes decided not to speak; she would tell him in her own time. He picked up his coffee and began to drink as Becca continued to stare at the knotted hankie in her hands. He heard the cat flap rattle and glanced up to see Spook dragging himself through it. The cat walked over to sit in front of the fireplace and stared at Becca, as though he too was waiting for an explanation.

'I was so tired when I got home, what with everything that has been happening to me, that I went to bed, but I couldn't sleep. Well, I was asleep but I wasn't. You know the kind of sleep I mean, when you must be asleep, but you remember everything that's going on?' She looked up at him at that point and he nodded, not wanting his voice to interrupt her train of thought.

Her gaze dropped down to the hankie, which she was now patting down flat on her lap.

'God, the dreams I was having were so clear and vivid at the time; that it was like I was actually living it, not dreaming it. But I can't for the life of me remember what they were now. All I know is that they scared the shit out of me and something happened in them that woke me up, but I can't remember what.' Becca went quiet again and Jakes watched her, as her brow knitted and her fists squeezed into tight balls and then she relaxed again.

'It's no good,' she said. 'I can't remember. I woke up though and, man, I was thirsty. I have never felt thirst like it, but it wasn't thirst for a drink, it was for something else. That's the last thing I remember until I woke up on the kitchen floor.' She sat up straight and exhaled deeply, as though by telling him this, she had purged herself of something.

'So, you can't remember what you did to quench your thirst?' Jakes asked.

'No, nothing.'

'You didn't go into the bathroom to get water?'

'No, I told you, it wasn't that kind of thirst and besides, I always have a glass of water next to my bed.'

'Describe the thirst to me.'

'Oh, I don't know,' Becca said. 'It's almost impossible to describe. It's more like a hunger than a thirst, I guess. Like you're hungry, but it's not food you want, it's a drink. But it's not a drink like water, juice or alcohol. It's something else, but I don't know what.' Becca thumped her knees in frustration and then started rubbing at the dressing on her neck again.

'I really do think you should let the air get to that.'

'Trust me, it doesn't help.' But she took the dressing off anyway. Jakes stared at the wounds on her neck. They were raw and inflamed and were exactly the same as those on the body in the crypt. Jakes decided not to mention them yet, he would get to that.

'So, tell me about when you woke up on the kitchen floor.'

'What do you mean?'

'Well, describe to me how you felt, what you saw, what you did.'

'Oh, yeah, sorry. Mmm, well I woke up and I was slumped on the floor. I guess I must have fallen.'

'What makes you say that?' Jakes interrupted.

'Because I'd gashed my head,' Becca replied, indicating a blemish free expanse of skin.

'Forgive me, Becca, but there is no cut anywhere on your head.'

'What? There must be.' Becca rushed into the hallway to look in the mirror.

'There was this morning, Inspector, I swear to you, because I had blood on my fingers when I touched it and my head hurt like a bitch…' Becca stopped in her tracks for a minute, as though she had remembered something, but then she came and sat down.

'What is it?' Jakes asked.

'Nothing much, just that when I was cleaning the wound this morning, it almost seemed like it had started healing.'

'How do you mean?'

'Well, once I had cleaned the blood off it there was no more oozing out, no redness or bruising, only a clean thin line. I thought I'd got off lightly.

As I said, when I tried to move, my head really hurt. I saw that the fridge door was open and that there was an open packet of meat on the counter which, when I managed to drag myself to my feet, I saw was empty. Oh, and then there was Spook and that's it. The phone rang, I answered and it was Dick. I got dressed and went to the site.' Becca leaned into the sofa then.

'What about Spook?'

'He was acting all weird. He wouldn't come near me and when I tried to go near him, he hissed at me and ran off.'

'And he's only been acting like this today?'

'Well, yeah, although he has been watching me a lot these last few days.'

'What do you mean?'

'You know, just sitting and staring at me. It kind of creeps me out.'

'What about this empty packet of meat then? You or the cat?'

'What do you think, Inspector?'

'Well, I…' Jakes broke off as a shadow loomed over him. He looked up to find Becca leaning over him, the tip of her tongue tracing the outline of her lips, her eyes dark pools once again.

'I think that will do for now,' he said and slid away from her. He stood up and straightened his coat and went to leave the room, only to find her centimetres away from him. He hadn't seen or heard her move.

'Are you all right, Inspector?' she asked, her head cocked to one side, her index finger caressing his neck.

'I'm f-f-fine. I just have to be somewhere,' he said and marched towards the front door. He turned before he left and his heart lurched. Becca was standing in the living room doorway, toes turned in, hankie twisted between her hands, eyes downcast.

'I'll be in touch,' he said. Becca nodded and fixed him with her black stare, a wicked smile on her face.

The door slammed behind him and Becca collapsed onto the floor.

CHAPTER 21

Becca groaned as she opened her eyes. She couldn't feel her legs. She pushed herself up and back so she was sitting, taking the weight off her lower limbs. As she did so, the prickling sensation started and she screwed her face up against the discomfort, as she rubbed her legs to help the blood recirculate.

Once feeling had returned, she pulled herself up using the doorframe for support and crept over to the sofa and sat down. The sun, in its descent, bathed the room in a warm orange glow, the same shade as the two eyes that were fixed on her. Spook still held his spot in front of the fireplace, the same spot he had occupied when Inspector Jakes had been there.

'Oh, God!' Becca groaned. *What on earth was he going to think of her?* At the very least he'd think she was on drugs, the way she'd talked to him and more importantly what she'd told him. At least she'd held back from the really juicy stuff. She shook her head and flopped against the cushions, feeling the heat rise in her cheeks as she remembered what she'd told him. She also remembered several dark periods, one of which resulted in the pins and needles she was still recovering from. *What had happened to her?* She replayed Jake's visit, trying to remember the first black spot.

He had been telling her to take the dressing off her neck and she remembered feeling a rush of anger and then nothing. The next thing she remembered was finding him looking around her apartment. Then it had happened again, but this time he had been asking who had eaten the raw meat – the implication clearly being her. When she woke up, a few minutes ago, she was alone in a heap on the floor.

As she thought about the marks on her neck, she felt a flash of heat surge through her body and her vision clouded. That was what had happened earlier, when Jakes was with her and then she'd… Becca's hand fluttered up to cover her gaping mouth and her stomach flipped as the dark period suddenly became light. *Oh no*, she thought, she'd all but threatened a police officer that afternoon, for absolutely no reason.

Becca wracked her brain trying to fix on some trigger point for her "flip out", but she couldn't. Her mind settled on the marks and the steak. She felt the heat rise in her body and her vision start to cloud. She rushed into the hallway and looked in the mirror and screamed. Staring back at her was the blackest set of eyes she'd ever seen.

CHAPTER 22

It's got to be drugs, Jakes thought to himself, as he drove back to the station. *What else could explain the apparent switching between personalities that he'd witnessed that afternoon? Schizophrenia?* He dismissed that thought. Something in his gut said it wasn't right and his gut was usually spot on.

'What about drugs then?' he glanced down at his protruding stomach, but got no response.

Drugs would explain the state she was in when she arrived at the site earlier that day. Or, should he say, a major come down from a binge could explain it and would most likely have still been affecting her that afternoon. He had a feeling though, his gut starting to churn, that drugs weren't the answer either, not conventional drugs anyway. After all, he'd never heard of any that could change the colour of someone's eyes. He shuddered as he remembered the blackness of Becca's eyes when she'd acted out. He'd give Jan a call when he got to the station. She'd know. Jan knew everything. A warm feeling flooded his body as he thought of her and he smiled.

Jakes entered the squad room ten minutes later and looked around for Robinson. He was nowhere to be seen; his desk an oasis of calm amidst the chaos going on in the rest of the room. Jakes marvelled at how his partner managed to achieve this and suspected it was probably OCD.

He continued on to his own office, slamming the door behind him, and walked around his desk and settled himself into his worn leather chair. Jakes faced the glowing screen in front of him, took a deep breath and called up a search engine.

'So far, so good,' he said and typed in the words *drugs that change eye colour* and hit the return key. Thousands of hits. A quick scan of the first few pages only served to increase his heart rate and cause him to slacken his tie.

'Dammit!' Jakes thumped his desk with his fist and grabbed the phone.

'Jan, it's Jakes. I've got…'

'Well, good evening, Frank. You haven't been to see me in a while. How are you?'

'Yes, I'm good thanks, I…' He felt the flush creeping up his neck at the sound of her smoky voice.

'I miss your little visits, you know.' Jan filled the silence and chuckled, her throaty laugh sending shivers through Jakes' body.

'Look, I'd love to chat.' Jakes regained his composure and focused on what he was calling her for. 'It's just that I'm in the middle of something and I could do with picking that vast brain of yours.'

'Oh, I'm sorry, yes of course,' Jan said, her voice snapping into the authoritative business voice that stirred things deep inside him; things he'd thought long dead. 'What is it you need to know, Frank?' Jan prompted after the line had gone silent for a while.

'Oh, yes, well, there's this case and… well, to cut a long story short, do you know of any drug that can change a person's eye colour?'

'Well, there are cases of eye colour changing with some medicines, but…'

'Not prescription drugs, Jan, narcotics?'

'Not that I've heard of. I could do some research, if you need it. Why?'

'Well, I was questioning a witness who'd been acting a bit weird, as if she was high, and she seemed to completely change personalities in a matter of seconds, her eyes turning black as coal. It lasted a short while and then she returned to normal, seemingly unaware of what had happened to her.'

'Sounds more like something out of *The Exorcist*, Frank.' Jan laughed again, making his insides churn.

'What do you mean?' he said, realising too late that he had been a bit sharp with her. What she had said, though, had flipped a switch in his brain; a switch that had been flicking on and off since he'd been called to the Ramply Homes site earlier.

'...well, you're the horror nut, Frank, you should know these things. Eyes changing colour are quite common in these films, sometimes it's the only way us poor unsuspecting mugs can tell that the character is a monster....'

Jakes had stopped listening, lost in his thoughts.

'Thanks, Jan. I've got some bloods I'd like you to run for me, so I'll see you shortly.' She was still talking as he replaced the receiver.

He leaned back in his chair, sifting through his repertoire of horror films in his mind, calling up as many films about possession and vampires as he could. Where had vampires come from? His mind was connecting some dots – the eye colour change, the bite marks – when the ringing of the phone brought him back to reality. He shook his head to clear his thoughts and laughed to himself. He must be going mad too, but his gut didn't seem to think so.

'Jakes,' he said when he picked up the receiver.

'Errmm, hello, Inspector Jakes. It's Becca Martin.'

'Hello, Miss Martin, what can I...'

'Becca, please. Look, errmm, I wanted to apologise for my behaviour this afternoon. I don't know what came over me. I think what's happened over the last few days has..,' she broke off and Jakes was about to jump in when she continued.

'Anyway, you never did ask me what you came to ask about, did you?'

'And what was that?' he said, his mind on her comment about events over the "last few days".

'Well, you came to ask me about what went on at the site this morning, didn't you?'

'Ahh, yes, that's right.'

'Well, if I haven't scared you off, please feel free to come back...if you're brave enough.'

Jakes pulled the phone away from his ear, as the dial tone sounded, and stared at it.

CHAPTER 23

What a day, thought Jim Smith as he climbed into his car and relaxed. As if the police invading the site hadn't been enough, but then the press had turned up and had badgered them for most of the day, thrusting microphones into everyone's face, asking questions no one could answer. The icing on the cake, though, had been the weather. It had been raining nonstop all day and he was soaked. Despite his waterproofs, the blasted rain had found a suitable gap and he'd had no change of clothes. *Yep, lousy day.*

He closed his eyes and rested his head against his headrest. Every bone in his body ached; every muscle was taught. An image of Amanda giving him a deep sensual massage crept into his mind and he smiled. *Not much chance of that anymore,* he thought, as two screaming five year olds hurtled into his fantasy. Not since the twins were born, anyway. Jim opened his eyes and smiled at the faces in the photograph pinned to his dashboard. Two white blonde heads with gappy grins and intense blue eyes were on either side of his wife of ten years. Amanda's sapphire eyes smiled at the camera as she rested her head on Sam's and had her arm draped around Jack.

Jim did his customary pre-departure check – keys, wallet, lunch-box. *Damn!* He knew he'd forgotten something. He opened the car door and eased himself out. God, he was tired. Still, if he didn't take it home, Amanda would go mad.

He trudged back towards the church, but as he passed the entrance to the crypt he thought he heard a noise. It was difficult to hear due to the hammering rain, so he stopped and listened. Sure enough, coming from the crypt, he heard grating noises. Jim squinted through the rain looking for the officer on duty, but couldn't see him. *Probably sneaked off for a coffee and a fag,* he thought and didn't blame him.

Jim was about to go and track the officer down, when he heard the grating noise echoing up from the bowels of the church. It seemed a shame for them both to get soaked when it was probably one of those damn reporters. He decided to check it out first. Jim ducked under the crime scene tape and pushed open the door at the top of the stairs.

'Oi! You lot! Get the hell out of here now!' he shouted. Jim stood still for what seemed like hours and listened, but the basement was silent. Not a shuffle, not a scrape, not a sound. He grabbed the torch out of his utility belt and descended the stairs. He'd find the sneaky bastards. As he descended, he let the beam of light explore the various crevasses of the room, but it found nothing. Finally, the beam hit the sarcophagus.

'How the hell..,' said Jim and let his voice trail off as he walked over to the huge stone casket. The lid was wide open. Jim leaned over and shone his torch inside, but it was empty. He stepped back and walked around to the other side, his interest in any intruders now long gone. He rested all his weight against the lid and pushed, but it didn't move an inch. He tried again, using every ounce of his strength.

'You won't be able to move it,' a deep voice sounded behind him and Jim thought he was going to have a heart attack. He whirled round to see a tall dark haired man standing behind him.

'Who the hell are you?' Jim said, more than a little unnerved by the stranger's deep-set eyes and threatening stance.

'My name is Antony Cardover,' Antony said and extended his hand, but Jim didn't take it. He just stared at him.

'What are you doing down here?' Jim's composure was crumbling as his torch highlighted the chalky white pallor of Antony's skin.

'I reside here.'

'What…?'

'In that sarcophagus. That is, I did reside here.'

Before Jim could ask any more questions, Antony gripped him around the throat and lifted him off the floor. Jim heard his spine protest as the full weight of his two hundred pounds was borne by his neck. He yelped as a sharp stab in the side of his throat caused his pulse to double its speed and he felt his eyes begin to bulge as a warm liquid started to trickle down his neck. Jim stared in horror as Antony licked blood, his blood, from the thumb whose sharp nail had pierced his artery. He tried to fight back, the picture of his family forefront in his mind, as Antony pulled him closer, but, to his horror, he found he was paralysed. He tried to scream, but it was muffled as two sharp objects punctured the skin on his neck.

Jim heard his heart thundering in his chest as his blood pounded round his body. He tried to move his head, to drag it away from the animal that was tearing at his flesh, but he couldn't. Antony held him fast. The pain ebbed through Jim's body causing a sweat to break out. He started to feel woozy and blinked repeatedly to clear his vision, but it was no good. He was numb, anaesthetised almost and his vision was becoming cloudier. Soon black and white dots sprang before his eyes and tears slid down his face as he whispered goodbye to his family.

Antony flung the body to the floor, blood dripping from his chin. The red cells coursed through his veins. At last, his strength was enough. He marched up the steps and out of the church. He followed the path to the edge of the churchyard and as he crossed the boundary, it was as if he had burst through a transparent screen. The earth seemed to shudder as he passed back into the population.

CHAPTER 24

Becca sat on the sofa staring out of the patio windows at the darkening evening, when she shuddered and her vision clouded. A moment later her eyesight cleared, but she was left with a heavy feeling in the pit of her stomach. Something was very wrong, she knew this, but she didn't know why.

She glanced at the clock. It was almost seven in the evening. It didn't look like the Inspector was going to come back. Becca sighed and looked at the phone she'd been cradling in her hands. She stared at it, her face expressionless and watched as her thumbs punched in the numbers. She then put the phone to her ear and waited. It was answered immediately.

'Rebecca?' an agitated voice said.

'Yeah, Mum, it's me,' replied Becca. A long awkward silence followed. Becca's mind drifted to the day she'd left, ten years before. The last time she'd seen her mother.

Ginnie Martin had remained downstairs after Becca had stormed off. As she'd thumped down the stairs dragging a hefty suitcase behind her, Ginnie had been standing next to the front door; her arms folded; her expression closed; her eyes cold. Becca's heart had sunk. She had loved her mother intensely. She'd loved the wiry red hair, which had always seemed in need of a good pair of scissors; she'd loved her paint-spattered clothes; she'd even loved her wacky ideas and her equally wacky friends. But what she'd loved most of all had been her mother's fairness and her ability not to judge. Yet, judging is exactly what she'd done and all because Becca hadn't wanted to be a witch. Christ, she had had enough problems trying to fit in without all that. It had been as if her mother had been obsessed with the need for her to become a witch. Becca had never been able to understand why and she'd been damned if she was going to ask.

'Are you sure this is what you want?' Becca had said as she'd faced Ginnie.

'I want you to accept who you are, Rebecca. It's you that has chosen, not me.'

'Whatever,' Becca had said and had then walked out.

She hadn't seen or heard from her mother until this week.

'Rebecca? Are you still there?' Ginnie said, her voice high and tight.

'What do you want, Mum?'

'I want you to come and see me immediately.'

'Why?'

'Because there is something I need to tell you, something I should have told you a long time ago.'

'Why can't you tell me now, over the phone?'

'I'd rather do it face to face.'

'But…'

'No buts, Rebecca. Just come. Tomorrow.' With that, the line went dead.

Becca put the phone down and let her gaze drift to the photograph of her, her mother and her grandmother. Absently, she fingered the delicate chain around her neck, which carried a small key. The key fitted a box, a box her grandmother had given her on her sixteenth birthday.

The snap of the cat flap broke her reverie and she watched Spook come in and sit a safe distance from her.

'Tea time is it, buddy?' she asked and his ears pricked up. 'C'mon then.' Becca pushed herself off the sofa and wandered towards the kitchen. She felt a little tug at her heart when he didn't come and weave in and out of her legs, as was customary. Instead, he waited until she had left the room and then he followed.

Becca filled his bowl with biscuits, but he waited in the doorway until she'd moved away before going to eat. She decided to ignore his behaviour. He'd come round eventually. She wandered over to the fridge and studied the contents. She grabbed some eggs, some mushrooms and some cheese and started to make herself an omelette. Her mind drifted to the key around her neck and, in turn, to her sixteenth birthday. The day she'd first learned of its existence.

Becca had lain awake, staring out at the azure sky through the half open curtains. Birthdays had been just another day for Becca. She had had no real friends and so hadn't had anyone to share her day with, no one to have fun with and, more specifically, no one to invite to a party. Not that her mother had ever offered to throw her a party anyway. Ginnie Martin had never agreed with children's parties. As far as she had been concerned, they'd just been an excuse for children to behave atrociously and eat junk food without getting into trouble and that, in Ginnie's book, had been unacceptable. As a result, Becca had never been allowed to go to any. This had been one of the reasons she had never had any friends. The other had been her family or, more specifically, her family history. It had been no secret in Carlford, that Becca's grandmother had been a witch. Although the adults of the town had frequently gone to see her to cure various ailments, the younger generation had treated her with contempt. She had always been a target for practical jokers, but for some reason it had never bothered her. Instead, she had played them at their own game. Halloween had always been a particular favourite for the pranksters, but Rosalind had always given as good as she'd got, casting temporary spells on her persecutors.

Becca's solitude had stemmed from people's fear of what she was and of what she could do. The eternal ignorance and misunderstanding of witchcraft had made people afraid of her. Having no friends hadn't really bothered Becca that much. She had always enjoyed her own company and her hobbies were all ones she could do alone. Still, it would have been nice to have had someone she could talk to, Becca had mused, as she'd lain in bed that morning, hoping her mother had got her what she had asked for. She heard a soft knock at the door.

'Come in,' she had said and had pushed herself up into a sitting position.

'Good morning, darling. Happy sixteenth birthday,' Ginnie had said, as she'd placed a tray laden with melon, cereal, toast, orange juice and tea on Becca's knee. She'd planted a kiss on Becca's forehead and then she'd gone over and opened the curtains and the window.

'It's such a beautiful day. How about we go for a long walk later?' Ginnie had said, but Becca hadn't answered.

'So, how does it feel to be sixteen then?' Ginnie hadn't questioned Becca's silence. She'd turned to look at her daughter, but Becca had simply shrugged her shoulders.

'Well, I'm sure it will be a lovely day,' she'd continued, undeterred. 'Now, eat your breakfast and then come downstairs and open your presents. Your grandmother will be here shortly.' With that, Ginnie had left Becca alone.

Becca had wolfed her breakfast down and had got dressed as quickly as she could, a small ripple of birthday excitement finally weaving through her veins. She had bounced downstairs and had almost stood on Tilly, their big fat black cat, who had always slept along one of the steps.

'One day, Tilly,' Becca had said as she'd ruffled the cat's ears. Tilly had merely opened one eye, yawned and then had closed it again.

'I swear that cat gets lazier every day,' Becca had said as she'd walked into the kitchen. 'Thanks for breakfast, Mum.' She'd given her mother a kiss on the cheek.

'You're welcome. I don't suppose you thought to bring your tray back down?'

'Err, no, sorry, I forgot,' Becca had said, picking at some grapes on the counter. 'I'll get it later. When's grandma coming?'

'She's here. She's in the living room. I'm making some tea and then we can start your birthday properly,' Ginnie had said with a twinkle in her eye. 'You take the cups and I'll bring the rest.'

Becca had picked up the tray and had taken it into the living room. Her grandmother had been standing by the patio doors that led to the untidy and overgrown garden.

'Hi, Grandma.' Becca had set the tray on the cluttered coffee table and had gone to hug her grandmother.

'Ah, happy birthday, Becca, dear. How do you feel today?' Rosalind had held her grand-daughter at arm's length to look at her.

'The same as any other day.' She'd always marvelled at how young and spry her grandmother had been. Although she'd been sixty-five back then, she'd looked ten years younger. Her rich auburn hair had always been tied back in a bun and she'd always worn trousers and twin sets. She'd reminded Becca of Audrey Hepburn. She had been so poised and proper, *unlike her daughter*, Becca had thought, as Ginnie, all unkempt and harassed, had come into the room.

'Right, shall we start then?' Ginnie had said, clapping her hands together. 'Mum?' She'd looked at Rosalind, who had come and sat on the old sofa next to Becca.

'What's going on?' Becca had said, an uneasy feeling settling over her.

'Now that you're sixteen, there are things that you need to understand about who you are,' Ginnie had said and had then fallen silent.

'What do you mean "who I am"?' Becca had said, her insides tight.

'Becca, sweetheart, it's nothing to be worried about,' Rosalind had said. 'It won't come as a big surprise as you are already aware of me.'

'So, you're trying to tell me I'm a witch?'

'Yes, we are,' Rosalind had said.

'Well, that's hardly a surprise, is it? I mean, I've spent most of my life being picked on because of it, so I'd always assumed I was.'

'Well, that's good. Ginnie, can you get the trunk, please.'

'What do you mean "that's good"? It just confirms the fact that I'm a freak,' Becca had jumped up and turned to face them.

'Rebecca, sit down!' Rosalind had said and Becca had obeyed and stared, wide-eyed, as her mother had dragged an ancient looking chest into the middle of the room.

'What the hell is that?'

'Language, Rebecca,' Ginnie had said.

'That,' Rosalind had started, casting a warning look to her daughter, 'contains your ancestry, your heritage and now that you are of age, it is time that it became yours.'

'Time what became mine?'

'This, my dear,' Rosalind had said as she'd opened the trunk. 'It was passed to me by my grandmother and to her by her grandmother and now I am passing it to you.'

Becca had peered inside the trunk, her curiosity having got the better of her, and had dropped to her knees and started rummaging around inside it.

'Why haven't you given this to Mum?'

'The gift doesn't endow each generation. Unfortunately, your mother isn't lucky enough to have those powers, but you do.'

'What powers?' Becca had asked as she'd dragged a heavy leather book out of the trunk.

'The powers to cast those.' Rosalind had indicated the book. Becca had opened it up to find pages and pages of what had appeared to be, to her, cooking instructions.

'What are they?'

'Oh, for God's sake, Rebecca!' Ginnie had said.

'It's a book of spells, rituals and charms,' Rosalind had said, silencing Ginnie with a wave of her hand. 'Or, should I say, it is "THE" book. It is known as the *Book of Shadows* or the *Grimoire*.' Becca had regarded her grandmother and raised her eyebrows in amusement.

'I suppose it's the equivalent of the Oxford English Dictionary. It contains all the spells that have ever been written and tried, and some that have never been used. It is many centuries old and has been handed down through our family.'

'How do you know?' Becca had said as she'd caressed the parchment of the pages and gazed at the intricate script.

'I don't for certain,' Rosalind had said. 'It's just that our family is one of the oldest families in the country to have ties to the Craft. The inscription in the back of the book indicates that it is, at least, one of the first copies.'

'What time have we got to meet the others?' Ginnie had interrupted.

'Oh, not until three,' Rosalind had said.

'Meet who?' Becca had asked, pulling a black cloak out of the trunk.

'The rest of the coven. Now, the cloak, your mother and I made especially for you, for your induction.'

'What coven? What induction?' Becca had said; the trunk forgotten.

'Well, I am a member of a coven, as are all practising witches. As you are now of age, you can join the coven and begin to learn the craft you have been born into.'

'What? And wear this? The Halloween costume? I don't think so.' She'd thrown the cloak back into the trunk. 'What if I don't want to be a witch?' she'd stared at her grandmother defiantly.

'Rebecca! How dare you!' Ginnie had said.

'It's all right, Virginia. Becca is only in shock. She will be fine,' Rosalind had said and had taken Becca's hand. 'Look at me, Rebecca.' Becca had obeyed. 'You will come with me to meet the coven this afternoon and then we will go out for your birthday meal, as planned. Okay?' Becca had nodded.

'There is one last thing I need to make you aware of and then I will leave you to go through the rest of the trunk at your leisure,' Rosalind had said as she'd handed Becca a cup of tea. 'Here, drink this while I find it.'

Becca had taken the cup and saucer from her grandmother and had watched as Rosalind had knelt before the trunk and sifted through its contents.

'Ah, here it is,' she'd said and had pulled out a dusty wooden box.

Becca had stared at the box and had put her tea down and reached for it, believing it to be some kind of music or jewellery box. She had wiped the dust away with her fingers to reveal intricate carvings on the sides and some sort of writing on the lid. As she'd tilted the box to get a better look at the writing, her grandmother had dampened her hopes.

'Don't ever open it, Becca,' she'd said. 'Not unless the time is right.'

Becca had stopped studying the box and had turned to her grandmother.

'What do you mean, "don't open it"?'

'Exactly what I said.'

'What's the point in giving me a present if I can't open it?' Becca had been more than a little disappointed in her birthday so far.

'It's not really a present, sweetheart,' Ginnie had said. 'None of it is. It's more an endowment from your grandmother to you.'

'But, it's my birthday,' she'd said as tears had slid down her cheeks.

'I'm aware of that, Becca, and we'll get to that soon, but first I need you to listen,' Rosalind had said, in her no-nonsense voice. 'The box must not be opened until the time is right and…'

'But, when is that?'

'You will know when, Becca. The inscription on the lid states that "you will know when". I sincerely hope it doesn't come in your lifetime, but if it does, everything you need is in that box.'

'Need to know about what?'

Rosalind and Ginnie had exchanged a look and Becca had seen Ginnie shake her head.

'What?' Becca had said.

'That's a story for another day,' Rosalind had said and had taken the box from her and had put it in her bag.

'You will get it once I am gone,' she'd said in response to Becca's astonished look. 'Along with this,' she'd continued, revealing a small key on a chain around her neck. 'Until then, it is my responsibility. In the meantime, you have a lot to learn. Now, on with the real birthday presents.'

She shook her head as she remembered that day. There was nothing like having your mind blown, in one sitting. *What had happened to that chest?* Becca wondered. It must be at her mother's with the little box.

She took her omelette over to the table, perched on the edge of her chair and started to eat, her mind still logged into the past. She stared outside and watched Spook as she absently ate her food.

Suddenly, she froze, her fork halfway to her mouth, her breath caught in her chest. She stared at Spook as he cowered down in the garden, his ears back, his teeth bared. The hairs on the back of Becca's neck were now upright and she shivered, as a sudden draught wrapped itself around her. She caught the scent of him as the draught moved through her towards the patio doors and she saw a dark shadow advance towards the threatened cat. The fork dropped from her hand as she raced towards the patio doors. She yanked the handle, but it was locked. She fumbled for the key. She always left it in the lock. It wasn't there.

'Noooooo!' she screamed as the shadowy figure crouched down in front of Spook and leaned in really close to him.

'Leave him alone!' Becca shouted and banged on the glass, hoping to scare Spook, but it was almost like he was in a trance. He didn't move a muscle. He didn't even try to lash out.

Becca picked up a chair and smashed it as hard as she could against the glass, but it bounced off. She dropped to the floor sobbing as she watched the figure reach out towards Spook. Suddenly the cat took off and the figure stood up and stared at Becca.

'Noooooo!' Becca screamed again, as she stared into the eyes of Antony Cardover.

CHAPTER 25

Antony stood on the pavement outside the cemetery and breathed deeply, pulling fresh air into his non-functioning lungs. Old habits, he mused, as he stared around him. Never had he thought he would have the chance of freedom again. Never, not since his showdown with Anna. Not for the first time, he wondered what had happened to the feisty old woman. Antony thought back to that night, the night he had assumed would be his route to freedom, but which had instead turned into his route to hell.

In the end he'd stayed away for over a year, a lot longer than he'd intended. He'd needed to. He'd had to get control of himself and his thirst. He'd partially succeeded, but his anger had still burned as brightly as the day he'd been betrayed. He hadn't been able to stand it any longer and had known that the only cure would be revenge. So he'd returned to the village of his betrayal, a year to the day since he'd left.

He'd worn a cloak with a large hood that shielded him from prying eyes and had seated himself in a corner of the Inn to observe. Nothing had changed. The same drunken faces had been littered about the place and he'd smiled in satisfaction to see that the old warlock had been right – his enemies had indeed returned.

His anger had flared as he'd watched the ease with which they'd been laughing and joking, without any care in the world. *Well, that was about to change*, he'd thought and a smile of satisfaction had lit up his ashen face.

He'd waited patiently, safely hidden away in a dark corner, until they'd all left and then he'd left as he had one more place to visit before he'd been able to begin. Antony had needed to make sure that she was there, so that his redemption could be completed.

It hadn't taken him long. Their cottage had been away from the village, so he had known that Anna and Isabella would never be able to hear what he was going to do to the rest of the villagers. He'd needed to see her, to make sure she'd been there because he could never get his life back without her. He'd kept to the edges of the woods as he'd made his way to Anna's, so as not to be seen.

The cottage had seemed the same as he'd remembered. Nothing had changed. It had still been ramshackle and about to fall down and he'd remembered promising Anna that he would fix the place up for her. He'd shrugged at the memory and had sidled up to the window at the side of the house, which looked into the parlour. He'd seen Anna asleep in a chair in front of the fire, a cat curled up on her lap. He'd strained his neck to see if anyone else was in the room, but there hadn't been. He'd leaned against the boarding of the house and had started to reconstruct the plan in his mind, when he'd heard footsteps and her voice calling Anna. He'd glanced through the window just in time to see Isabella wake Anna.

For a moment he'd simply stared at his wife, a smile across his lips, awed as always by her beauty. She'd moved so gracefully. The gentle line of her neck, her full lips, her dark eyes and her mass of black curls had all brought back memories for him. Memories of happier times. Times when things had been good between them, before she'd… He'd thumped the side of the house at the thought of her betrayal and had scarcely managed to duck out of sight as both women had looked towards the window.

That had been too close and so he'd wasted no more time there, but had instead headed back towards the village, revenge on his mind.

He'd focused on the task at hand. His hatred and resentment towards the men who had been part of Isabella's betrayal sent the energy coursing through his body.

Fuelled by the demon, Antony had stormed into the village. People had stopped in their tracks and stared at him, the recognition soon replaced by fear as they'd watched him. Antony, not knowing and, more importantly, not caring where his betrayers had lived, had raised his boot to the first front door and had kicked it open.

The splintering of the wood had ripped through the quiet night. The door had banged against the wall and he had walked in, fists clenched, eyes red, teeth bared and hatred pumping. He had seen before him a young couple and two small children at the dinner table. The man had immediately come around the table, placing a barrier between Antony and his family. The man had not been one of Isabella's lovers, but Antony had been too far-gone to care. Without a word he'd strode forward and had swiped his left hand, as though it had been a sword, across the man's neck. His razor sharp nails had slashed straight through the tissue severing an artery. Blood spurted. The man gasped. Antony laughed. The wife screamed. The silence had been broken.

As the man had collapsed to the floor, Antony had upended the table with one swipe of his hand. He had yanked the two children from their mother's protective grasp and had held them by the neck, one in each hand, and had squeezed. The sound of breaking bone had echoed in the hollow room. The woman had started screaming again and dropping the children at his feet, Antony had grabbed her and plunged his teeth into her neck. She had struggled a little, but there had been no heart in it. He'd drawn her blood into his body, had felt the beat of her heart slowing as he'd drained the life force out of her. Just before her heart had stopped he'd torn himself away and had hurled the body against the wall. He'd turned and strode out of the house and into the street, blood dripping from his chin.

He'd stopped outside and had started laughing at the sight before him. The whole village had been there, disturbed by the screaming. The men had been armed with pitchforks, hammers and any other weapon they had been able to find. The women had cowered behind their men. As Antony had stepped forward, they had all stepped backward.

'Who dares to challenge me?' his voice had boomed. Silence.

'Who dares to try and stop me?' he'd shouted again.

He'd seen movement to his left and had thrust his arm out, lifting the man into the air by his neck and holding him there as he'd pressed the sharp point of his thumbnail into the man's jugular. He'd felt the skin yield and the warm blood had begun to flow down his arm. The man had screamed in pain, but Antony had silenced him by twisting his head quickly to one side and snapping his neck. He'd flung the body into the crowd, knocking several people to the ground, and had advanced towards them.

'Who's next?' he'd said. 'Because I will get you all eventually.' He'd lunged at the crowd and had grabbed a young man and plunged his teeth into his neck. He drew deeply on his victim and then he'd thrown the body to one side. People had started to scream and run for cover.

Antony had laughed to himself as he'd watched them scurrying into their homes and closing the doors. That hadn't been enough to keep him out. It had only been family he had needed an invitation to visit, the warlock had said.

He'd strode straight to the next house and shoved the door open, just as the owner had been hurrying to close it. The sheer force had shattered the man's skull against the wall and as Antony had walked into the house, the door had slammed behind him and the man had collapsed to the floor, pieces of skull and brain remaining embedded in the wall in his wake. Antony had grabbed for the man's wife, had ripped open her dress and had slashed her across the chest before sinking his teeth into the gaping wound and drawing the blood straight from her heart. Not a sound had passed her lips. There hadn't been time.

He'd gone from house to house, not caring who had been inside, and had killed whoever had stood in front of him. He hadn't cared who they were and he hadn't felt an ounce of remorse as he'd ripped the head from the body of a man he'd considered a friend only a year before.

His thirst sated, his anger almost spent, Antony had left behind the remnants of the village he had once called home. He'd one more score to settle and then he would have his life back. That's what the warlock had said. Once Isabella and her descendants had been killed, he would be free. He would be a man again, not the monster he had changed into. Since Isabella and he hadn't had any children, his freedom had been imminent.

The warm night had contrasted with the storm raging within him as he'd started walking towards Anna's cottage. His gaze had remained fixed as he'd made the journey, running through the rest of his plan in his mind as he went. He couldn't simply barge in, he had to be invited – there had been some things that just had to be got around. He'd known that Isabella would never just invite him in and so he'd had to come up with a ruse. As he'd drawn close to the cottage, Antony had pulled the hood over his head so that his face had been totally hidden. Standing before the solid oak door he'd knocked and waited. He'd heard footsteps and then a scared voice.

'Who is it?'

Antony had smiled to himself. *This was going to be too easy*, he'd thought.

'It's Father Tom, Isabella. May I come in?' Antony had said, his accent perfect.

'Oh, Father, yes, yes, of course. Come in, come in.' As Isabella had opened the door, Antony had grabbed her by the throat and had dragged her outside.

'Hello, my dear,' he'd said as he'd stared down into the face he'd once loved.

'Oh, no,' Isabella had said, her eyes wide, her hands clasped around his arm as he'd grasped her by the throat.

'Where's Anna?' he'd said.

'She's g-g-gone out,' Isabella had said, her eyes starting to close at the restriction on her airflow.

'Where?' he'd said.

'Let me g-g-go, p-p-please, you're h-h-hurting me,' Isabella had said, choking under his tightening grip.

'Where is she, bitch?' he'd dragged her to him until she'd been so close he could smell her fear. Tears had seeped from her eyes, but his emotions hadn't wavered.

'WHERE IS SHE?' he'd said again. Her tears had continued to flow and her lips had started to turn blue as he held her.

'She's g-g-gone to f-f-find you,' she'd exhaled and her head had lolled. Antony had thrown her to the ground.

'Where?' he'd asked as she'd sat in the dirt, rubbing her neck.

'The c-c-cemetery,' she'd replied and had pushed herself to her feet.

'What the hell has she gone there for?'

'I d-d-don't k-k-know,' she'd said, backing away from him.

Antony had laughed out loud and had then fixed his stare on Isabella.

'Where do you think you're going, bitch?' He'd advanced towards her and had grabbed her by the hair. 'It's you I've come for and I want her to see what I'm going to do to you.'

Isabella had screamed as he'd dragged her behind him by her hair. It had been about half a mile to the cemetery and he'd heard her whimpering as she'd stumbled along behind him. It'd made him smile. He'd bet she had never whimpered like this when she'd been betraying him. Bitch! He'd yanked her hair harder, just to hear her scream, and as they'd passed through the cemetery gates, he'd flung her to the ground.

'Come and get me, old woman!' he'd shouted into the night. He'd then turned round and stared at his wife.

'So, what was it that made you want to betray me, Isabella? What exactly was it that I wasn't giving you? Come on, tell me because I honestly can't think of anything that you were lacking.' He'd knelt over her, his face inches from hers. She'd pushed herself backwards to try and escape him, but he'd easily stopped her.

He'd grabbed her legs and had dragged her towards him. She'd kicked and screamed, but his hold had been vice-like.

'Did you put up this much of a fight with them?' he'd said, but she'd not answered him. She'd closed her eyes and cried, battling against him as he'd pinned her arms to the ground.

'Is this how you like it, bitch? Is this what you wanted from them? What I didn't give you? Is it? Answer me?'

'No!' Isabella had cried. 'It wasn't like that, I promise you.'

'Funny, but I don't believe you,' he'd said and had shoved her skirts up above her waist and released himself from his trousers.

'I believe I was too good to you and all along all you wanted was this,' he'd emphasised what he was doing by forcing himself inside her and he'd smiled in satisfaction as she'd screamed.

'Is this the way you like it?' he'd grunted as he'd thrust himself inside her, harder and harder and watched the pained expression on her face – the grimace; the tears.

'Noooooo!' she'd screamed and had opened her eyes wide and stared straight at him. 'You were never there, that's what it was all about,' she'd shouted as he'd continued to violate her. He'd stared into those defiant eyes, but still he'd felt nothing.

'Antony! Leave her alone.' Anna's voice had hurtled through the night.

'Why, old woman? Isn't this what the slut enjoys?' He'd then leaned in and kissed Isabella, tearing her lips with his teeth.

'Antony!' Anna had shouted, but he'd ignored her. Instead he'd carved a heart on Isabella's breast with his nail. He'd then sunk his teeth into the wound and had drawn the traitorous blood deep into his soul. Isabella had screamed and Anna had grabbed at him, but he'd shoved her out of the way. He'd felt the strong beat of Isabella's heart start to slow as he drew the life out of her.

'Antony!' Anna had shouted once again.

'All right,' he'd grunted and had dragged himself out of her. He'd stood and faced Anna, buttoning himself up as he'd done so.

'What do you want, old woman?'

'I want you to stop what you're doing to this village and I want you to leave and never come back.'

Antony had laughed. 'And why, pray tell, should I do as you ask?'

'Because your fight is not with them,' Anna had replied.

'Of course it is. It was members of this village that took advantage of MY WIFE.'

'Those are a few misguided men, not the entire village. They don't deserve what you have done.'

'They are all accomplices. Now let me finish what I came here to do and then I will be gone.' He'd turned away from Anna and had grabbed Isabella around the throat and had hauled her to her feet. He'd turned towards Anna, her daughter brandished in front of him.

Antony had stared at the tiny old woman before him, her clothes hanging off her near skeletal frame. She'd always been good to him, had Anna, she'd always been fair and a distant part of his soul had felt sad for what his actions were going to do to her. He'd shaken his head and had pushed such useless sentiments aside. Anna would be better off without the trouble

122

making harlot anyway. So he'd actually be doing her a favour. By getting rid of Isabella, he'd be freeing both of them.

Antony remembered the agony in Anna's screams when he'd snapped Isabella's neck. No matter what she had done, Anna had loved her fiercely. Neither of them had been freed after all.

Antony had felt nothing as he'd turned away from them both and had started to walk away. He'd wondered how long it would take before the monster would leave him, when he'd heard Anna's chanting.

He shouldn't have underestimated her power. That had been his first mistake. His next had been his naivety. *Why had he assumed Isabella had been barren? Arrogance?* She'd certainly been with enough men to produce a child.

As the vines had encircled his neck and his eyes had met Anna's, he'd known the truth. He'd known the curse hadn't been broken; nor would it be. Isabella had borne a child. The relief he'd seen in Anna's eyes had said it all.

Antony shuddered as he remembered the feeling as he'd been entombed. But not anymore. He scrutinised his surroundings as he walked through the town of Carlford. He understood nothing of what surrounded him, but then again, it didn't interest him. Not yet, anyway. He had a job to finish, a four hundred year old job. He just needed to regain his strength.

He closed his eyes and focused his mind. He knew who she was, he always had. He just didn't know where to find her. He could see her in her kitchen. His focus followed her gaze outside to her cat. His mind took him to the cat, her precious cat and he smiled as he watched it cower in front of him. In his mind he knelt down in front of the cat, which was now hissing and spitting at him and he reached out to touch it.

'Boo!' he said and the cat turned and fled. He laughed out loud, drawing the attention of several passers-by, but he was somewhere else. He turned now and faced the kitchen where she stood at the window, a fallen chair on the floor beside her, tears streaming down her face. He smiled at her and blew her a kiss and then brought his mind back to the street he was walking down.

Now, to the task at hand. Regaining his strength. He focused his attention on the people milling around the streets and smiled. This wouldn't take long. He caught the eye of a young woman who reminded him of Isabella.

'Good evening,' he said, taking her arm and dragging her down an alleyway.

CHAPTER 26

'Jakes,' he said, cradling the phone against his shoulder, as he tried to light a cigarette and steer the car at the same time.

'Inspector, it's Becca, Becca Martin.'

'Dammit!' Jakes said as the lit cigarette fell into his lap and instantly burned a hole in his one good pair of trousers.

'Oh, sorry, is this a bad time?'

'No, no, it's just…never mind. What can I do for you, Becca?' he said as he plucked the cigarette from the smouldering fabric and flicked it out of the car window.

'S-S-something's happened. Can you come?'

'What's happened?'

'Please, Inspector, I'm scared and…' Jakes heard a sob and then the line went quiet.

'I'm on my way.'

When he arrived, Becca was huddled on the doorstep of the apartment building, legs drawn tight into her chest, rocking back and forth.

'Thanks for coming back,' she said. 'Especially after earlier.'

Jakes stood a little distance from her, not quite sure which "personality" he was addressing.

'Would you like to come in?' she pushed herself up and stepped inside and held the door open for him. Jakes followed her into the apartment and into the kitchen where he could smell fresh coffee brewing. Becca filled the two mugs from the steaming cafetière and handed one to him before she headed into the living room and sat on the sofa, cross legged, her back against the side so she could look at him.

Jakes sat down at the other end and turned as best he could to look at her. She hadn't uttered a word since they'd entered the apartment and he was starting to feel a bit uneasy. He looked at her and she was watching him over the rim of her coffee mug. Her eyes were a bright green in the lamplight and he relaxed a little.

'What happened?' he asked as he took a sip of the delicious smelling coffee.

'When?'

'You said something had happened this evening.'

'Yes, it did, but so much has happened over the last few days that I don't know whether I'm coming or going.' She fell silent again.

Jakes looked down at the floor, trying to collect his thoughts, wondering how he might draw it out of her.

'Becca, were you drinking last night or had you, perhaps, smoked something not entirely legal?'

'No, why?'

'You're not going to get into trouble or anything. I'm more interested in the body we found this morning.'

'No, really, on both counts,' she said. 'Why?'

'When I saw you at the site, you certainly seemed to be under the influence of something...' Jakes left the sentence unfinished.

'No, I hadn't been drinking and I don't do drugs. Never have, never will. I just felt woozy, as though I was going to faint. I guess the knock on the head did it to me because I still had a splitting headache.'

'Knock on the head?'

'Yeah, I told you earlier.'

'Ah, yes.'

'Anyway, that place always makes me feel weird. Ever since I first set foot in that cemetery, things have been happening to me. Weird stuff. My mum seems to know something's going on, but she won't tell me and…'

'Hang on, hang on,' Jakes said, his palms raised in a gesture to stop her continuing. 'What weird stuff and what's your mother got to do with it?'

'I can answer the second bit easily. I don't know what my mother has to do with it. I had a weird call after my first day at the site, after I'd heard his voice for the first time, but I've not been able to speak to her…'

'Who's voice?' Jakes interrupted.

'Oh, hhmmm, I'd rather not say.'

'Why not?'

'Coz you really will think I'm on something if I tell you and, besides, you wouldn't believe me anyway.'

'Try me.'

'Look, Inspector,' she eventually said. 'I've been having weird dreams, visions and experiences ever since I started working at that site and they got even worse once they dug that coffin up, especially after I touched it.' Becca rubbed the palms of her hands together and studied them, a gesture that did not go unnoticed by Jakes.

'Tell me what happened, Becca, maybe I can help you.'

'Ha! By getting the men in the white coats round? No one would believe me, Inspector. I shouldn't have called. It's just, tonight; he seemed so real, he…' She stopped herself and looked down at her hands.

'Please, Becca, I can't help if you don't tell me.'

'You won't believe me,' she said and tears were spilling down her cheeks as she looked at him.

'You'd be surprised what I believe, Becca, trust me.'

Becca watched him over the rim of her mug. It was as if she was weighing him up; deciding whether or not she could trust him; assessing whether she would be incriminating herself. Jakes was starting to feel a bit uncomfortable under such intense scrutiny. Her expression started to change, as though an inner turmoil had been resolved; for the better.

'I…' She stopped again and studied him, her gaze roving his face and then her shoulders sagged and she sighed.

'You mentioned that things had been worse since you touched the sarcophagus? Tell me what you mean,' Jakes prompted.

'Please just listen, then, and please don't laugh at me.'

'I won't,' he said. 'I promise.' He studied her and he saw what he thought was a glimmer of hope cross her face.

'Well, it's like I'm drawn to it, but when I touch it, it's as though I've been burned, like the day they dug it up.'

'What happened?'

Becca told him the story and the whole time she paced up and down in front of the fireplace, wringing her hands.

'Is that what happened to you today?'

'Not exactly. I got burned, yes, but it was when I fell and my hands touched the ground. There were definitely burn marks on my hands, but they healed so quickly…'

'How did you get those marks on your neck? I don't believe they're insect bites and they look remarkably similar to those on the victim this morning.' Becca reached up to touch her neck and winced.

Tears formed in the corners of her eyes and Jakes watched as she brushed them away with the back of her hand. 'I don't know how I got mine. I-I-I had a bad dream, like I told you, a few nights ago and when I woke up, they were there.'

'What was your dream about?'

'A man and a woman. I was the woman in the dream, except it wasn't me, if you understand what I mean. He called me Isabella.'

'Who was he?' Jakes asked, alarm bells already sounding in his head at the name Isabella.

'Antony, Antony Cardover.'

'What?'

'Antony Cardover,' Becca repeated, not picking up on Jakes' recognition. 'I've seen him since. A few times. That's when my neck hurts the most.'

Jakes was only half listening to her now. She was right, what she was telling him was truly unbelievable and would certainly have some of his colleagues calling the loony bin to have her committed, but something was niggling him about what she was saying. He almost had a feeling of déjà vu, but not quite. Yet, he had heard a similar tale before, he was sure of it. What she was saying, together with the niggles he'd been having since he'd seen the sarcophagus, seemed to be trying to unlock some long buried part of his memory.

'Inspector, are you okay?' Jakes realised he hadn't heard her finish speaking.

'Yes, yes, I'm fine. I'm sorry, Becca, did you say you'd seen him, this Antony Cardover?'

'Yes.'

'Where?'

'At college, but no one else did. Then here, the other night. I threw a glass at him. That's why..,' she drifted off, indicating the mess that remained on the floor. 'He was also here tonight, that's why I called you, he looked like he was going to kill Spook and I got scared and…'

'He was in this room?'

'No. Outside, both times. I honestly thought he was going to hurt Spook and I got scared, what with the other times and the rest…'

'Understandably,' Jakes said, his mind elsewhere. Antony Cardover. Isabella. He had heard those names before, but his memory was refusing to yield the answers. Suddenly, he stood up.

'Look, I need to go, Becca, but if you think of anything else or if anything else happens, please call me,' he said and handed her his card. 'Call anytime. I meant what I said. I want to help you if I can.'

Becca fingered the card and followed Jakes to the door. He let himself out and she double bolted the door after him. She was more than a little puzzled by how calmly he had accepted what she had told him. If she didn't know better, she would think he had heard of Antony and Isabella.

CHAPTER 27

Jakes was in a world of his own as he drove from Becca's apartment. He didn't bother going back to the station. What he needed was at home.

He parked in the only available space and waited for five minutes, for a break in the traffic, before he could get out of the car. He walked the two hundred metres to his tenement block, the name Antony Cardover churning through his mind. Still, nothing was coming forward. As he put his key in the door, he found that it had been forced open, again. This was the third time in as many weeks. Clearly, the landlord was incapable of dealing with it. He made a mental note to file a report the next time he was at the station.

The entrance hall stank of cats and he automatically held his breath as he grabbed his mail and climbed the first two flights of stairs. On the third, he couldn't hold it any longer and doubled over as he filled his lungs with the rancid air. He then walked the remaining six flights, dragging himself along by the rail. As he reached the top, the lift "pinged" and his next-door neighbour walked out.

'Evening, Frank.'

'Evening, Arthur,' said Jakes, wheezing.

'You know, you really should use the lift. You'll give yourself a heart attack one day,' Arthur said.

Jakes raised his hand in acknowledgement and shuddered at the thought of climbing in a lift and the doors closing and sealing him in. He shook his head to clear the "penned in" feeling and opened his front door.

Christ, he needed to clean up in here, he thought, as he walked down the murky hallway into the kitchen and opened the window wide. He turned round and surveyed the mountain of unwashed pots and empty takeaway containers, which covered every available surface.

Disgusted, he grabbed a black refuse bag from under the sink and swept the takeaway cartons into it. He then dragged the bag through into the living room, kicking over empty cans of coke, his fix since he'd given up the booze. He swept the contents of the coffee table into the bag as well.

He started to pick up the empty cans when his gaze alighted on the single photograph on the sideboard and he felt the familiar pain in his chest. He dropped the bag and went over and picked up the photo, running his fingers over the three faces in it. It was the last time they'd all been together, only a week before she'd left and taken the kids with her. He thought back to that fateful day, as he often did, and shuddered.

He'd been working late and, as usual, had called for a drink on the way home. One drink had inevitably led to another and another and he'd got drawn into the football match that was on the TV and the bets that went with it. He'd rolled home about ten thirty and when he'd opened the door to his 1930's semi, he'd seen the suitcases in the hallway.

'Where the hell have you been?' Jean had asked as she'd walked out of the kitchen, her arms folded over her chest.

'Been working late…on a case,' he'd said and had tripped on the doormat as he'd staggered in through the front door.

'Don't lie to me, Frank Jakes. I know where you've been. I can smell you from here,' she'd said, her dark eyes almost black in the dimly lit hallway.

'Only 'ad a couple, jus t' unwind,' he'd said and had tried to hug her, but she'd sidestepped him and he'd lost his balance and fallen flat on his face.

'You're a disgrace,' she'd said and had grabbed her coat off the banister. 'C'mon you two, time to go,' she'd called upstairs.

'Where you going?'

'Away from you. You'll hear from my solicitor in due course.'

'Why?' he'd said and pushed himself up to seated.

'Why?' she'd said, rounding on him at last, years of pent up fury visible on her face. 'Why? I'll tell you why. I have had enough of this.' She'd gestured to his drunken form lying on the floor. 'Every night it's the same. You're not even man enough to admit where you've been. You still lie after all these years. Do you honestly think I'm stupid enough not to know?'

He'd opened his mouth to reply, but nothing had come out.

'And the last straw was today, when these came.' He'd squinted at the letters she'd been brandishing and could barely make out the words 'Final Demand' stamped on the top one. 'You'd promised me you'd stopped. You swore on the lives of your children that you wouldn't put this family through any more crap, so I assumed these were simply a mistake and phoned the bank. Do you know what they said? Do you?'

He'd stared at her, his wife of twenty years, and he'd shaken his head.

'They said that there was nothing there. That the account was empty. I asked them to transfer money from the savings, but they said that was empty too. Empty!' she'd shouted at him and had thrown the bills in his face. 'Well, they're your problem now. C'mon kids,' she'd said and had pulled coats around his children, John aged twelve and Elizabeth aged ten. He'd watched as she'd opened the front door and they'd trooped out.

'I nearly won,' he'd muttered as the front door had slammed. He'd fallen asleep where he'd lain.

Jakes wiped a tear away from his eye and put the photo down. He glanced around the cluttered room and stopped at his overstuffed bookcase. His mind snapped back to the reason he'd come home and he walked over to it and grabbed a thick volume off the shelf. He pulled a chair out from the dining room table, dropped the book on the table and sat down.

He automatically reached for an available can of coke, not caring that it was warm, and gulped down the fizzy liquid, belching as he came up for air.

He'd nearly reached the end of the book, when a drawing caught his eye. He stared at it, the can halfway to his mouth. *Could it be the same one?* He squinted at the picture, but couldn't quite make out the detail. It certainly appeared to be the same one. He'd have to check it out tomorrow.

He glanced from the picture to the narrative accompanying it and read about Antony Cardover and a feud that led to his demise. His lids felt heavy and he closed them for a moment, allowing the sensation of near sleep to wash over him. He needed to get to bed, but his mind conjured up the image of the stone sarcophagus again. It had to be the same one.

CHAPTER 28

Jakes jolted awake and winced at the glaring sunlight streaming through his open curtains. He lifted his head off the table and massaged his stiff neck with one hand. He sat up and stretched, the odour of his own sweat making him wrinkle his nose in disgust.

'Time for a shower,' he muttered and got up from the table. He made his way to the bathroom, kicking over the open sack of rubbish as he went.

He stood under the hot jets, feeling the needles jabbing at his skull and numbing his skin in the process. He let his thoughts drift until his sleep fuddled mind started to clear and the picture of the sarcophagus came into focus. He needed to make sure. He turned the shower off, climbed out and grabbed a damp towel off the floor.

He dried himself on the way to his bedroom and picked up some boxer shorts off the floor and his suit trousers from the back of a chair. He yanked open his wardrobe door and rifled through the contents, but no clean shirt appeared. He turned round and surveyed the floor, littered with dirty laundry. He seized a crumpled heap of cloth off the floor and smelt it, then threw it back and grabbed another and inhaled. *That would have to do,* he thought, and got dressed. He picked up the first two socks he could find and pulled them on, before sliding his feet into his only pair of shoes. Grabbing a tie and his coat on the way passed, he headed out of the front door to his car.

'Shit!' he muttered as he pulled the parking ticket off his windscreen and stuffed it in the glove compartment with the others. He wove in and out of the protesting traffic on his way to the site, his mind focused on identifying the sarcophagus. Once he knew for sure it was the same one, he then needed to find a link between Antony and Becca. There must be one. Why else was she having such vivid dreams about him?

He screeched to a halt outside the churchyard and saw that Ramply was already there. Although the crime scene techs had finished, the area was still sealed off. He nodded to the officer on duty and headed straight for the crypt. He picked up a torch from the entrance and descended the steps to stand in front of the stone casket. He shone his light on the sides to illuminate the markings and squatted down to get a better look at the decayed carvings, rubbing his fingers over them. They certainly appeared to be the same ones, but the drawing hadn't been very clear. The narrative had mentioned about the "church window" style carvings on the ends of the sarcophagus, though. Jakes stood up, his knees protesting at the strain. He heard footsteps running up the gravel path to the entrance to the crypt.

'Jakes! Jakes! Jakes, are you there?' He heard Robinson's voice shout.

'What's up?' Jakes said and continued to move around the sarcophagus, his torchlight examining every last inch of the closed lid.

'Three murders last night.' Robinson's vagueness caused Jakes to point the torch at him and raise his eyebrows. Robinson pulled his notebook out of his pocket and started scanning his notes.

'There were three murders in town last night. According to the SOCs, all three had the same wounds as our vic from yesterday. The press are going mad, saying we've got a serial killer on our hands,' he said.

'Great, just what we need. O'Halloran will be breathing down our necks before we know it,' Jakes said, thoughts of the Chief Superintendent making his stomach churn. 'How do you know, by the way?'

'Know what?' Robinson said.

'That the wounds are the same. Have you seen the bodies?' Jakes said, already aware of the answer.

'Well, no, I haven't, but Collins said…'

'Collins wasn't here yesterday,' interrupted Jakes. 'So he has no idea either.' Jakes carried on walking around the sarcophagus and as his light illuminated the carving on the foot of the tomb, he tripped on something large in front of him.

'Shit!' Jakes said and pointed his light at the object at his feet. 'We've got another body.'

'What? I know, that's what I've been trying to tell you,' said Robinson.

'Here,' Jakes said, moving out of the way so that Robinson could see. He flipped open his mobile phone. 'It's Jakes. Get the crew back down to the Ramply Homes site. We've got another body.' He closed the phone and pulled some latex gloves out of his coat pocket and squatted down, wincing as his knees made a grinding sound.

He gently held the man's chin and turned his head. The puncture marks assailed his vision, the blood still glistening in the torchlight.

'Same as yesterday,' muttered Jakes.

'So are the ones in town,' said Robinson.

'Go and check them out. We need to be one hundred per cent sure,' Jakes said. Robinson turned and left. From his lower position, Jakes didn't notice, his torchlight was focused on the newly broken seal of the sarcophagus.

CHAPTER 29

Becca lay in bed watching the morning sunlight filter through the voile curtains, creating mottled patterns on the oak floor. Her gaze drifted to Spook, curled up in a ball by his cat flap. Her eyes filled with tears as she remembered the previous night.

'Spook?' she said and watched his grey ears turn towards her. 'C'mon, baby,' she crooned and he opened his orange eyes and focused them on her. 'Mummy needs a hug, Spook,' she said and clicked her fingers. He stood up and stretched lazily before sauntering over to her outstretched hand. He rubbed his head around her fingers and tears welled up in her eyes again. Just as she reached out to try and pick him up, he seemed to remember and he backed away from her and jumped through his cat flap.

Becca sighed and flopped back against her feather pillows. Her left hand stroked the key around her neck and her mind turned to thoughts of her grandmother. A pain pulled at her heartstrings. She wished her grandmother was here now. She'd be able to deal with all this. She'd been good at dealing with problems. She'd certainly managed to get Becca practising magic, despite the whole coven initiation debacle.

Her sixteenth birthday had gone from bad to worse. She'd thought that inheriting a trunk, a spell book and a "curse" had been bad enough, but they had been nothing compared to what had happened to her at the coven that same afternoon.

Becca had laughed out loud as she'd walked into the cave that served as the coven's meeting place. Talk about the stereotypical horror movie setting.

'Rebecca, have some respect,' Rosalind had said.

'Sorry,' she'd said and had stared around the cave at the flaming lanterns hung on the walls, the dozen women hidden by black hooded cloaks and the stone plinth in the centre of the group.

Becca had shuddered and had turned to her grandmother for reassurance, but Rosalind had already melted into the unidentifiable group of hooded figures.

'Welcome, Rebecca,' a voice had said and one of the women had stepped forward, her hands outstretched.

Becca, hands clasped together in front of her, eyes darting from one member of the group to another searching for Rosalind, had hesitantly started to move towards the faceless woman. She'd stopped, the plinth between them, hands remaining clasped in front of her.

'Our sister, Rosalind, seeks to induct you into our coven. You, like all of us, are chosen to carry the gift and to use it to protect those not so blessed, from the evils that exist in this world. You will learn, through guidance from your sisters, how to hone and channel your power for the good of all. Do you understand?'

Becca had nodded, incapable of replying for fear she would burst into tears.

'The purpose of your visit today is for you to pledge yourself to your sisters and to upholding the responsibilities of your gift. Your pledge will involve an initiation, which will bring you together with the companions of our craft and the eternal guardians of our secrets.'

Becca's head had snapped round, as she'd heard the faint mewling and she'd gasped as a tiny grey kitten had been set down on the plinth in front of her. She'd watched the poor creature shaking as it had huddled down on the cold stone and, instinctively, she'd gone to pick it up, but hands had grabbed her arms and had held her firm.

'What are you doing? Let go of me!' she'd said and had tried to twist out of their grasp.

'Rebecca, be still, this won't take long,' Rosalind's voice had sounded in the faceless group.

'Grandma, what...' but she had been interrupted by the high pitched mewl from the kitten. 'Noooooo!' she'd screamed, straining against her captors, and stared in horror as one of the group plunged a dagger into the kitten's chest and opened up its tiny ribcage. Tears had poured down her cheeks and she'd slumped to the floor, sobbing, her captors' grasp never yielding.

'How could you? What the hell is this place? What are you?' she'd said, choking back the sobs.

'Hold still, Rebecca, we've all done this. It is perfectly normal,' Rosalind had said.

'Normal! You've just murdered a defenceless kitten. How the hell can that be normal,' she'd sobbed. 'And, for what?'

'For you, my dear,' the woman who'd first addressed her had said. 'Now, drink this.'

Becca had examined the thick red liquid in the goblet and had felt her stomach clench and her gag reflex kick in.

'No way,' she'd said and had clenched her jaw as the goblet had been placed to her lips and her head tilted backwards. The blood had run down her chin as Becca had refused to open her mouth.

'Let me,' Rosalind had said and the hold on Becca's right arm had been released before being taken up again by someone else. Becca had looked up into her grandmother's face, being careful not to open her lips.

'Rebecca, listen to me,' Rosalind had said and had forced Becca to look at her. 'As heinous as you think this ritual is, it is crucial. This sacrifice brings us together with our feline partners. Together we act as Guardians, protecting the innocent from the evil that exists. Now, you need to drink this. It is part of who you are and an important step in who you will become.' Rosalind had clasped Becca's jaw with one hand and had squeezed hard, while her other hand had positioned the goblet over Becca's mouth.

'Owww!' Becca had yelped and, with perfect timing, Rosalind had poured the blood into Becca's mouth and had held her head back so she'd had no alternative but to swallow.

'How could you?' Becca spat as she'd tried to cough the blood back up. She'd had to resort to sticking her fingers down her throat to make herself sick, but to no avail. 'I can't believe you'd do this to me! I hate you!' she'd shouted and had fled from the cave.

Becca shuddered at the memory and felt a pang of sadness for the grey kitten.

Her mother, predictably, had been horrified. Not at what had happened to her, but at Becca's refusal to embrace the whole experience. They'd fallen out soon after that and Becca, for want of somewhere else to go, had gone to live with her grandmother.

Rosalind hadn't mentioned the coven again and had treated Becca as normal, as though the incident had never happened. Becca had soon started to relax in her grandmother's company. She had never managed to stay mad at her for long; she'd loved her too much.

Rosalind had introduced Becca to meditation as a way of calming her mind and becoming at one with her spirit. Becca had struggled at first, not being able to sit still for more than a couple of minutes without getting agitated and fidgety. Rosalind had remained calm and everyday had encouraged Becca to try again. Eventually, she had introduced a candle and this had brought Becca on in leaps and bounds. Becca had been mesmerised by the flame and was soon able to sit, transfixed, for hours at a time, without a thought troubling her mind. She had finally learned to relax and, to some extent, let go of the anger she'd felt towards her mother.

Becca's grandmother had soon changed the candle for a pencil and, because it had no real movement to keep her attention, Becca's mind soon started to imagine the pencil levitating and spinning round. One day, the pencil had quivered and had so shocked Becca that her concentration had been broken and she had been unable to carry on. She'd told her grandmother and Rosalind had smiled.

'You can do anything when you put your mind to it, Becca,' she'd said.

'But why couldn't I do it again?' Becca had said.

'You can't force these things, my dear. You will do it again, but you have to make sure your mind is in the right place.'

'Well, how will I know when that is?'

'The pencil will move for you,' Rosalind had said.

For the next week, Becca had been unable to get the pencil to move. Just when she'd resigned herself to the fact that she must've imagined it, the pencil had budged again. Forcing herself to stay calm, Becca had pictured the pencil rising off the floor. After a few minutes, Becca had seen one end of the pencil start to twitch and lift off the floor. A surge of excitement had run through her and the pencil had immediately dropped to the floor.

Taking a deep breath, Becca had closed her eyes and had pictured the pencil rising up off the floor and levitating in front of her.

'Well done, Rebecca,' she'd heard her grandmother whisper. 'You've done it!'

Becca's eyes had flown open and she'd stared at the pencil hovering in the air, in front of her. She'd glanced at her grandmother and had grinned, causing the pencil to dip a little.

'Always keep the image in your mind. That's the trick. Never let it go.'

Becca had been enthralled and had practised levitation on anything and everything, much to her grandmother's amusement and, sometimes, annoyance.

Her interest piqued, Becca had soon begun to ask Rosalind to show her more. She'd enjoyed the power she'd felt when moving those objects and she'd wanted to be able to do more.

'I'm not going back to the coven though,' Becca had said one day, as they were mixing a remedy for one of Rosalind's neighbours.

'But you should go back. You are part of them and they are part of you.'

Becca had shivered at the memory of her initiation and the helpless kitten.

'Never,' she'd said. 'If you make me go, I'll stop practising altogether.'

'Okay, okay. If that's what you want,' Rosalind had said, much too readily for Becca's liking.

'It is,' Becca had replied. They'd then worked together in silence for the rest of the day.

Rosalind had never spoken to Becca of the coven again and Becca had carried on with her magic until the day she'd found her grandmother dead.

Becca had gone into her grandmother's room with a cup of peppermint tea for her, as she'd done every Sunday morning. She'd known she'd been dead, simply by looking at her.

Rosalind's skin had had a greyish tinge to it, her brow smooth and relaxed, for the first time ever, and her lips had been turning blue. Becca had placed the tea on the bedside table and had sat on the side of the bed and regarded the woman she'd loved so fiercely, tears spilling down her cheeks.

She'd taken hold of her grandmother's hand and had shivered in response. She'd sat there for over an hour, just looking at her grandmother and crying. Then she'd stood up and had placed a kiss on her forehead, shuddering at the temperature. She'd left the room and had closed the door behind her. Becca had then picked up the phone and had dialled.

'Hello? This better not be one...'

'Mum, it's me. Grandma's dead,' she'd said and had put the phone down. She'd walked to her room and had grabbed a suitcase from under the bed and had started to pack. The last thing she'd put in had been the photo of the three of them, dressed as witches. That had been a happy day.

Becca had sat at the bottom of the stairs and had waited. Within half an hour, her mother had arrived accompanied by a doctor. Becca had moved out of the way as they'd raced passed her up the stairs and then she'd got up and walked out of the house.

She hadn't gone to the funeral, nor had she contacted her mother straight away. She hadn't felt the need to do either. Nor had she practised magic again. It had reminded her too much of her grandmother and the pain had always been too raw.

Once she'd settled, she'd sent a note to her mother advising her that she was safe and where she was, but she hadn't asked to see her and her mother hadn't sought to contact Becca; not until her twenty first birthday.

Becca had been woken by a knock at the door and had opened it to find a parcel, wrapped simply in brown paper, on her doorstep. She'd unwrapped it to find the wooden box that her grandmother had shown her on her sixteenth birthday and a small metal key on a chain, that she'd remembered her grandmother wearing. There had been no note. Becca had rubbed her fingers across the inscription on the lid, which said "you will know when". She'd remembered her grandmother saying that Becca would receive the box on her death. That had been two years previously. *Where had it been since then?* Becca had assumed that her mother had kept it and, later that day, she'd mailed the box back to her mother, but had kept the key. *Why?* Because it had been the only piece of jewellery that her grandmother had ever worn. She'd never heard from her mother again, until now.

Becca sighed again and snuggled back under the duvet. She was not looking forward to seeing her mother. The phone rang, but she ignored it.

'Rebecca! I know you're there! Pick up the phone!' Dick's voice cut through the apartment, courtesy of the answer-phone.

Becca groaned and pulled a pillow over her head so she couldn't hear him and then felt guilty about skipping work again.

Almost at the point where she was suffocating, Becca lifted the pillow. Silence reigned. She groaned again and threw the pillow on the floor and swung her right leg out of bed. Such was her reluctance to go and see her mother that it took her almost five minutes to slide out from under the duvet. The resonating ring of the alarm clock ending her mission with a thud.

'Shit!' she muttered as her knee connected with the solid oak floor. She sat there staring out of the window, listening to the persistent ring of the alarm clock. Not moving her eyes from the nothingness she was staring at, Becca reached out her right hand and smacked it down on top of the clock. No sooner had the ringing stopped than she heard it.

'B...E...C...C...A...' His voice echoed and the hairs on the back of her neck stood on end and she shivered. Her hand came up to the bite marks on her neck, which had started tingling. She pulled her hand away and examined her damp fingertips. They were covered in blood.

She jumped up and raced into the bathroom, but when she looked in the mirror, the wounds were healing nicely.

CHAPTER 30

Becca sat and stared. She'd already been there over half an hour, but she couldn't bring herself to get out of the car. A few people had passed by, looking at her in that "trying not to be nosey" way that people had, but no one recognised her. Well, it had been over a decade since she'd last been here.

The front of the house was immaculate. The windows sparkled on either side of the royal blue front door and the render was a pristine white. The lawn was cut short and shaped and the flower beds were teeming with neat rows of rainbow coloured flowers. Even the patchwork pathway was freshly power washed, so that not even the bravest weed dared to trespass. It made Becca smile as she knew that the inside of the house was a complete contrast to this order. Despite not caring what people thought of her, Ginnie Martin did respect the wishes of the village and their desire to win "Village of the Year" for the umpteenth year.

Becca looked up and down the tree lined street. Her mother's house looked the same as all the others, yet it was different. It wasn't a difference that was palpable, but more of a feeling that you got when you passed in front. More correctly, it was the way that it made you feel as you passed by. As a child, Becca had seen naughty children turn into angels; tired looking businessmen become infused with energy; and heartbroken lovers start smiling again. The house had an aura; a power of some kind. It healed people.

'It didn't work on mum and I though, did it,' Becca sighed as she thought about the distance that had grown between them.

Becca smiled again at an image of her mother dressed in her usual gypsy attire, her hair in braids, and her feet bare, humming to herself as she painted another masterpiece that she probably wouldn't sell. Ginnie Martin had only ever sold enough paintings to keep a roof over her head and food on the table. She'd never sold her "best" paintings because, for some reason, she'd always wanted to keep them for herself. The thing was, she'd never got around to putting them on the wall, so the house had always been strewn with loose canvasses. Becca wondered whether it was still like this or whether her mother had changed over the years.

There had only ever been one room that Becca had not been allowed into as a child and this had been Ginnie's "hobby room". Ginnie may not have been able to do magic, but she had an acute sixth sense which she'd developed naturally as she'd grown up. Her "hobby" had been as a medium and tarot reader and the forbidden room was where she took her clients. Ginnie hadn't charged for her services until Rosalind had pointed out that she was spending more time doing readings for people, which didn't pay the bills, than painting, which did.

To her credit, Ginnie had taken on board what Rosalind had said and had introduced a charge for her readings and had restricted the times to evenings and weekends. Becca wondered whether her mother still had her "hobby". She glanced at her battered old Timex watch, a present from her father on her tenth birthday. It was already ten o'clock. She couldn't sit out here all day.

She shoved open the door to her beloved old Fiesta and hauled herself out. She took her time locking the car then plodded across the road, only to stand at the end of the crazy-paved path looking up at the window above the front door. That had been her bedroom and had stretched along to the left of the front of the house with an en-suite bathroom to the back. It had originally been two rooms, but Ginnie had had it knocked through to give

Becca her own "living quarters", as her grandmother had called them. Becca wondered whether her room would still be hers or whether Ginnie would have thrown all Becca's things away. She couldn't blame her if she had.

Becca dragged herself up the path to the front door and, as there was no bell – her mother didn't believe in them – she took hold of the brass knocker and knocked hard. She waited for a few minutes and then knocked again. Still there was no answer and no movement from inside the house. Becca ventured around the side of the house and opened the pristine wooden gate.

It was almost like she'd crossed into the wilderness, with the gate acting as the barrier between the two worlds. Becca closed the gate behind her and started wading her way through the waist high weeds and grasses which had overgrown the path leading to the rear of the house.

The back garden resembled a meadow left to go wild, a far cry from the plain cropped lawn and neat borders of her childhood. The lawn had merged into the borders and wild flowers ran amuck amongst the knee high grasses. The large garden was bordered all around by sycamores and hawthorns, interspersed with hazelnut trees. In pride of place in the middle of the garden rose a huge laburnum tree and it was here that Becca headed.

As she drew nearer she heard the familiar melody of "Greensleeves" being hummed, in that slightly off key manner that was so typical of her mother. Becca stopped a few feet away and as the breeze rippled through the tendrils of the tree, she caught a glimpse of her mother for the first time in ten years. Ginnie was perched on a stool in front of an easel, facing the tree's thick trunk, her back to Becca. Her wild mass of red hair was pulled back and speared by a cross of paintbrushes, whose blue and yellow dregs had run down to mix in her hair. She wore her ancient paint smeared smock over a tatty pair of jeans. She was in a world of her own, concocting another masterpiece from the dark recesses of her mind.

Becca parted the curtain in front of her and went to stand behind her mother. Ginnie remained elsewhere. The colours and patterns on the canvass reminded Becca of the chaos that currently surrounded her.

'Very appropriate,' Becca said, causing Ginnie to jump and smear vermillion across the canvass, completely ruining it.

'Rebecca! You came!' Ginnie said and jumped up, her masterpiece forgotten, as she knocked the easel over in her haste to see her daughter. Ginnie reached her arms out to embrace her, but Becca shrank away.

'So, what's this about, Mum?' she said, starting to walk towards the house.

'Please, Rebecca, don't be like that. It's been so long since I've seen…'

'This isn't a social call, Mum. You asked me to come and I'm here, so what's this about.' Becca faced her mother, her hands planted on her hips. She felt a twinge of guilt as she saw Ginnie's shoulders drop and the smile disappear from her face. 'Look, I'm sorry, it's just…'

'No, you're right, Rebecca, I did ask you to come, but I don't wish to talk about it out here. Go on inside, I'll be in shortly. I just need to clear up out here.' Ginnie smiled at Becca, but Becca could see it was forced and she saw the glitter of tears in her mother's eyes. She felt terrible as she turned and carried on towards the house. It had been so long and there was so much angst between the two of them that Becca just couldn't pretend it didn't exist. *Perhaps when this was over, they could talk,* she thought.

Becca opened the back door and felt as if she'd stepped into a time warp. Nothing had changed, except that there was more clutter than Becca remembered. The kitchen units were the same yellow covered chipboard that had always been there. The Formica was coming away in places, where the water had found its way into the cracks; inevitable after so many years of use. The matching table still stood in the middle of the room, heaped with paintbrushes, tubes of oils and acrylics, dirty rags and brush cleaners. The four metal legged chairs were stacked on top of each other in one corner, the stuffing protruding out of the torn yellow vinyl seat. Dead potted plants lined the windowsill behind the stainless steel sink, which was crammed with several days' worth of washing up.

Becca glanced at the peeling wallpaper and faded linoleum floor, as she wandered through into the hallway. As predicted, canvasses were stacked against the blown vinyl walls, their vibrant colours in sharp contrast to the chocolate brown carpet.

She pushed open the lounge door to find it would only go halfway. As she squeezed through and looked behind it, she found more canvasses. The décor in here was slightly more modern than the previous rooms and Becca remembered her and her mother painting the lined walls the universal colour of magnolia. Ginnie had then bought a beautiful beige carpet and was going to invest in a new leather sofa, but that obviously hadn't happened. Becca sat down on the faded pink velour sofa, whose springs had given way many years ago, and waited for her mother.

Becca heard the back door open and her mother stumble over the doorstep with her load. The door then slammed shut, as though kicked, and then there was a hubbub of noise, as the painting apparel was obviously dumped. The slightly too high melody of "Greensleeves" drifted through the house as Becca heard her mother filling the kettle and then clattering around with what she assumed were cups.

Becca sank into the collapsed sofa and started to play with a loose thread hanging from its arm. She stared at the gas fire in front of her. There was no television in Ginnie's house, as she didn't believe in them, never had; nor was there a radio or a CD player. All Ginnie had was an old turntable, which she'd had since she was a girl, and an immense collection of vinyl records which, in true Ginnie style, lay strewn across the living room floor by the turntable.

'Damn!' Ginnie said, breaking Becca's reverie, as she tried to push the door open with the tray. Becca got up and moved the canvasses back slightly so that the door would open further.

'Thanks, love,' Ginnie said, tea stains now adding to the rainbow of colours on her smock. She walked over to the sofa and set the tray down on top of the array of magazines and books scattered across the coffee table. She patted the cushion next to her for Becca, who hesitated for a moment and then came and sat down.

'So, tell me what's been happening with you,' Ginnie said as she handed Becca a cup and saucer.

'Mum, as I said, this isn't a social visit,' Becca said, guilt stabbing her insides as she saw the pained look on Ginnie's face again.

'Doesn't do any harm to catch up, first,' Ginnie continued, her voice stilted.

'Why, after all these years, are you suddenly interested in my life?' Becca said, staring into her teacup.

'I've always been interested in your life, Rebecca,' Ginnie said.

'Well, you've got a funny way of showing it.'

'It's you who chose to leave, Rebecca, not me.'

'Yeah, but it's you who chose never to speak to me again.' Becca sank back into the sofa, her cup and saucer still in her hands. Ginnie reached for the teapot and refilled Becca's cup. The two women lapsed into silence.

'Are you still painting?' Ginnie asked after a few minutes.

'Why didn't you speak to me the day gran died?' Becca said. Silence ensued again.

'I don't know,' Ginnie eventually said, taking hold of Becca's hand, but Becca pulled away.

'You just ran passed me as if I wasn't even there. Why?'

'I don't know. I was upset. Part of me refused to believe you, didn't want to believe you, thought that maybe you were…'

'What? You thought I would say my own grandmother, whom I loved more than anything else in the world, was dead, just to get you to come

151

round?' Becca stared at her mother, her brow furrowed, her lips curled back in a sneer.

'No, it wasn't that... oh, I don't know.'

'So, what was it like then, Mum? How bad was it for you? So bad, that you chose to ignore your own daughter?'

'That's not fair, Rebecca. You'd gone by the time I'd come back downstairs and you made no effort to contact me.'

'I sent you a note telling you where I was and that I was okay.'

'Yes. You sent a note. A note that asked no questions and implied that it required nothing in return.'

'You could've got in touch,' Becca said, her arms folded across her chest.

'So could you,' Ginnie whispered. Both women lapsed into silence and drank their tea. *Stalemate*, thought Becca, as she glanced at her mother over the top of her cup.

'So, why did you want to see me?' Becca finally asked.

'To tell you about your ancestry and a very unpleasant man who is...'

'If it's about Antony Cardover, I already know,' Becca said, a smug smile on her face.

'Yes, you are probably aware of some of it, but I guarantee you don't know the full story.'

'What makes you say that? I've read the books.'

Ginnie smiled. 'You'll only be familiar with what the historians know about. But that isn't the full story. The real story was never recorded in any history books, because no one ever really knew the full details. No one, that is, except the family. People knew what had happened and what he had become, but they never knew the price he had had to pay.'

Her interest now piqued, Becca let the smart retort die on her lips and settled back to listen to what her mother had to say.

Ginnie proceeded to tell Becca the real story, the sun tracking its path across the sky as she did so. She told Becca about Antony's upbringing by his carpenter father, Julius, his mother having died in childbirth. Becca learned how an untalented young man had been forced to take over the business when his father fell ill and how he had turned it around and made it a roaring success after his father had died. Julius had been known as the "Chippendale" of his time and Antony also managed to attain such status.

Becca was told that it was while Julius had been ill that Antony had met Isabella. Anna had been treating Julius and had brought Isabella along with her one day. Antony had fallen in love with her as soon as he saw her and no amount of warning had discouraged him from marrying her.

To Becca, it sounded like a historic soap opera, especially when she learned of Isabella's betrayal, but she soon sobered as her mother told her of Antony's deal with the warlock.

'What do you mean by "eternal hell"?' Becca halted Ginnie's story telling.

'Antony Cardover was turned into a form of vampire, an immortal creature without a soul, whose constant thirst for blood would…'

'Shit!' Becca said and raised her hand to touch her neck, the wounds covered by a silk scarf.

'Rebecca!' Ginnie chastised. 'Anyway….are you all right? You've gone very pale,' Ginnie reached out to touch Becca's face, but Becca pulled away.

'I'm fine, but why didn't anyone try and stop this Ebenezer guy?'

'No one knew where to find him. He always found you. His house was hidden in the woods, an empty abandoned ruin to most passers-by. For those in despair or anger, though, it was a welcoming haven. Ebenezer would befriend you, in his ancient little old man persona, lulling you into a false sense of security and then he would take your soul, using it to keep himself young. It wouldn't surprise me if he was still around somewhere today.'

'If few people ever survived an encounter with him, how do you know what he did to them?' Becca said.

'There were some survivors, who used to put their own spin on the story, but whenever someone had had an encounter with Ebenezer, a little boy would appear to the family of the victim the next day and tell the tale. He would then disappear, never to be seen again, until the next person visited Ebenezer.'

'Surely, someone must have got hold of this boy and got Ebenezer's whereabouts out of him?'

'Oh they tried,' Ginnie said, 'but the boy did literally just disappear into thin air.'

'That's bullshit!'

'Watch your mouth, young lady. You forget, Becca, times were different then. People believed in the power of magic and because of such magic, legendary monsters such as vampires and werewolves became a reality. In this day and age, people would laugh if a vampire walked up to them, believing it was just some idiot dressed up in a costume. That's what films and television have done – trivialised something which, in reality, is a very serious issue.'

'So, you believe that vampires exist?'

'Of course they exist, as do werewolves. They exist as much today as they did back then, the same as witches. They blend in more today as our society both accepts and ignores those who are different. Many of these people are in mental institutions and their "condition" treated as some form of schizophrenia.'

'But you just said we are more accepting of those that are different.'

'Yes, until they upset the status quo and that's when they are removed.'

Becca fell silent, her mind on the wounds on her neck and the possible implications. Small waves of panic were rippling through her body, but she wanted to hear the rest of the story before telling her mother what had happened to her. That's if she told her mother. She hadn't decided yet.

'So, what did the boy say about Antony?' Becca prompted.

'Oh, yes, well, Antony had apparently sold his soul for the chance of revenge on all those who had humiliated him, including his wife. The boy unusually didn't say what Antony had become, but he did say that the only way Antony would ever find peace again would be to destroy Isabella and all her descendants. The villagers were very disturbed by what was said, as they knew that many of the men in the village had had a hand in Isabella's betrayal. The men involved left the village for a while, until it blew over. The village braced itself for Antony's revenge, but it never came. It didn't come for a whole year and, by that point, they had forgotten all about it and the sinners had returned, every last one of them. None of them were in the least bit prepared for the revenge Antony had planned.

During that year, though, Isabella had had a baby. A baby whose safekeeping Anna entrusted to Carla, the young girl who had lived with her for many years. It was Carla who managed to escape to Anna's sister with the baby, the day they took Anna away. Antony knew nothing about the baby.'

'But, why didn't she just tell Antony? You know, when he came back?'

'When Antony came back, he was a different man, more like a monster. He was trapped with a curse and only one way of escaping it. Besides, Antony wasn't the father. One of Isabella's dalliances had that honour. The night of Antony's return is well documented in the history books.'

'I know, Father Michael told me the story of how he'd murdered over half the village.'

'Yes, and who did they call on to try and stop him?'

'Anna,' Becca said.

'The woman whom they had all turned against, because of her craft. Bloody hypocrites!' Ginnie snapped, shocking Becca, as she'd never heard her mother swear before.

'After they'd got her to deal with Antony, after she had had to witness the murder of her own daughter, they… Becca, are you okay?'

'I-I-I saw that,' Becca said.

'Saw what?'

'I-I-Isabella being killed in a d-d-dream. I was her. I…'

'What on earth are you talking about?'

'I had a dream. This man was attacking me, screaming at me, raping me.' Tears streamed down Becca's face as she remembered the dream that had started the nightmare. 'That's where I got this,' she said and untied the scarf around her neck.

'Got what?' Ginnie asked, not moving from where she was sitting. She was looking at Becca as if she'd gone mad.

'These,' Becca said and turned to show her mother the wounds on her neck. She watched Ginnie's jaw tense as she looked at the marks.

'Tell me the truth, Rebecca. How did you get those marks?'

'I told you. I had a dream. While he was raping me, he bit my neck. The pain was like nothing I've ever felt before. Then she came, Anna, and he let me go while he argued with her, but then he grabbed hold of me by the throat and then I woke up. I know Anna put a spell on him and stuff. Father Michael told me that, but I don't know what it has to do with me,' Becca regarded her mother. Ginnie was staring into space.

'Mum, are you okay?'

'Mmmm, what, oh yes,' Ginnie said focusing back on Becca. She gripped Becca's chin and turned her head, so she could get a better look at the marks. She ran her fingers over them and Becca winced and pulled away.

'It's worse than I thought,' Ginnie muttered.

'What is?' Becca said, but Ginnie didn't answer.

'Have you had any more dreams like this?'

'What? No, but I did remember the story grandma told of Anna and how she got dragged away and burned at the stake.' Ginnie's attention snapped back again, as though jolted by an unpleasant memory.

'But none about Antony?'

'Not really. Not dreams anyway. I've had visions and heard his voice and other weird stuff. Mum, what's going on?'

'Tell me about the visions and "stuff", everything that's been going on,' Ginnie said, the tone in her voice prompting Becca to obey.

She leant against the sofa, away from Ginnie's intense scrutiny, and stared up at the ceiling. Taking a deep breath, she told Ginnie about the churchyard and the sarcophagus, about her visions and about hearing his voice. She told her about the morning she woke up on the kitchen floor, about Spook's behaviour since and about seeing Antony, the previous night, intimidating Spook. Finally, she told her about the dead body. Ginnie had been pacing the room as Becca talked, but she stopped at the mention of the body.

'How many dead bodies?'

'One, in the crypt, why?'

'He is regaining his strength. Whilst he is weak you stand a better chance of defeating him, but when he is strong…' Her voice trailed off.

'Wait a minute,' Becca said. 'What the hell are you talking about?'

'Stopping Antony,' Ginnie said, surprise etched on her face.

'Why me? What's it got to do with me?'

'Everything.'

'Why?'

'Because you and I are the last surviving descendants of Isabella Cardover.'

CHAPTER 31

What a day, Jakes thought as he leaned back in his chair and stretched. He glanced out of the grimy windows of his office and saw that the sun was setting. It was late; it was the middle of summer and he was the only one left in the station. *Not an uncommon event*, he mused.

Not for the first time, Jakes found himself envious of his partner. Robinson may not have been the best officer, but he had the family thing all sewn up. He had a stunning wife, who most men would call perfect, even though it wasn't PC anymore.

Gillian Robinson was a woman obsessed with everything 1950s. From her beliefs about a woman's place, to the way she dressed and did her hair and makeup. It was as if you'd stepped back in time when you met her. Her beliefs suited her husband, Paul, and his image of himself as the controller and provider. Gillian didn't do anything without Paul's say so and he loved to come into the station bragging about the latest request that he'd denied. It was no secret that, although Gillian obeyed Paul to his face, she did the things she wanted to do anyway. Paul was the only one who had no idea.

The Robinsons had two little girls, Jessica and Emily, both aged five. They were the image of their mother, with their light blonde hair and angelic faces. They certainly appeared to be the picture perfect family and Robinson, for all his faults, always put them before the job. He was consistently out of the station by six and no one could ever get hold of him out of hours. Although colleagues complained about this all the time, they secretly admired him for it. It was no secret that his rigid attitude would never earn him further promotion, but he didn't seem concerned. *Yep, the perfect family*, thought Jakes, *but then again, that's what people used to say about him.*

Robinson had become Jakes' partner by default. He had been transferred in from another station, following a bust up with a colleague, and had been assigned to Jakes – no discussion; no argument; no option. The rest of the station had taken a sigh of relief. With his history of drinking and gambling, coupled with his old fashioned ways of working, Jakes was not a popular member of the force and many felt he should be sacked. His superiors didn't agree. For all his weaknesses, Jakes never let them affect his work and that was all they cared about. His success rate with his cases was far higher than any of his colleagues so, as far as his superiors were concerned, he could carry on as he was.

Jakes looked down at the case files on his desk. Two were from the Ramply Homes site and the others were the murders that had occurred in the town the previous night, murders with exactly the same wounds as the Ramply Homes ones.

'I told you the MO was the same,' Robinson had said as he'd dropped the crime scene photos onto Jakes' desk. 'Two puncture wounds on the neck, just like the others.'

'I never said they weren't,' Jakes had said, studying the photos.

'Yes, you did.'

'No, I didn't. I merely asked you if you were sure.'

'Okay, but, Collins was right wasn't he?'

'You're missing the whole point, Robinson. You, as the lead investigator on a crime, have to go and check things out for yourself. Collins wasn't even present at the crime scene. You were going purely on hearsay and that isn't the way to go about things.'

'He'd heard it from someone who was at the scene, so it was accurate,' Robinson had said, arms folded across his chest like a petulant child. Jakes had sighed and had looked at his partner.

'But neither of them had been to the Ramply Homes crime scene had they? So they had no way of knowing that the crimes were the same, had they?' Robinson had opened his mouth at that point to speak, but had thought better of it.

'Now, I've got work to do, if you don't mind,' Jakes had said and had turned his back on Robinson. He'd heard the younger man leave a few minutes later.

He'd had his fill of idiots today. Robinson hadn't been the first.

After Robinson had left the crypt that morning, Jakes had resumed his examination of the sarcophagus. He had been almost positive that it was the same one depicted in the book and, hence, contained the remains of Antony Cardover.

He had been more than a little shocked to finally discover that the sarcophagus really existed. He'd always assumed the story had been some kind of local fairy tale. The story he'd been told had certainly had a fairy tale spin put on it.

As a child, his mother had told him the tale of Antony and Isabella. Her story bore little resemblance to the truth, except for the stone sarcophagus. This had been the one constant. Jakes had to admit that, fairy tale or not, the story had intrigued him and had sparked his interest in local history and in legends and folklore. It hadn't been until he had been in his early twenties, whilst rifling through an antiques shop that he had come across a book which had told the real story of Antony and Isabella Cardover. It had been weird because, despite his interest in folklore and legends, there had still been a huge part of him that hadn't believed there was any truth in them. Until now.

Jakes had been examining the broken seal around the lid and had been trying to lift it without any success, when he'd heard a commotion outside. He hadn't looked up; presuming the officer on duty would deal with whatever it was.

'Detective Inspector Jakes?' a high pitched voice had whined and Jakes had sighed. He'd pushed himself up, his knees groaning in response and had headed up the steps.

'Mr Ramply, you shouldn't be at my crime scene' Jakes had said as he'd exited the crypt and faced the small man. He'd propelled Dick away from the cordoned off area, waving away the apologies of the officer. 'Now, what can I do for you, Mr Ramply?'

'Is there a reason you are here again today? It's just that I have contractors who are currently doing nothing, yet still expecting to be paid and I don't like that,' Dick had said as he'd faced Jakes; his hands on his hips; his chin thrust out.

'Mr Ramply, as you were told yesterday, this is a crime scene and until that changes, no one will be allowed down here,' Jakes had said.

'But, I thought you'd finished. The little chaps with the boxes left yesterday and the only person who's still here is Officer what's his name back there. By the way, he's not very talkative.'

'Mr Ramply,' Jakes had said, 'the investigation is still ongoing and so the crime scene needs to remain intact.'

'For how long?' Dick had stamped his foot like a child and had folded his arms across his chest. Jakes had shaken his head and had bitten down on his lip to suppress the angry retort.

'Mr Ramply, a man was murdered here the night before last and, by the looks of it, last night as well, so..,' he'd held his hand up to stop Dick from speaking, 'so, until we get to the bottom of these and have finished our investigations here, this church is out of bounds to the workmen.'

'Who was killed last night then?' Dick had asked, his morbid curiosity having momentarily won the battle against his need to make money.

'I don't know yet, I'm waiting…'

'I might know. Can I see?' Dick had tried to dodge passed the stocky man and under the tape, but Jakes had blocked him.

'No, Mr Ramply, you can't.'

'Fine, if you're going to be like that.'

Dick had stalked off and Jakes had headed back to the crypt and, again, had tried to lift the lid of the sarcophagus, but it hadn't shifted at all. He had thrust his hands in his pockets and had felt some folded pieces of paper. He had pulled them out and focused his torch on them. They'd been the rubbings he'd taken from the sarcophagus. He'd forgotten all about them. He'd been about to leave the cellar and go and see if this wording was referred to in the book when he'd remembered the dead body. Dammit!

Jakes leant back in his chair and rubbed his eyes. The press were having a field day. Their theory that a serial killer was on the loose was gathering momentum and Jakes had nothing to disprove it. *At least they hadn't given him a name yet*, he thought. *What would they call him,* Jakes wondered, *Son of Dracula.*

He snorted at this and then stared down at the photographs spread out in front of him. Each one showed the wounds on each of the victims. Each had two puncture marks on the left hand side of their neck. Each set of punctures were the same distance apart and measured the same diameter. Each victim had been drained almost entirely of blood. There had been no other marks or wounds on any of the bodies. To Jakes they appeared to be bite marks, the sort of bite marks Bram Stoker had written about. But what other explanation was there? The sarcophagus; the story behind it; the bodies.

They all said "vampire". Jakes laughed to himself as he thought about what his colleagues would say if he told them that a vampire was on the loose.

'They'd lock me up and throw away the key,' he muttered and pushed away from the desk and stood up. Time to prove his theory. He grabbed the papers with the stone rubbings on them and left the station.

CHAPTER 32

Jakes dropped his keys in the bowl on the hall table, went through into the kitchen and dumped a takeaway bag on the kitchen table. He opened and closed cupboard doors and then turned to the mound of pots requiring washing up, rooting through the sink until he located a relatively clean plate.

He emptied the contents of two foil containers on to his plate and inhaled the aroma of chicken vindaloo. Grabbing a fork off the side, Jakes picked the plate up and plucked a can of coke out of the fridge. He walked through into the other room and set his dinner down on the table, ignoring the spilled rubbish bag once again.

Jakes picked up the book he'd been looking at the previous night. He turned to the relevant pages again and began to read as he forked his curry into his mouth, at a pace that would make most people gag. Every four or five mouthfuls he took a large gulp of coke and then carried on. He skimmed through the story of Antony and Isabella. He still marvelled at how he'd forgotten it.

Anna Martindale had been the witch who'd eventually stopped Antony. *What a fate had befallen her for her troubles*, Jakes thought, as he remembered reading of Anna's demise at the hands of the villagers. He pushed that story from his mind as it wasn't important at the minute. Finding out how she had stopped Antony, on the other hand, was.

The book said that Anna had waited for Antony in the churchyard. It had been the only place strong enough to hold him. She'd known he'd come eventually. He would want to flaunt Isabella in front of her. Isabella had caused this mess and so she had to be instrumental in sorting it out. Anna had had to witness the murder of her own daughter at his hands, yet she still managed to stop him.

The first spell she had cast had caused thick vines to shoot up out of the ground and wrap themselves around him, rendering him immobile. Once his body had been lifted into the stone casket, Anna had cast a second spell that had sealed the lid with an enchantment which could not be broken whilst the casket remain buried in consecrated ground. Just before she had left the cemetery she had pressed her hands against the stone. The carvings in the stone had apparently appeared at her touch.

Jakes stared at the last line in the narrative:

UNDER NO CIRCUMSTANCES MUST THE SARCOPHAGUS BE REMOVED FROM CONSECRATED GROUND

The book didn't say why, it merely said not to remove it. Jakes sat back as he thought about the sarcophagus and about the Ramply Homes site. He remembered the rubbings he had brought home with him and went back into the kitchen, where he vaguely remembered dropping his coat. Fumbling in his coat pocket, he pulled out the sheets of paper and made his way back into the living room.

He spread the pages next to the book and stared at them before transferring his attention back to the book. The book stated the spell which sealed Antony's tomb had been etched into the stone. Jakes glanced back at the pages of rubbings. They definitely read like a spell to him. The sarcophagus in the Ramply Homes church basement had to be that of Antony Cardover.

Jakes leaned back in his chair and tried to process what it all meant. The sarcophagus could not be moved from the church's ground, which it hadn't been, so the spells, according to the book, should still hold. *Even if they didn't work anymore, it had been four hundred years after all, why would he escape and how? His body must be dust by now, surely? And, anyway, what on earth did it have to do with Becca Martin?* The thoughts swirled round in Jakes' mind making him dizzy.

Through the fog, Jakes remembered the photograph on Becca's living room wall, which depicted her, her mother and her grandmother dressed as witches. *I wonder*, he thought, and sat up straight, his mind clear all of a sudden, but then he slumped back shaking his head. *No, they can't be, she never had any children…or none that anyone knew about.*

His brain was in overdrive now. He would need to try and construct a family tree and try to find out whether Isabella did actually give birth to a child and whether, as his thoughts had initially concluded from Becca's photograph, Becca and her family are descended from that child. That would at least provide a connection between Antony and Becca, even if he still had to determine the reason why Antony was back.

As these thoughts skittered through his mind, Jakes' gaze fell on the last line of the narrative and on two words in particular. He felt his heart almost stop as realisation dawned.

CONSECRATED GROUND

The church and the churchyard were no longer classed as consecrated ground. The spells, in effect, were broken. Antony Cardover was, in theory, free. Jakes remembered the photos lying on his desk at the station. It seemed the "fairy story" was true after all.

CHAPTER 33

Becca sat on the floor in her mother's attic, staring at the trunk that her grandmother had given her on her sixteenth birthday. Her mother's words still bounced around in her head.

'What?' Becca had said, staring at her mother in shock.

'You and I are the last of Isabella's descendants. Unless there's something you're not telling me...?' Ginnie had said.

'W-w-what does that mean?' Becca had said, ignoring her mother's ridiculous suggestion.

'I told you,' Ginnie had started clearing up the tea things. 'You need to stop him before he regains his full strength; otherwise we will both be doomed.'

'Stop him? What are you talking about?' Becca had stared at her mother, her mouth agape.

'Oh for goodness sake, pull yourself together! Did your grandmother not tell you anything, Rebecca?' Ginnie had picked up the tray and had started walking towards the door.

'What the hell are you talking about?' Becca had shouted and had felt an uncontrollable rage course through her body as she had jumped up and faced her mother. She had felt the wounds on her neck throbbing and an overwhelming thirst overcome her – the same thirst as the night before her kitchen floor incident.

'Rebecca!' Ginnie had said and had whirled round to face her daughter.

'How dare..,' Ginnie had fallen silent; her brow furrowing; her face tensing.

'What's the matter now?' Becca had said as she'd seen a flicker of concern flash across her mother's usual stoic countenance. 'I only swore.'

'Your eyes.'

'What's wrong with my eyes?' Becca had said as she'd struggled to control the rage that had sprung up from nowhere. The thirst had been overpowering and her gaze was drawn to the veins in her mother's neck.

'They're black.' Ginnie had pointed to the mirror above the fireplace. Becca had turned and glanced at her reflection. Horrified, she'd stepped closer to the mirror, staring into the inky blackness that looked back at her.

'Oh my God,' she'd said and, dropping to her knees, she'd put her head in her hands and had started to cry. Almost immediately she'd felt the rage ebb away from her, taking the thirst with it.

'What's happening to me?' she'd said and Ginnie had crouched down beside her daughter and had wrapped her arms around her.

'I'm sorry, darling,' she'd said. 'I'm so sorry that this has to fall on you. If only it had happened when your grandmother was alive. She'd have seen the signs. She knew what to expect. She'd have dealt with it straight away. This would never have happened.'

'For God's sake, Mum, will you just tell me what's going on,' Becca had pushed away from her mother, but had held her by the upper arms.

Ginnie had detached herself from Becca's grip and had stood up. She'd crossed her arms over her chest and had rubbed her hands up and down them as she'd stared out of the patio windows, into the jungle beyond.

'Mum?' Becca had prompted, still sitting on the floor, rubbing the wounds on her neck to try and stop the throbbing.

'The deal Antony made with Ebenezer was for life, so to speak. When he was told he had to kill Isabella and all her descendants before he could be free, he'd thought it would be easy. As far as he knew, Isabella didn't have any children and so, as far as he was concerned, all he had to do was kill her.'

'But she did have a child, the one Anna sent away with Carla,' Becca had continued. Ginnie had nodded.

'Antony realised that something wasn't right after he'd killed Isabella and nothing changed. The anger and the demons were still in him. By this point, though, he could do nothing as Anna had begun to cast the spells that would hold him for four hundred years.'

'So, why's he decided on now?'

'There were three things containing Antony in his tomb – two spells and burial in consecrated ground. The spells cannot be broken whilst he is buried in hallowed ground so, all I can assume, is that he no longer is.'

'No, he isn't,' Becca had said.

'How do you know?'

'Because I've seen the sarcophagus. Remember? It's...' Becca had drifted off, her mouth agape. Ginnie had stared over at her daughter.

'You've seen it? How?'

'At the site...where I work...dug up...in the cellar...he's going to kill us, isn't he?' Lucidity had returned and Becca had turned and faced her mother as she'd asked.

'He must kill all of Isabella's descendants to regain his soul and become human again. What site are you talking about? How have you managed to see the sarcophagus? It's been buried for over four hundred years.'

'Well, it isn't anymore,' Becca had sighed. 'I told you this on the phone. Don't you listen? It was unearthed a few days ago and instead of reburying it at another church with the others, Dick decided he wanted to keep it to showcase. So, now it's in the cellar until building work is completed,' Becca had said, her mind elsewhere.

'Who's Dick? And what do you mean "it's in the cellar"? What cellar?'

'Dick Ramply, my boss? The crypt of the church…so you and I…'

'You mean you work for Ramply Homes?' Ginnie had said.

'Yes, why?'

'Don't you know that he's a crook? His houses are shoddy and fall apart after a couple of years. He has no concern for the environment when he sources his materials and…'

'Mum! Can we get back to the point?' Ginnie had fallen silent and Becca had sat and stared at her, waiting for an answer to her earlier question.

'Well?' Becca had prompted.

'Well what?'

'Is he or is he not going to kill us?'

'He needs to kill her descendants, yes.'

'And we are her last descendants?'

'Yes.'

'So, he's going to kill us?'

'If you want to put it like that…'

'How else do you want me to put it, Mum? We have some psycho vampire whack job out there looking for us because his wife cheated on him way back when!' Becca had shouted and then they'd both fallen silent.

'What are we going to do?' Becca had finally asked.

'It's not a case of what *we're* going to do, but what *you're* going to do.'

'Gee thanks, Mum. But, if I'm not mistaken, you're on his hit list too.'

'I know that, but I don't have the power to stop him. Only you do.'

'That's bullshit!'

'No, it isn't. Remember the wooden box that your grandmother showed you on your sixteenth birthday?' Ginnie had asked and Becca had nodded, fingering the key around her neck.

'That box has been passed down through the generations. It is what is in that box that will tell you how to stop him.'

'Where is it?'

'What?'

'The box!'

'In the trunk, your trunk, in the attic.'

Becca sighed and ran her hand over the warped lid of the trunk. She still felt dazed. How could some ancient vampire want, or should she say, need to kill her? Vampires didn't exist. They were characters in gothic novels, folklore and dodgy movies. They weren't real. Yet, according to her mother they did exist or, at least, one did.

Becca reached up and scratched the wounds on her neck and winced. She could feel them pulsing and could feel the dampness there. She glanced at her watch. It was getting late and the sun would be going down soon. She shivered and hugged herself, staring into space. Part of her didn't believe the story her mother had told her, but part of her did.

'Rebecca? Tea's ready,' her mother's voice drifted up the attic steps.

'Okay,' Becca said, pulling the scarf more tightly around her neck to try and subdue the throbbing.

'Now, Rebecca, before it goes cold.'

'Coming.' Becca stood up and dusted down her battered jeans.

'Eat your food, Rebecca, don't play with it,' Ginnie chastised as Becca pushed a floret of broccoli around the other food on her plate.

'I'm not hungry,' she said and continued in her quest.

'I'd like you to stay here tonight,' Ginnie said.

'Why?'

'I'd feel better knowing you were safe.'

'Doesn't mean I'll be safe, or you for that matter, just because I stay here.'

'I know. I just don't want to be here alone. Will you stay, please?'

'Okay,' Becca sighed, pushing her chair away from the table.

'Where are you going?' Ginnie asked, her voice edged with panic.

'I need to find the box,' Becca said as she left the room.

Up in the attic, Becca didn't waste any more time. She threw open the lid of the trunk, which protested at the harsh treatment, and began to rummage through it. Memories of her sixteenth birthday flitted through her mind, but she pushed them away. She didn't have time for nostalgia. She wanted whatever was going on to be over. She wanted everything returned to normal.

Just as she was about to give up hope of finding the box, her fingers bashed against something on its end in the corner of the trunk. She picked it up and set it on the attic floor in front of her and sat and stared at it.

Becca ran her finger over the lid and the words *You will know when* emerged out of the dust. Taking the key from around her neck, she inserted it into the rusty lock and turned. Although there was a slight resistance, to Becca's surprise, the lock opened fairly easily. She lifted the lid and peered inside. Several pieces of parchment lay neatly folded, nestled in the deep purple velvet interior.

With the tips of her fingers, Becca gently removed the pieces of parchment and set them down on the floor in front of her. She then held the corner of each piece down with one finger and carefully unfolded them, until all three were open before her. She stared at them and a shiver ran up her spine.

The first one showed drawings of church windows and Becca's mind raced as she tried to place them. She had seen them before, but where? Her gaze drifted to the other two pieces. Both were covered in intricate writing, which Becca struggled to read properly in the dim attic light. She picked up one of the pieces of parchment, no longer caring about the age, and tilted it towards the window, to pick up the additional light of the moon. She skimmed the script and then moved on to the next piece. The words read as

172

poems, but Becca knew better. They were spells. Becca's heart sank as she realised that they must be the spells used to contain Antony Cardover, almost half a millennium ago.

If they were the spells, then the drawings must be the etchings on his sarcophagus. She picked up the page of drawings and studied them. She couldn't be one hundred per cent sure. A faint glimmer of hope fluttered through her. Hope that this was all a misunderstanding. Hope that she was merely having bad dreams. Hope that her mother's story was just that; a story.

In her desire for it all to be untrue, Becca conveniently forgot about her hallucinations, her thirst and, most of all, the marks on her neck. She grabbed the pieces of paper and the box and, leaving everything else behind, she dashed down the stairs, nearly knocking her mother over.

'Rebecca, what's the rush? Where are you going?' But Becca didn't answer. She slammed the front door behind her and ran down the path towards her car.

She didn't see the man standing in the shadows.

CHAPTER 34

He was restless tonight. The cellar felt like another prison as he waited for the last rays of sunlight to disappear. He had to move fast now. He had to get the girl before she realised what was going on. He had known Anna pretty well and he knew she would have left instructions of some kind behind for the bitch's offspring. He punched the wall as he remembered the deception, but didn't notice the fractured stone crumbling to the floor.

He'd been so naïve. First, he had been taken in by the old warlock and then he'd been deceived, yet again, by his slut of a wife. For some stupid reason, it had never even occurred to him that Isabella might have had a child in the year he'd been gone. Just because he'd never managed to get her pregnant, didn't mean that someone else hadn't. He'd simply assumed there had been something wrong with her. He shook his head as he thought about that final night, yet again.

He'd dropped Isabella at his feet and had turned to walk away. He'd made plans to leave Carlford that night, to start again somewhere else, where no one knew him or knew of him. Once the curse had been lifted he'd be able to put everything behind him and move on. It would never have happened if that bitch hadn't humiliated him and he'd felt the rage still bubbling deep within him.

The old man had told him that the curse would lift as soon as Isabella and all her descendants had been destroyed. Well, Isabella was dead and so far he'd felt no change. In fact, the demon inside him had seemed to be even more restless and images had started to flash through his mind.

He'd stopped and dropped onto his haunches to try and steady himself as the flashing images had begun to make him dizzy. A short distance away he'd heard Anna's chanting, but he hadn't been listening, he'd been trying to focus on the images.

He'd closed his eyes and taken a deep breath to try and steady himself, but the rage within him had made it difficult. He'd forced himself to focus and, slowly, the images had begun to take shape and to merge. As a clear picture had settled in his mind, the rage had exploded within him and he'd felt the demon take over once more. He'd jumped up and had turned to face Anna, at the same time as a bolt of lightning had struck the ground in front of him, knocking him off his feet.

'Where is the slut's bastard child?' he'd bellowed into the night, as he'd floundered in the mud struggling to gain grip, but Anna had appeared not to hear as she'd continued chanting. He'd watched as a crack in the earth had opened before him and he'd thrown his head back and laughed.

'Just what do you think that's going to do, old woman? Swallow me whole?' He hadn't seen the vines as they'd shot out of the crack, but he'd felt their tug as they'd wrapped themselves around his ankles. *Excellent*, he'd thought and had sat forward, grabbed the thick stems and had used their strength to haul himself to his feet. Once upright, he'd snapped the bindings like firewood.

Antony had stridden over to Anna. The old witch had continued to ignore him as he'd towered over her; as he'd spat in her face; as he'd whispered in her ear; and even as he'd thrown the heavy vines back in her face. He'd clenched his fists and set his jaw, his anger at boiling point once again. He'd known, however, that he wouldn't get anything out of the her.

Perhaps it was time to pay young Carla a visit, he'd thought and had turned to leave when he'd been struck in the back and thrown to the ground. The force had stunned him and by the time he'd come to, vines had been lashing themselves around him once again. He'd tried to fight; to break free; with all of his strength he had, but somehow the bitch had made them stronger. As he'd fought, he'd locked eyes with Anna.

'These won't hold me forever!' he'd shouted. As the vines had shrouded his face, he'd sworn he'd seen relief in the old woman's eyes.

As soon as the last rays disappeared, Antony strode up the cellar steps into the darkening evening. When Becca had crossed the threshold into the cemetery, he'd felt the tremor. He'd closed his eyes and he'd cleared his mind and he'd seen her. She was the image of Isabella. Now he had to find her and destroy her. The resemblance to Isabella would make it so much easier and more enjoyable.

He closed his eyes and focused his mind on the bite marks he'd left on her neck. To him they were like a homing beacon. They enabled him to find her anywhere. He smiled as he got an image of her eating a meal with an older woman. They looked alike, apart from their colouring. The older woman must be the mother. A smile spread across Antony's chiselled face as he realised he had two of them to get rid of.

'B...E...C...C...A..,' he murmured, as he raised his arms to the sky and his body morphed into a hanger of bats and disappeared into the gathering night.

Antony reformed outside Becca's mother's house. He walked around the perimeter until he reached the kitchen window, where there was a light on. He peered in, careful not to be seen, and saw the woman he presumed to be Becca's mother standing at the sink, washing up. Becca was nowhere to be seen, but he knew she was in the house, he could feel her. He stared

176

intently at Becca's mother and then closed his eyes and focused on her.

'G…I…N…N…I…E..,' he breathed, opening his eyes. Ginnie glanced up from the sink and stared straight out of the window at the spot where, moments before, Antony had stood.

He went back round to the front of the house pondering the best mode of entry when he heard Ginnie's raised voice addressing Becca. He drew back into the shadows by the front door and waited. A few minutes later he heard the front door open and someone come out, slamming the door behind them. He watched as Becca ran down the garden path. For the second time that night Antony smiled. He waited a couple of minutes and then he knocked on the door.

'Come in,' came Ginnie's voice. 'You don't have to knock, silly.'

Antony opened the front door, stepped inside the house and closed the door quietly behind him. He stood in the hallway and looked around him. Discarded canvasses were everywhere, stacked up against the walls, making parts of the hallway very narrow. So, this was where Becca got her artistic flair from. He shuddered as an unfamiliar feeling swept through his body. Pride. What the hell was he feeling proud for? These people weren't related to him. They were related to that slut of a wife. His anger surged again.

'Becca? Is that you?' Ginnie called and Antony walked towards the kitchen where he could see a light was still on.

'Hello, Ginnie,' Antony said as he stood in the doorway. Ginnie jumped at the sound of his voice and dropped the plate she was holding. It smashed all over the kitchen floor.

'W-w-who are you?' Ginnie said as she whirled round to face him.

'Oh, I think you already know that,' Antony watched her eyebrows pucker into a quizzical frown.

'N-n-no, I'm sorry, I d-d-don't,' she said and braced herself against the sink, her arms spread wide. Antony watched in amusement as she tried to manoeuvre her hand towards the carving knife that was lying on the draining board.

'I'm sure you do, Ginnie. Haven't you and your lovely daughter, Becca, been talking about me for most of the day?' He walked towards her as he watched the colour drain from her face and her mouth drop open, but no words came out.

'Let me refresh your memory. I'm Antony Cardover,' he said and picked up the carving knife and offered it to Ginnie. 'Go on. Take it. See if it works.'

Slowly Ginnie took the knife and pointed it towards him, her eyes never leaving his face.

'Well?' he said, spreading his arms wide and standing in front of her. 'Go ahead. Stab me.' Ginnie didn't move. She stood rigid, rooted to the spot in front of the sink.

In one swift movement, Antony grabbed the knife out of her hand and thrust it through his heart. Ginnie's hands flew to her mouth to muffle a scream as her eyes widened in shock.

'See. Nothing. You cannot kill me. You don't have the power,' he said as he spread his arms wide again, the carving knife protruding from his chest. 'Did you honestly think it would be that easy? If it were, why would the old woman have imprisoned me in that tomb? Why not simply run a stake through my heart? There is only one way I can be cured and you already know what that is, don't you?' he stared into Ginnie's eyes as he asked, but she didn't move.

'Don't you!' he shouted, making her jump and she nodded.

'And how is that, exactly?' he asked, yanking the knife out of his chest and throwing it down onto the floor. 'See. No harm done.' He lifted his shirt to reveal a taut unmarked torso.

'So,' he said, placing his hands on the sink, either side of Ginnie and leaning close into her, his lips inches from her neck. 'What is the only way that I can be cured, Virginia?' he whispered. He heard her whimper and smelt the odour of ammonia as she started to shake. A smile played across his lips as he brushed them gently up and down her carotid artery.

'Tell me, Virginia, and maybe you'll be okay.'

'I-I-I need to d-d-die,' she whimpered and leant her head against his chest, as though seeking comfort.

'That's right, Virginia, you do. And who else?' he said, kissing her neck and feeling goose bumps erupt across her skin.

'M-m-my d-d-daughter,' she said and then she looked directly at him. 'Please don't.' He studied the dark pleading eyes, so much like the dead slut's.

'You know I can't do that,' he said and pushed away from her and walked to the other end of the kitchen. He turned round to face her.

'But, I want to play a little game with young Rebecca,' he said and started walking towards her once more. Ginnie remained still; tense, fearful, her gaze following his every move.

'Or, should I say, I want you to play a little game with her.' Antony stood in front of Ginnie and took her head in his hands, massaging her scalp as he did so. Her eyes widened as his lips brushed against hers and then moved towards her ear again.

'I'd like you to tell her that the story of me is just that – a story. I want you to tell her that everything you talked about this afternoon, because I know you did, was just fiction.' He caressed her neck with his tongue and she shuddered. He smiled and pulled back to look at her.

'Do you think you could do that for me, Virginia?'

'Why would I help you?' she said, her voice growing stronger, fire suddenly filling her eyes.

'Because you will have no choice,' he smiled at her, causing her to shudder again.

'I always have a choice,' she said and pushed against him with all her weight. He staggered backwards at the unexpected force and Ginnie made a run for the hallway.

Oh, how he loved a chase. Before she'd even made it to the doorway, he was standing in front of it, blocking her exit. She screamed and spun round, running now in the opposite direction, towards the back door. Antony laughed out loud.

'Do you honestly think you can get away from me, Virginia?' he asked as he stood between her and the door. Ginnie collapsed in a heap on the floor and started to sob.

'Please. Why can't you just leave us alone?' she begged as she looked up at him, tears streaming down her cheeks.

'You know I can't do that,' he said, crouching down in front of her and running the elongated nail of his index finger along her jaw line.

'But why?' she pleaded. 'We don't want any trouble…' Her voice trailed off and she stared down at the floor.

'Bad genes on your part mean that's never going to happen. You and Rebecca are my key to freedom and that's all that matters to me,' he said and he felt the rage surge inside him and his vision change. He then inspected Ginnie and all he could see were the veins running through her body. Her heartbeat pulsed inside his head and he could feel the familiar hunger building.

'It's just your bad luck to be descended from such a harlot.' He lunged for her, grabbing her head and dragging her towards him. She screamed and flailed her arms, but she was no match for his strength.

He growled and sank his teeth into her neck. Her heart was pounding, making the oxygenated blood drain from her body all the more quickly. She tried to push him out of the way, but he could feel her strength waning.

Just before her heart stopped, he tore himself away and slit his wrist with his nail and then forced the bleeding limb into her mouth. She turned her head away from him, her lips clenched together, but he grabbed her jaw and squeezed until, with a yelp, she yielded. He held his wrist over her now open mouth and watched the blood dribble into it. She tried to spit it out at first, but it wasn't long before instinct took over and she gripped his arm with both hands and drew on him hungrily. He grimaced at the pain, but he let her feed. He could feel the thundering of blood through his body and it was getting louder and louder. Just as the pounding reached a crescendo, he shoved her away from him and fell against the kitchen wall.

Ginnie collapsed in a heap on the floor and he closed his eyes and waited for the pounding to settle. He had to wait now. It wouldn't take long. So, he sat and he watched her.

Antony jumped and his eyes flew open as a piercing scream echoed through the house. He glanced up at the kitchen clock. Hell! He must have fallen asleep. He was weaker than he thought. He would need to feed soon. They both would.

He watched Ginnie, writhing on the floor. He remembered the pain she was going through. It was not pleasant.

'It will pass,' he said to her as he stood up and walked passed her and glanced out of the kitchen window. The night was clear and the moon was almost full. Tomorrow it would be at its peak; full and ripe. *How poetic,* he thought and smiled to himself.

'We'll both need to feed before dawn,' he said and looked over at her. She was still. She was calm. She had awoken.

'Are you ready, Ginnie?' he asked and held out his hand to her. She reached up and took it. He pulled her to her feet to scrutinise her. Virginia Martin was certainly a different woman to the one he'd first encountered. The once frizzy red hair was now a lustrous mass of auburn spirals, which hung long down her back. Her skin, once dull and lined, now resembled porcelain with a slight glow to her cheeks. Her lips were now full and crimson, where before they had been pale and thin. Her eyes remained the same, though. They were Isabella's eyes. Deep dark pools that drew you in. Antony glanced away from her quickly and turned towards the door, too many memories flooding his mind.

'Come, there is a lot to do before dawn.'

CHAPTER 35

So, if Antony was free, who or what was he after? There must have been a reason why he had been kept under such tight security and why he hadn't been killed way back when. The answers to both these problems must be somewhere; they had to be.

As Jakes pondered this, his gaze rested on the unopened bottle of Jim Beam that he kept locked in a glass cabinet – a test of his sobriety. The bottle stood as a constant reminder of the life he'd thrown away and of everything he'd lost. Whenever he was faced with a difficult case, Jakes always spent time looking at this bottle. It sought to calm him; to still his thoughts and focus his mind. It didn't fail him now.

Jakes pushed his chair backwards, stood up and started to scan the collection of volumes on his bookshelf. He pulled various titles from the shelves and dropped them on to the table behind him.

He sat down again, muttering to himself, and started flicking through the indexes of the books he'd selected. Every so often he would delve into the depths and scan down the pages and every time he would come up, shaking his head. As he slammed the last volume shut, he cursed and put his head in his hands. *It must be somewhere; it had to be.* Abruptly, he stood up and grabbed his coat as he left the house.

Lucky for him, the public library was only ten minutes away. As he huffed and puffed up the grandiose stone steps, Jakes prayed that it would be open. At the top he stopped and bent forward, his hands resting on his knees, drawing air into his screaming lungs. *This place better be open*, he thought again. He looked at his watch – it was nine o'clock – then he straightened himself up and headed for the entrance. He glanced at the opening hours on the door as he pushed it open. He had one hour.

Jakes cursed himself again for not having a computer at home and found himself a vacant machine. He didn't have time for the books; which was a shame, because for a small library, they had a phenomenal collection of books on local history, folklore and even the occult.

Jakes slowly typed Anna's name into the search engine and hit return. He waited a few seconds until the results appeared and then started to scan down them. There were thousands. He'd never get through all these. He slammed his hand onto the desk in frustration, catching the attention of the librarian. She frowned at him and marched over, pushing her glasses up on her nose and patting her coiffed grey hair down. Jakes rolled his eyes. *Here we go*, he thought, *now I'll never get anything done.*

'What are you looking for? I'll probably be able to find it quicker than you,' she said. Jakes snorted with amusement and she frowned at him again.

'Why don't you just tell me what you want and we'll see, shall we?' she said. Not wanting a fight and, more importantly, not having the time for one, Jakes sighed.

'I'm trying to find out about Anna Martindale. She was a very powerful witch who was burnt at the stake about four hundred years ago…' His voice drifted off as he watched her fingers fly across the keyboard. 'Well, actually, it's not only her, but, more importantly, her daughter, Isabella and also, maybe, a young girl who lived with them. The girl's name was Carla. I have no idea what her last name was,' he said.

She stopped and he thought she was going to say something, but she didn't. She started typing again and Jakes sat back and watched as she flicked through website after website, hitting the print icon every so often.

'I'll go and get your printouts and…' she drifted off.

'And what?' Jakes said, a little too abruptly, he thought, when he saw the pinched look on her face. 'Sorry…Marion,' he said, glancing at her name badge. 'This information is for a case I'm working on and it's perplexing me, to say the least.'

'Well, why didn't you say that when you came in. Things might have gone more smoothly, Inspector…?'

'Yes?'

'Your name, Inspector. I'm not in the habit of dealing with people whom I am not acquainted with.'

'Oh, right, Jakes. My name is Jakes.'

'Very well, Inspector Jakes, give me a moment, I have something that will probably be of interest to you.'

She stalked off back to her station and Jakes sighed, rubbing his eyes with his thumb and forefinger. Women, would he ever work them out? He heaved himself up and headed towards the empty station where he had seen Marion headed. Puzzled, he leaned over to see if she had passed out and was lying in need of help behind her desk. Why he thought of that he had no idea, but she wasn't there anyway. He was just about to call out, when she appeared from a room beyond her desk.

'This may be of use to you,' she said and thrust a bound ream of papers into his hand.

'What is it?'

'It's a copy of a diary that came to us as part of a house clearance about ten years ago. The diary itself is in a poor state, hence the copy, but as it's for a case, I will allow you to borrow it, as long as you return it when you are finished.'

'Why will it be of use to me?'

'Goodness, you are an exasperating man! Why do you think? It refers to the people you've just been enquiring about. To be more precise, I believe it is a diary that was kept by a young lady by the name of Carla Emerson.'

'Carla who.......oh, really? That's fantastic!' Jakes said, the penny finally dropping. 'Thanks. You're a lifesaver.' Jakes leaned over her desk and planted a kiss on her waxy cheek.

Marion pursed her lips and gave him a curt nod and then glanced at her watch. 'You'll have to leave now, Inspector, it's closing time.'

Jakes nodded and turned to leave.

'Don't forget the rest of your research.'

'Ah, yes, right, thanks again, Marion,' he said as he took the papers from her and headed for the door.

Back at home, Jakes made himself a strong black coffee and settled down in his threadbare armchair to read the reams of information that Marion had given him. He switched on the lamp on the table beside him and the dank room was illuminated in a harsh yellow light. *Christ*, he thought, he really needed to clean the place up. He took a swig of his coffee and winced as the scolding liquid burnt the insides of his mouth. He definitely wasn't used to hot drinks.

He thought about starting with the information on Anna and Isabella, but as the story had never been documented in any books, why should the internet be any different? A diary, on the other hand, could well hold all the information he needed and more. He picked up the sheaf of papers and stared at the curling writing on the front page:

The Diary of Carla ~~Adams~~ Emerson

Jakes turned the page and started to read.

CHAPTER 36

Carla Adams was orphaned at the age of seven and Anna took her into her home. Anna was treating Carla's mother for a disease that she hadn't come across before and she was losing the battle. By the time Rebecca Adams died, Carla was already part of the Martindale family and Anna didn't see any reason to change that. Rebecca Adams had been poor and no one else seemed interested in the well being of the child, so no questions were asked.

Anna had a daughter, Isabella, whom she gave birth to soon after the tragic death of her husband. Isabella was fifteen when Carla came to live with them and she took the orphan under her wing, much to Anna's surprise.

Carla idolised Isabella and followed her around everywhere. Isabella's creamy skin, dark eyes and dark curly hair mesmerised Carla. Carla thought that Izzy was the most beautiful person she had ever seen. She was the complete opposite of Carla. Where Izzy was tall and shapely, Carla was short and bone thin. Her white blonde hair and pale freckled skin contrasted sharply with Izzy's dark beauty. Carla's clear blue eyes were almost transparent.

Carla always felt ugly and awkward in Izzy's presence and so she always kept herself in the background. As such, Carla never made any friends. Izzy and Anna were all she had. Izzy, on the other hand, was extremely popular and spent little time at home in the evenings. Izzy would come home and wake Carla up to tell her stories about what had been happening in the village. These tales always revolved around Isabella and always involved boys. Izzy made it sound so wonderful and Carla lapped up every word. Too young to know any better, she dreamed of the day when she would be old enough to do the same.

Anna's home was on the edge of the woods, a good distance from the main village. Her profession meant that she wasn't allowed to live in or spend a lot of time in the village. Witchcraft was the devil's work and people's ignorance meant that Anna led a very lonely existence, following the death of her husband. Despite their fear of witchcraft, people always came to see Anna when they needed help. Whether it was a cure for an ailment or a solution for misbehaved children or wayward husbands, Anna never bore a grudge and always did everything she could to help. Many a traumatised husband came to her in desperation and smuggled her into their homes to help with the birth of their children.

The only person who ever came to visit Anna, as a friend, was Father Tom. He and Anna had grown up together and Father Tom had been Anna's husband, John's, best friend. Neither of them held their professions against each other. No one in the village knew about their friendship because Anna did not want Father Tom to be treated in the same way as the villagers treated her.

The same ostracism was never extended to Isabella. Whether they believed her to be a witch or not, the villagers loved her. She was beautiful and fragile. People simply stared at her in awe and treated her as though she was someone special. Izzy, being the type of person she was, just drank it all in and played up to it.

Izzy changed once she started seeing Antony. For a period of time he became everything she appeared to care about and she had no interest in anyone or anything else, including Carla.

Carla was devastated at being cast aside in such a way and cried for weeks. Anna did her best to comfort her.

'Isabella may be beautiful on the outside, Carla, but inside she is not so,'

Anna said to Carla, on a day when she was particularly upset.

'I-I-I don't understand,' Carla said, regarding Anna through tear-filled eyes.

'She isn't a kind person, my dear. What lurks within Isabella is dark and selfish. Everything she does is to benefit herself. She never has, nor will she ever do anything for anyone else,' Anna said and shook her head and sighed. 'You, Carla, are very different. You are a very pretty girl and you have a good heart. You will understand more as you get older.' She took the young girl's hand and squeezed it tight.

'But she is so popular. Everyone loves her. I want to be just like her…' Carla trailed off as though lost in an image of herself.

'No, Carla, you stay as you are. You do not want to be like Isabella. People don't know her. Antony doesn't really know her, but he will, one day, and I pity him that day.' Anna looked at Carla, only to be greeted by a quizzical expression.

'Oh, Carla. All people fall in love with are Isabella's looks. They fall for an image of what they imagine her to be and she can fool them because they don't know her. Not many people do. Even you are only just starting to get to know her. She'll be back when she starts to get bored, which she will.' Anna went quiet for few minutes and Carla was about to go to her room when she spoke again.

'Isabella will bring ruin on this family, of that I am sure. How she will do it is less clear, but she will destroy us. Now, now, don't be frightened, child,' Anna said, at the look of fright on Carla's face. 'You, young lady, will be fine. Now, off you go, I have things I need to do.'

Over the next few years Carla learned to live with her own company. She remained a shy, isolated child, who preferred to be with Anna than with people her own age, but gradually the pain of Isabella's abandonment diminished. Izzy visited them and was her normal gushing self with Carla, but with Anna's help, Carla learnt to take it at face value and not to read more into it because, once Izzy left, they did not see or hear from her until the next time she wanted something. Isabella's visits, as Anna explained, were for her own purposes and nothing more. Whether it was food, a remedy, help, repairs to clothes or money, Isabella always wanted something.

Antony was different. He dropped in on them several times a week, just to say hello and to see how they were. He had to visit the village or other villages for materials or to deliver orders and he always called in on them. Often he brought gifts – shawls or herbs for Anna and carved wooden animals that he had made himself, for Carla. Carla worshipped Antony. He was like the big brother that she'd never had.

Sometimes Carla went to watch Antony work. His workshop was like a second home to her. She'd sit on a stool by the ever burning fire and watch him at his bench under the window, hunched over his latest piece. She loved the way the sunlight caught his hair, somehow illuminating the sawdust that speckled it. Most of all, though, Carla loved the smells – the raw muskiness of Antony as he sweated under his leather apron; the comforting scent of freshly worked wood; and the eye-watering aroma of varnish.

The floor, strewn with chips of cut wood from the broad-axe and curly shavings from the plane, was peppered with sawdust, which Carla drew pictures in. Antony never swept up. The walls were adorned with the tools of his trade – broad-axe, chisels, mallets, plane, handsaws – and Carla liked to watch him work with them all. Antony always showed her how he did things and sometimes he would even let her have a go. He had helped her make a stool , which now took pride of place in Anna's parlour.

It was during one of these visits that Carla noticed that something was wrong between Antony and Isabella. Carla was in the store room looking for some nails when she heard the door to the workshop slam.

'Hello, Isabella,' she heard Antony say, weariness edging his voice. Carla was about to rush out to see Izzy when she heard the tone in her voice and decided to stay where she was.

'I'm bored,' Isabella said and stamped her foot. Carla opened the door a touch so she was able to see both of them. Isabella was standing there with her hands on her hips, while Antony was crouched over his latest creation, his head bowed. It almost seemed, to Carla, as though he was bowing down before her.

'Why are you bored?' Antony continued to work the piece of wood in front of him. He didn't look up at his wife.

'Because there's nothing to do and you won't spend any time with me,' she said and stamped her foot again.

'Izzy, we've been through all this,' he said and looked up at her.

'I've got to work hard and build this business back up otherwise we won't have any money to live on,' she mimicked, a sneer turning her usually beautiful face into an ugly grimace.

'Would you rather we were poor and had nowhere to live?' Antony shouted and jumped up off the stool to face her, his fists clenched, spittle flying from his mouth. 'What in God's name is wrong with you?'

'You never spend any time with me,' Isabella shouted at him, her dark eyes, almost black in her anger. 'All you care about is this stupid business.'

'This "stupid" business is what keeps you in your fancy clothes and keeps a roof over our heads, Isabella,' he said through gritted teeth.

'Yes, well, maybe I want a man who pays attention to me all the time,' she said, raised her nose into the air and started to turn away from him. Antony grabbed her by the tops of her arms and shook her.

'What the hell is the matter with you? What do you want from me? I am doing the best that I can for you. All of this is for you,' he said looking around his workshop.

'What I want,' Isabella said, shrugging out of his grip, 'is a real man. A man who knows how to appreciate me. A man who knows how to treat me.

A man who knows how to keep me satisfied.' She laughed to herself.

'How dare you, you ungrateful bitch!' Antony slapped Isabella hard across the face. Carla gasped and immediately clamped her hand over her mouth, worried that they might have heard her.

Isabella crumpled to the floor, tears flowing freely down her cheeks, her hand pressed against her reddened cheek.

'How could you?' she whispered.

Antony dropped to the floor in front of her.

'I'm sorry, Izzy, I'm sorry, but you made me so angry. I'm sorry, I'm sorry,' he tried to pull her into his arms, but she pushed him away and stood up, her tears and hurt suddenly gone.

'As I said, I want a real man. One who can stand by his actions. Not like you. You're pathetic!' she spat at him and turned on her heel and left the workshop.

Carla stayed where she was, not sure when the best time was to come out. Antony had clearly forgotten that she was there. She watched him as he slumped back on his haunches and placed his head in his hands. She watched as his body shook. Unable to stand it anymore, she left the store room, went and wrapped her arms around him and pulled him towards her. She held him while he cried, neither of them saying a word. When he finally stopped crying, Carla simply left. She knew, without being told, that he wanted to be alone.

She didn't see him after that and three weeks later he disappeared.

Isabella came crying to them one night, appearing to be totally distraught. Carla had learnt to ignore her natural instinct to go and comfort Isabella and instead held back and let Anna take the lead.

'What on earth is the matter, child?' Anna said and patted the chair next to the fire for Isabella to sit down.

'I can't go back,' Isabella sobbed, dabbing at her eyes with a handkerchief.

'He'll kill me if I do.' She looked up at her mother with such sorrow in her eyes that Carla ached to go to her, but she didn't. She stayed where she was.

'Why? What have you done?' Anna said, her expression suddenly closed and hard.

'What do you mean what I've done? What about what he's done? It's all his fault, you know!' Isabella said, her tears suddenly gone, her eyes flashing.

'I simply asked what you'd done because I have no doubt, Isabella, that you have done something to provoke him.'

'Mother! How could you?' Isabella jumped out of her chair and headed for the bedrooms.

'Sit down,' Anna said, her hands on her hips, her eyes cold in her wrinkled face. Isabella carried on walking. 'Now!' Anna said and something in her voice made Isabella turn round. She sat down, knees together, hands on her knees, head bowed.

'Now, young lady, you are not going anywhere until you tell me exactly what you've done to Antony.' Anna stood in front of her daughter and stared down at her.

'I haven't done…'

'Don't lie to me, my girl,' Anna said. 'I know you and I know Antony, so spit it out.'

'But, I didn't…'

'Isabella, I'm warning you. I will force you to tell me, but I'd rather not.'

'I-I-think I know,' Carla said, emerging from her hiding place in the bedroom doorway.

'What do you know? You're only a kid,' Isabella said and the look of spite cut Carla to the core.

'Be quiet! Come on, child, what is it that you think you know?' Anna asked, her voice gentle, as she coaxed Carla to come forward.

'I-I was at the workshop a few weeks ago and I heard Izzy come in and they started to shout at each other…' Carla trailed off as she turned to look at Isabella and found her staring daggers back at her. She was shaking her head to try to discourage Carla from continuing.

'What were they arguing about, child?' Anna encouraged and Carla looked away from Isabella's angry face and into the eyes of the woman who had been a mother to her now, for many years.

'I-I-I'm not sure, but…'

'See, she doesn't know anything and I've already told you…' Anna waved her hand in front of Isabella's face and muttered something under her breath, cutting Isabella off mid sentence.

'Now, Carla, tell me what you heard,' Anna said, ignoring Isabella's silent protestations. Carla looked at Isabella and her eyes widened in fright.

'It's okay, Carla. Just tell me what you heard. I will deal with Isabella.'

'I-I just heard her say that he never spent any time with her and that she would go and find someone who would. Antony tried to explain about needing to work to look after her, but she wouldn't listen. She said he wasn't a real man and he hit her. He didn't mean to, but she just laughed when he apologised and said again that he wasn't a real man and then she left. Antony was really upset. I put my arm around him and he cried. I could tell that he wanted to be on his own, so I left. I never saw him after that and now I probably never will…' Carla broke off and started crying. Anna pulled her into her arms and Carla caught a glimpse of Isabella's face. It was purple with rage and she waved a clenched fist at Carla, but Carla turned away and buried her head in Anna's shoulder.

'There, there, child. You've done the right thing. Now, off you go to your room. I need to speak to Isabella.' Anna ushered her away, but Carla didn't close the door. She wanted to hear what was said. She could see Anna's face, but only the back of Isabella's head, from where she was standing.

Anna waved her hand in front of Isabella's face again and Carla saw her lips move as she muttered the counter spell.

'How dare you do magic on me like that!' Isabella shouted as she jumped up and towered over Anna.

'Sit down, Isabella,' Anna said and Isabella fell into the chair as though she'd been pushed.

'Now, I want you to tell me exactly why you spoke to Antony the way you did that day and don't even think about lying, or I will place a truth spell on you.' Anna stared down at her daughter and Isabella leaned back in the chair and began to rock back and forth.

'He deserved it,' Isabella said.

'Deserved what, exactly?' Isabella didn't reply.

'Okay, what was the argument, which Carla overheard, about?'

'He doesn't love me anymore.'

'What on earth makes you think he doesn't love you? Everything that man does is for you. He adores you.' Anna raised her arms to the heavens at this point and shook her head in amazement.

'He never spends any time with me. All he cares about is work. All he cares about is his stupid wood.' Carla saw Isabella fold her arms and she knew that she was pouting as well. Izzy always did that to try and get her own way, but Anna had never fallen for it in the past and Carla doubted that she would this time.

'For goodness sake, Isabella! The man is only trying to make a future for the two of you. Can't you see that?'

'But he never spends any time with me.' Isabella stamped her foot.

'It's about time you grew up, young lady, and stopped being so selfish. Antony has worked his fingers to the bone to rebuild that business and make it into the success that it is. He's done it all for you, so you can have your nice clothes and so that, one day, you can have a family. He is building a solid foundation for you to have an easy life and all you can do is complain that you are not getting the attention you want.'

'Well, what's wrong with that?'

'You are not a child anymore. If you were any kind of wife you would be helping him, not thwarting him. But, then again, I'd never expect anything else from you. I did warn him.'

'You did what?' Isabella said and stood up to face her mother. Carla could see her clearly then and saw the rage and hatred on Isabella's face, but Anna remained calm and composed, her pale eyes staring right up into her daughter's.

'I warned him about you. The day he asked me for your hand in marriage, but he wasn't interested in what I had to say. He was too taken in by you and by the picture he'd created of you.'

'What...exactly...did...you...say...to...him...Mother?' Isabella said through gritted teeth, her head bent so she was inches from her mother's face.

'I told him what a spoilt and selfish person you are. I warned him not to be taken in by the way you look because, in your case, beauty is only skin deep. I told him that eventually you will break his heart. By the look of it, I was right, wasn't I?' Anna stared up at Isabella, not an inch of fear or intimidation registering on her face.

'How dare you say that about me. How could you? You're supposed to be my mother. You're supposed to love me.' Isabella turned away and walked towards the kitchen, out of Carla's line of vision. Carla watched Anna as her shoulders dropped and she lowered her head and slowly sank into the chair, looking all of her sixty years.

'I do love you, Isabella, but I am under no illusion about the sort of person you are and what you are capable of.' Anna glanced up then and Carla presumed she was looking at Isabella. 'So, I know that if you'd said to him that you were going to find someone who would spend time with you; then I have no doubt that's exactly what you did. Why you would be so blind and stupid is beyond me. Antony is a good man, why can't you see that?'

'Because he doesn't spend any time with me. He's stopped telling me how beautiful I am. He's stopped…'

'He's stopped worshipping you. Is that what all this is about? You are a grown woman, Isabella Cardover, and it's about time that you realised that the world does not revolve around you. You are not the sole reason for people's existence, young lady.'

'But he stopped…'

'So, you just went right out and found your adoration elsewhere, did you?' Anna jumped out of the chair, suddenly infused with energy, and disappeared out of sight.

'Well, why shouldn't I?' Isabella's petulant voice shouted and then she yelped as Carla heard a slap.

'How dare you..,' Isabella started to say.

'I dare because I am your mother and I should have done it a long time ago. Maybe then you wouldn't have turned out like you have. I am ashamed of you. You are Antony's wife and you should have behaved as such, but no, you needed people, or should I say men, fawning over you all the time for you to feel loved. You can't comprehend what love is and you don't deserve to!' Carla heard Anna spit at Isabella and then she hobbled to the chair and sat down.

'So, why can't you go back and sort it out?' Anna asked.

'I can't, he'll kill me,' Isabella said. 'I heard how angry he was when he found out about the others, he just…'

'Others? You mean you were carrying on with more than one?' Anna shouted and was out of the chair again. 'My God, I realise you are many things, but I never thought you were a slut. My own daughter; a slut.' Anna shook her head, turned to face the fireplace and reached her hand out, as though to support herself. Silence followed and Carla held her breath, waiting for someone to speak.

'Get out of my house and don't come back,' Anna whispered, after a few minutes.

'I'm sorry? What did you say?' Isabella's arrogance astounded Carla.

'I said, get out of my house!' Anna whirled round to face Isabella. 'I never want to lay eyes on you again.'

'You don't mean that, you're just...'

'Oh, I do mean it. Leave now and don't come back.' Anna hobbled over to the front door, opened it and then stood back. Carla saw Isabella come into view as she walked towards Anna, her arms outstretched.

'But I have nowhere...'

'I don't care. Now go.' Carla watched as Anna pushed Isabella out of the door and locked it behind her. She came to sit back down, her head resting against the back of the chair, a sob escaping her throat.

Carla, tears in her own eyes, ran to the old woman and put her arms around her and held her, whilst she cried.

CHAPTER 37

It was about a week later when he'd finally appeared on their doorstep. For Carla, it had been a week of watching Anna living on her nerves. They hadn't heard any more from Isabella and Carla couldn't work out whether Anna was relieved or upset. She never said. She simply went about her days as normal.

Carla was in the back, putting some laundry away, when she heard the loud bang and then the front door splinter and fall. She ran out of the bedroom to find Antony striding into the cottage. She was about to run to him and hug him, when she registered the look on his face. She stopped in her tracks in the middle of the living room and stared. He didn't even see her as he strode passed her and threw all the doors open in the little house.

'Where is the harlot?' he shouted.

'She isn't here, Antony,' Anna said. Carla marvelled at how calm Anna was, while Antony upended their furniture and yanked out drawers in his futile search.

'Where are you hiding her, Anna?' he said as his rantings finally took him to the kitchen where Anna was baking.

'I'm not hiding her anywhere,' Anna said and faced him. Carla stared at Antony, as his body shook with the rage it was obvious he was struggling to control. She jumped when he slammed his fist onto the wooden table, causing the mixing bowl to crash to the floor.

'Liar!' He grabbed Anna by the throat and pinned her to the wall. Carla screamed and started forward, but a look from Anna stopped her. Antony didn't seem to have heard her scream.

'Where is that lying, scheming, selfish slut of a daughter of yours?'

'I have no idea where she is, Antony. She came here asking to stay and I said no. After that, she left and that is all I know.'

Carla watched as Antony stared at Anna for a long time before letting her go. He then turned round and looked around the house at the mess he'd made. His face never registered Carla's presence. Then he left.

Carla started to cry and she ran to Anna. The old woman held her tight while she cried.

CHAPTER 38

They didn't hear from Antony after that nor did they see Isabella, not for several months anyway. Anna forbade the mention of Isabella's name in the house and withdrew into herself, concentrating on helping the people who came to see her. She lost interest in everything else and, in the evenings, Carla watched her rocking backwards and forwards in her rocking chair staring into space, the cat her constant companion. She barely acknowledged Carla anymore, although she always cooked her meals and laundered her clothes.

Carla grew lonely. Despite being a quiet child who always enjoyed her own company, Carla needed to interact with others every once in a while. Anna, Izzy and Antony had always filled this need, but now she'd lost all of them. She found herself being drawn towards the village and civilisation. Nobody had seen Carla since her mother had died and so nobody recognised her. She wasn't familiar with any of the children her own age because Anna had not allowed her to attend the local school.

'I don't want you being picked on because of what I am,' she'd said one day when Carla had asked why she no longer went to school.

'Why, what are you?' Carla had asked, full of the directness and innocence of a child. Anna had sighed at this point and had turned back to the stew she'd been cooking.

'Are you a monster or something?' Carla had persisted, her breath caught in her throat as she'd contemplated the likelihood.

'No, child, I'm not a monster, although some people would disagree,' Anna had said.

'I don't understand what you mean,' Carla had said and Isabella had jumped up from her place at the table at this point.

'Oh, just tell her, Mother!' Anna had carried on stirring the stew. 'Mother's a witch, Carla, a big scary witch who'll turn you into a frog if you don't do as she says,' Isabella had said and had made a face at Carla, who had screamed and had started to cry.

'Isabella!' Anna had shouted, swinging round to face her daughter, ladle in hand. 'Now you've frightened the child. There was no need for that.' Isabella had smirked, shrugged and plonked herself back down at the table.

'Leave us alone while I talk to Carla,' Anna had said and had gone over to comfort a now sobbing Carla.

'What am I supposed to do while you toughen up the orphan?' Isabella had said, stamping her foot. Anna hadn't replied, but had simply stared at Isabella who'd then flounced off, slamming the bedroom door behind her.

'Now, child, sit down and we'll have a little talk, shall we?' Anna had said and had pulled one of the kitchen chairs out for her. Carla hadn't answered, but had simply sat down on the chair, her eyes never once leaving Anna's face. Silence had reigned between them for a few minutes as Anna had put down her ladle and had made herself comfortable, in a chair opposite Carla.

'Are you really a witch?' Carla's small voice had asked, her breath still laboured as she'd continued to try and hold it in. Anna had paused and had then smiled at Carla. The smile had been warm and had made Carla relax again and made her remember the kind old lady who had cared for her mother for so long.

'Yes, child, I am, but not the sort of witch that Isabella referred to.'

'But I thought that all witches were scary. That's what mother and father used to say,' Carla had said, her small hands twisting and turning in her lap.

'There are witches who are not entirely good and who use their magic to harm others, but I am not like that. I used my magic to help your mother,' Anna had said.

'But mother died.'

'Yes, child, your mother did die, but not because of anything that I gave her. Your mother was a very sick woman and by the time she came to me there was nothing I could do except try to make her more comfortable.'

'But, if you can do magic, you can do anything. You could've saved mother, but you didn't,' Carla had said and had felt tears fall down her cheeks as she'd thought of her mother and how sick she'd been. 'Why didn't you make a spell to make her better?' she'd whispered and had then started sobbing. She'd heard Anna get up and come around the table to her and she'd felt the old woman's arms surround her. How could Anna be a witch? She'd been too nice and kind.

'There, there, child. I'm afraid that white magic doesn't work like that. It can heal, but it has its limits. Maybe if she'd come to me sooner…' She'd let the sentence die and Carla hadn't asked any more questions.

Over the years Carla had seen the good that Anna's magic had done in healing people and had gradually learned to accept its limitations. She'd learned to respect Anna for the way she'd selflessly offered her services to others.

'Why do you do it, Anna?' she'd said shortly before Antony had disappeared.

'Why do I do what, child?' Anna had asked, deeply engrossed in making a lotion for a burn.

'Why do you help them, when they won't even let you live in the village?'

'Carla, it is always important to treat people in the same way that you would like to be treated,' Anna had replied simply and Carla had pondered this for a while.

'Have you always lived here?'

'No, I grew up in the village with Father Tom and the other children our age.' Carla had been surprised by this and had stopped what she had been doing and had faced Anna.

'So, what happened? How did you end up living here?'

'As soon as they found out that I was a witch, they forced my father to take us out of the village.'

'But why?'

'People are afraid of what they don't understand, child. It's an age old story and instead of learning about it, they immediately brand it as wrong or evil and dispose of it. It will get far worse before it gets better, but I believe that one day, a long time from now, people will be more accepting of those who are different.' Carla had nodded at this and had chewed on her bottom lip, a sign that she was thinking hard about what Anna had said.

'If you're a witch, does that mean Izzy's a witch too?' she'd asked after a few minutes.

'No, child, thank the lords above, Isabella is not a witch.'

'How do you know?'

'The craft always misses a generation, so my grandmother was a witch and any daughter that Isabella may have will be a witch, but neither my mother nor Isabella were blessed with the craft.'

'But, how do you know for sure that she isn't?'

'I just do. People with the gift of the craft have a certain temperament and a certain aura about them. I could tell simply by looking at Isabella that she wasn't blessed.' Carla had gone quiet again and had continued to help Anna prepare various lotions and tonics for her patients.

'What did you do?' Carla had asked eventually.

'What did I do when, child?'

'To get thrown out of the village. What did you do?'

'Oh, I made a boy go and jump in the lake,' Anna had said and Carla had started to giggle, which had brought a rare smile to Anna's wrinkled face.

'Why...did...you...do...that?' Carla had said, between giggles, and soon Anna had been chuckling away to herself as well.

'He'd been picking on one of the younger children and I'd become very angry about it. I remember staring at him and wishing I was strong enough to throw him into the lake. The next thing I knew, he stopped what he was doing and, as if he was walking in his sleep, he walked to the lake and jumped in. He couldn't swim, but a few of the other children managed to get him out. I just stood there and watched.'

'How did they know it was you?' Carla had said.

'My best friend, Emma, told them. She'd been standing next to me when she saw what the boy was doing and, apparently, I'd clenched my fists, lowered my chin, stared right at him and started chanting.'

'And she gave you away?'

'She was scared, child, she didn't know what I was doing, so she ran and told the schoolmaster, who sent me home. A few hours later the priest came to call and told us we had to leave the village.'

'How did you know what to do?'

'I don't know. It was already there, inside me. It happens like that sometimes. With other people, they have to learn to do spells, but they will always be able to do them, because they have the gift.'

Carla and Anna had continued to work, side by side, and the sun had started to go down before Carla had spoken again.

'Anna? Did your father punish you for what you did to that boy?' She'd asked because she'd remembered how her own father, before he'd left her and her mother, had beaten her mother and sometimes herself whenever they'd done the slightest thing wrong. If she'd done what Anna had done, her father would have whipped her until she had been raw.

'No, child, father didn't punish me. He knew what I was and he knew I'd done what I'd done to protect someone else. He sat me down then and explained to me about my heritage and how I needed to learn to control my power and to use it to help, not harm, others. I was twelve years old when this happened.' Anna had smiled at Carla and had patted her on the hand.

It was on one of her, now daily, visits to the village that Carla learned of Isabella's circumstances. Whenever she went into the village, she never spoke to anyone; she just sat by the fountain, content to watch the comings and goings of village life. No one ever seemed to notice her; they were always far too wrapped up in their daily lives to notice a skinny, fair haired girl, huddled on a seat near the fountain.

This suited Carla fine because she learned far more about what was going on in the village than she would have, had someone spoken to her. On this particular day, however, Carla thought her heart would stop beating as she held her breath from the minute she heard Isabella's name. The two women were standing about six feet away from Carla and, as usual, were completely oblivious to her presence. Carla, for her part, shrank as far into the background as she could and listened.

'…yes, what's her name, Isabelle or Isabella or something,' the baker's wife said.

'You mean, the old witch's daughter?' the woman with her, whom Carla had never seen before, replied.

'That's her. Well, you should see her. She's certainly come down a peg or two. Little Miss "I'm better than everyone else", is no longer so attractive to the men of this village.'

'At least we don't have to worry about her stealing our husbands anymore.'

'That's a shame. I was going to give her mine and let her wear him out!' the baker's wife said and both women burst out laughing.

'So, who's she managed to con into taking her in then, since she was turned away by most of the village?'

'Father Tom, who else,' the baker's wife said, rolling her eyes. 'She probably worked her magic on him too. He is a man after all.'

'Who do you think the father is?' the other woman said.

'Well, I think we all know who it isn't,' the baker's wife said. 'I wonder what ever happened to Antony Cardover. He wasn't a bad lot after all. He had a temper on him, but he really tried after his father passed away.'

'He was something to look at as well, wasn't he? Tall, dark and those eyes, they just...' Their voices disappeared as they walked away and Carla didn't dare move until she was certain that they'd gone.

As soon as she could, she started to run, faster and faster, until she reached home. She burst through the front door, causing Anna to drop the bottle she was holding. It smashed on the stone floor.

'Carla! What on earth is the...'

'Isabella's with child!' Carla interrupted and collapsed into a chair.

'Isabella's what?' Anna said, her hand rising to flutter around her throat.

'Going to have a baby,' Carla said, finally getting her breath back.

'Oh my God!' Anna whispered as she collapsed into a kitchen chair.

'Anna!' Carla said, alarmed by the sudden loss of colour in Anna's face.

'I'm all right, child, I'm all right,' she said, reaching over the table and patting Carla's hand. 'How do you know this, child?' Anna clasped Carla's hands and studied her.

'I'm not lying, Anna, I...'

'I know you're not lying, child. I just want to understand how you found out. Who told you?'

Carla hesitated at first, unsure whether to admit her visits to the village but, in the end, she just blurted it out.

'I overheard two women talking, in the square. I was by the fountain. I always sit there. I can see and hear everything from there.'

'You've been to the village? But why? You know how I feel about that.

You know what people think about us going into the village, Carla. Why would you deceive me?' Anna released Carla's hands and put her own hands over her face, her elbows resting on the table.

'I-I-I didn't deceive you, Anna.' Carla's urgent voice made Anna look up as the young girl rushed around the table to her. 'I-I-I just felt lonely. Antony's gone, Isabella's gone and you didn't seem to want me around. I-I-I just wanted some company. I'm so sorry, Anna. It won't happen again,' Carla said as she fell to her knees and buried her face in the grubby skirts of Anna's dress.

'There, there, child, don't cry,' Anna said as she stroked Carla's hair. 'You've done nothing wrong. I said, a long time ago, that Isabella would bring ruin on this family and she has.' Anna fell silent, but continued to stroke Carla's hair. Carla closed her eyes and savoured the gentle feeling. She'd missed this closeness to Anna.

'Where is she, child?' Anna said at last and Carla shuddered at the tone in her voice. It was dead, devoid of all emotion.

'They said that Father Tom had taken her in.'

'Ah, Tom,' Anna said, her voice softening. 'I should have known he would take pity on her. He always did have a weakness for that girl.' Anna moved to stand up, forcing Carla to move out of the way.

'What are you doing?'

'Going to get her.'

'But, I thought you didn't want to see her again.'

'I don't, but she is with child and so it is my responsibility to take care of her, until the baby comes.'

'What about after?' Carla said and Anna stopped in her tracks, her back to Carla.

'After...after will be a different matter. I...' A rap on the door interrupted Anna. The old lady looked at Carla, but Carla just shrugged her shoulders.

CHAPTER 39

Anna pushed her chair away from the kitchen table and hobbled to the door. Carla heard the gasp as Anna opened the front door and she rushed forward just as Anna closed the door again, leant her back against it and closed her eyes.

'Anna, what is it?' Carla asked; panic fluttering in her chest when she saw the now deathly pallor of Anna's skin.

'It's nothing, child,' Anna said as she opened her eyes and fixed Carla with a blank look. 'Go to your room, I have something that I need to deal with. It won't take long.'

'But...'

'Now, Carla!'

Carla, hurt by the harshness she heard in Anna's voice retreated, but, as was her custom, she kept her bedroom door ajar so she could see and hear what was going on.

From her hiding place, Carla watched as Anna opened the door and then stepped aside to admit the visitor. Fearing the worst, Carla shielded her gaze slightly, but then had to stifle a gasp when she saw who the visitor was.

So, he does exist, Carla thought to herself, as Anna allowed a young boy of about ten years old to enter the cottage. Carla knew who he was from the stories she'd heard on her visits to the village. He was the "Doom Bringer", according to the villagers. He was the corporeal representation of the death or downfall of a loved one. He didn't look very scary to Carla, but then he turned round so she could see his face and she shuddered.

Their visitor appeared to be close to death himself. His skin was chalky white and his lips had a bluish tinge to them, but it was his eyes that chilled Carla. They were dark, dead pools sunken into deep grey sockets. He didn't say a word as he handed Anna a rolled up piece of parchment and then he left the house.

Anna remained in the open doorway, the parchment clutched in her hand, tears already running down her face. She unrolled the parchment and Carla held her breath as Anna read it.

'Anna!' Carla shrieked as the old lady slumped to the stone floor, the parchment caught by a sudden gust of wind was sucked outside and the heavy oak door was slammed shut after it.

'Anna, are you all right?' Carla asked as she rushed over to help Anna to her feet.

'No, child, I'm not,' she said as she allowed Carla to propel her towards her armchair by the fire.

'Why? What's happened? What did the "Doom Bringer" have to tell us?'

'How do you know who he is? I thought…'

'I heard the villagers talking,' Carla interrupted. 'What did the letter say?'

'I-I-I can't tell you, child. It's better that you don't know.' Anna lapsed into silence then, her gaze transfixed on the dancing flames.

Carla watched the old lady and saw shadows cross her watery blue eyes. She opened her mouth to speak, but Anna cut her off.

'I said it's better you don't know and I mean it. Now, we need to go and get Isabella. I can't allow Father Tom to shoulder my burden any longer.' With that, Anna pushed herself out of the chair, pulled her shawl around her shoulders and prodded Carla towards the door.

CHAPTER 40

Father Tom opened the door to his two evening visitors.

'Ah, Anna, how nice it is to see you. And you, Carla. How are you both?'

'Hello, Tom,' Anna said and kissed him on the cheek, much to Carla's surprise. 'I'm afraid this isn't a social call. You know why I am here.'

'Yes. I was wondering how long it would take. Once I'd seen young Carla here, in the square, I knew it wouldn't be long before you found out,' he said, patting Carla affectionately on the head. Carla blushed. She honestly thought that no one had seen her.

'How far along is she?' Anna asked, her voice still devoid of emotion.

'The doctor says about six months, but there is no way of knowing for sure.' Anna merely nodded.

'Thank you for all your help, Tom and I'm sorry that this has fallen to you. What I don't understand is why you didn't tell me.'

'Isabella told me of your words. She told me she didn't want you to know.' Anna winced at the comment. 'Besides, I knew that you would come someday because a secret like this would have reached you eventually, even without Carla's help.' Carla blushed again, as Father Tom's gaze rested on her.

'Did she tell you the whole story?' Anna said.

'She didn't have to, Anna. I live in the village. I see everything that goes on and what I don't see, I soon get to hear about.' Anna studied the floor and Carla went to her and clasped her hand. She knew Anna felt awkward and wanted to comfort her.

'I'm sorry, Tom, I…'

'You don't have to explain, Anna. You did what you could. Unfortunately, some children are born bad and there is nothing you can do about it. Sit down and I'll go and wake her,' Father Tom took Anna's hand and led her over to a chair. Carla followed and sat down on the floor next to her.

Nothing prepared Carla for the Isabella who appeared in the living room. Gone was the lustrous curly hair and glowing complexion and gone was the voluptuous woman, who, six months ago, had been cast out of their lives. In her place stood a painfully thin girl with straggly hair and sallow skin. Her eyes were rimmed with dark circles and the sparkle was gone out of them, replaced by a deep seated resentment as she considered them. Her hands rested on top of what appeared to be, in her present condition, an abnormally distended belly.

'Oh my goodness, Isabella, what has happened to you?' Anna said, as she hobbled towards her daughter, arms outstretched. Isabella shrank away from her and stepped behind Father Tom.

'What do you want?' she said, her hatred bringing her dark eyes to life once again.

'We've come to take you home,' Anna said and reached out to touch her, but Isabella slapped her hand away, causing Anna to cry out.

'Home! Home!' Isabella shouted, her stance wide, her eyes wild. 'I don't have a home. You made sure of that.'

'What are you talking about? You could have gone back to the workshop after he left.'

'Ha! For about a month before I got thrown out of there because my dear husband was behind on the rent! Apparently, his "saintly" behaviour wasn't so "saintly" after all, since he'd managed to drink away all of his profits!'

'Why didn't you come to me?'

'You made it quite clear, Mother dear, that you never wanted to see me again.'

'Stop being so stubborn, Isabella. You know I'd never have left you out on the street,' Anna said and pulled back, away from her daughter. 'What do you take me for?'

'A mother who thinks more of her no good son in law than of her own daughter!'

'I'm not here to argue with you, Isabella. I'm here to take you home.'

'Why? Because I'm carrying someone's bastard child? It's not his, if that's what you're thinking. Antony, the Saint, couldn't even get that right!' Isabella shouted at Anna. Father Tom went to sit next to Carla and put his arms around her. Tears ran down Carla's cheeks and she felt her heart breaking as she listened to the hurtful things that Isabella was saying.

'Please, Izzy, stop it.' Anna said.

'Why, is it too embarrassing for you? Too ashamed to admit that your daughter doesn't even know who the father of her child is?' Isabella said and then started laughing hysterically.

Carla watched, open mouthed, as Anna walked over to Isabella and slapped her hard across the face. Isabella fell silent and pressed her hands to her now blood-red cheek. She stared wide-eyed at Anna.

'Now, you listen to me, my girl,' Anna started, her voice once again cold and hard. 'For a while there, I felt sorry for you, felt that this whole experience might have humanised you, felt that we could put the past behind us and start again, but I was wrong. You haven't changed. You're still the spiteful, selfish person you've always been and you're still a hussy. But, just because you are a poor excuse for a human being, I will not let that child suffer. Regardless of who the father is or isn't, that child is not to blame for any of this and it is for the sake of that child that I am here, not for you. So, I will look after you both until your child is born and until you've nursed it, but then you are on your own. More fool me for even thinking that you might have developed some humility.' Anna finished and turned her back on Isabella. 'Come on, child, it's time you were in bed,' she said to Carla.

'Tom, I'd be grateful if you could bring her to the cottage and I don't care how you get her there.' With that Anna left the house and Carla followed, looking at Isabella, still standing in the same place, as she walked passed.

CHAPTER 41

During the remaining months of Isabella's pregnancy, Carla helped Anna to look after her. Isabella was not an easy patient. She remained in bed for the whole time, shouting her orders through to Carla and throwing things back in her face. Carla's dislike for the person she'd once idolised grew and grew, until one day she finally saw Isabella for the person she really was.

'Carla, I need you. Come here!' Isabella screeched one morning while the rest of the house was still sleeping. Carla lay where she was, her eyes shut tight. She was willing herself back to sleep, for a while longer, so she wouldn't have to listen to that voice.

How could she have idolised Isabella so much? She shuddered, remembering the way she used to follow her around, constantly at her beck and call. She'd thought that Isabella was so beautiful and so perfect and all Carla had wanted was to be just like her.

'What an idiot,' Carla muttered to herself. She turned over in bed and pulled the covers over her head, but she was awake and no amount of trying would make her sleep again.

'NOW!' Isabella bellowed from the next room and Carla threw back the covers and sighed. She had better go and see what her ladyship wanted before she woke Anna, if she hadn't already.

Carla's thoughts drifted to Anna then and her heart ached. Isabella's presence was taking its toll on her. Anna no longer smiled and rarely said a word. It was far worse than when Isabella had left. At least then, Carla had been able to get through to her, had managed to make her laugh and engage her in conversation and even go for a walk, once in a while. Now, though, nothing worked. Anna had completely shut down. She was focused on one thing only and that was Isabella's baby. That was all that Anna seemed interested in. Carla's heart ached still as she thought of the shell that Anna had become.

'Carla, you little bitch, get in here, now!' Carla clenched her fists and took a deep breath to calm her temper. Anna didn't need to deal with any more bad feeling. She pushed her feet into her slippers, pulled a shawl around her shoulders against the chill of early morning and left her room, glancing quickly over to the other bed. Anna slept on.

'About time. Where have you been?' Isabella said when Carla appeared in her doorway.

'What do you want?' Carla said, having no intention of engaging her in conversation.

'How dare you speak to me like that, you little bitch!'

'What do you want, Isabella?' Carla asked again; weary with the older girl's constant demanding ways.

'Water. I'm thirsty. Fetch me some water and hurry up. You've kept me waiting long enough.'

'You woke me up for a glass of water,' Carla said, through gritted teeth, her patience finally snapping.

'Yes. You know I shouldn't strain myself. It might harm the baby.'

'Ha!' Carla snorted. 'Like you care what happens to that baby.'

'Of course I do.'

'Rubbish. All you care about is what will happen to you once it is born,' Carla said.

'Mama won't throw me out,' Isabella said.

'Oh, I think she will and I cannot wait,' Carla said and turned to go.

'What about my water?'

'Get it yourself, like the doctor advised,' Carla muttered.

'Come back here, right now!' Isabella screamed and, as Carla closed the door, she heard something smash against it and shatter all over the floor. She walked into her own bedroom to find that Anna was awake.

'What is it, child?' she asked, her voice tired and hoarse.

'Nothing, Anna, get some rest,' Carla said and kissed the old woman on the top of her head as she pulled the covers over her.

'Get back in here with my water, now!' Isabella's voice thundered through the walls and Carla shook her head and glanced at Anna, to see tears rolling down her cheeks.

'Don't worry, Anna, the baby will be here soon,' Carla said and Anna turned her watery eyes to her then.

'And that's when all our troubles will really begin, child.'

CHAPTER 42

'Aaargh!' The animalistic sound woke Carla from a deep sleep. She jumped out of bed and shook Anna to wake her.

'Anna, Anna, wake up! It's time,' Carla said and then rushed into the next room.

Isabella screamed again. Sweat drenched her forehead as she clutched the sides of the bed; her hair wild; her eyes rolled back so that the whites were visible. *Like a rabid dog*, Carla thought.

'Help me!' she shouted and then burst into tears. Carla stood in the doorway and stared. She'd never seen anything like this before. She felt her heart tighten every time Isabella bellowed like an injured animal.

'Hurry, Anna,' Carla called. 'Isabella's dying!' Carla bumped into the old woman as she turned back towards the other room.

'Stop fretting, child. She's not dying. She's having a baby. Here, take these. Put them around and underneath her and strip back that bedding,' Anna said, her voice calm, as she thrust a pile of sheets into Carla's arms.

Carla walked into Isabella's room and stood there for a moment, staring as Isabella writhed around on the bed.

'Hurry up, Carla. We may not have much time.' Anna's voice came from the kitchen and snapped Carla out of her reverie. She rushed forwards and dragged the bedclothes off a screaming Isabella. She started to arrange the sheets that Anna had given her.

'Izzy, lift yourself up so I can put these under you,' Carla said, her voice gentle and sympathetic. As Isabella rolled onto one side and Carla managed to push the clean sheet beneath her, she felt the wetness of the sheets underneath.

'Anna, Anna, the bed's wet. Something's wrong!' Carla shouted.

'Calm down, child, calm down,' Anna said as she bustled into the room with a bowl of steaming water and some smaller cloths. 'Now, get the rest of those sheets down and then go and hold her hand. She'll need you.'

Isabella's howls were getting worse and Carla felt her stomach tense.

'Is she going to be all right?' she whispered.

'Isabella will be fine, unfortunately.' Anna muttered the last word under her breath, but Carla heard her.

'Right, my girl,' she said to Isabella. 'For once in your life, I want you to do everything I say. It will be much easier for you, if you do.'

'Just make it stop, Mama. It hurts too much. I'm going to die.'

'You're not going to die. Now, open your legs and bend your knees.' Isabella did as she was told and Anna, with a strength that surprised Carla, dragged her down the bed so she could reach her more easily.

'Aaargh!'

'Maybe you'll learn your lesson from this. Hopefully this pain will make you think twice before you behave like that again.'

'Mama, make it stop!'

'Carla, take this and hold it across her forehead,' Anna said and threw a cold damp cloth over to her. Carla laid it across the forehead of the writhing Isabella, but she wasn't able to hold it still.

'Keep still, my girl, and do what I tell you. Carla, you must help her to do this. It is something I have found helps in these circumstances. I want you to take deep breaths and calm yourself down. Carla, do this with her,' Anna instructed. Carla immediately started to take deep breaths.

'Come on, Izzy, you can do this,' she urged, her voice gentle.

'I can't! Mama!' Isabella wailed.

'Yes, you can, my girl, and you will,' Anna said. 'Take regular deep breaths and then, when the pain comes, I want you to push hard.'

To Carla, the minutes that passed seemed like hours. She'd never seen anything like it and she certainly never wanted to see it again. She watched, as though in a trance, wiping Isabella's forehead and breathing with her, all the while Anna was shouting instructions at Isabella. None of them had eaten or drank anything all day and Carla was starting to feel the effects. She glanced out of the bedroom window, watching the sun drop below the horizon and shivered as the first chills of evening drifted through the ill fitting wood of the cottage.

'Right, Isabella, I can see the baby now. You're nearly there. I need you to push harder.' Anna's voice snapped Carla back to reality.

'Come on, Izzy, you can do it,' she whispered in her ear.

'I can't do it anymore, Mama. I'm too tired. I just want to sleep.'

'Nonsense, girl. You have no choice. Now, push and let's get this baby out.'

Isabella did as she was told and Carla stared in amazement as Anna pulled a blood covered baby out from between Isabella's legs. She smacked the baby on its back and a wail erupted from its tiny lungs.

Carla watched in fascination as Anna cut the cord from the baby and then cleaned it quickly and wrapped it in a clean cloth.

'Carla, come and take the baby while I see to Isabella,' Anna said and held the baby out to her. Carla took the baby and stared down at the tiny sleeping form.

'What is it?' she whispered.

'It's a girl,' Anna said. 'Now, off with you.' Carla left them alone and sat in the chair next to the fireplace and stared at the baby.

'Let's get the fire lit and make some supper.' Carla jumped at the sound of Anna's voice. She hadn't heard her come into the room.

'Can we call her Rebecca?' Carla asked.

'Rebecca?'

'After my mother.'

'Rebecca it is then,' Anna said, her voice final. 'Come on, put the baby in the crib and help me.'

'Rebecca,' Carla said and Anna looked up.

'She has a name, Anna. Her name is Rebecca and none of this is her fault.' Anna smiled and hugged Carla tight.

'How's Isabella?'

'She'll live,' Anna replied, her tone cold and she got up and busied herself in the kitchen.

CHAPTER 43

Life settled into a quiet routine after the birth of Rebecca. Carla and Anna took care of her while Isabella went back to being Isabella. Carla didn't understand how she could just ignore her own baby, but she did. She spent her time around the village, catching up where she'd left off.

Carla tried to get Anna to talk about it, but she refused. It was three months since Rebecca had been born and Anna had made no move to get rid of Isabella, nor had she made any attempt to speak to her. Anna had withdrawn into herself and Carla was constantly worried about her, but there was nothing she could do.

It wasn't only the subject of Isabella that bothered the old lady. Feelings in the village and in many of the nearby villages were changing towards people such as Anna. Carla didn't understand why and she couldn't find out from anywhere. People had stopped coming to Anna for help and many a night they heard the villagers shouting taunts of "die, witch, die" outside the cottage. Stones were even thrown at the doors and windows. Carla was scared, but tried to be strong for Anna's sake. The old woman simply sat in her chair by the fire and cried quietly to herself, muttering under her breath.

Isabella, being Isabella, was not in the least bit concerned.

'You've brought it all on yourself, Mother,' she said one night, as they ate a meagre meal of bread and broth. Anna continued eating without saying anything.

'Don't speak to Anna like that,' Carla said, her blood boiling.

'Well, she has,' Isabella said. 'Dabbling in all that hocus-pocus nonsense was always going to bring trouble in the end.'

'Don't forget that it's that "hocus-pocus nonsense" that has given you such a good life,' Carla said and slammed her spoon down on the table.

'Oh, please,' Isabella said. 'A good life. This is what you call a good life? You are so naïve, Carla.'

'How dare you!' Carla shouted, jumping out of her chair. 'After everything Anna has done for you!'

'Sit down, child,' Anna said. 'Do not waste your breath on her.'

'Spiteful old bitch,' Isabella said and got up and stormed off into her room, slamming the door behind her. Rebecca started to cry and Anna pushed herself up and hobbled over to the crib, next to the fire.

Carla heard voices outside and fear pulled at her heart. She'd just got up to go and look out of the window when there was a hammering at the door and she jumped. She turned to Anna, her eyes wide, but Anna simply nodded and stayed where she was. Carla crept to the front door, the hammering having continued, and opened it. One of the men from the village fell over the threshold into the cottage.

'Anna, Anna, we need your help!' he cried, his voice high and agitated. Isabella appeared in the doorway to her room, but didn't come any further. Anna remained near the fire, the baby's crib hidden next to her chair, the baby quiet once again.

'What is the matter, Jacob?' Anna asked and Carla noticed the weariness in her voice.

'It's Antony! He's back!' Jacob replied, still panting from his run from the village.

'Antony's back?' Carla asked, her heart filled with an overwhelming joy, but Anna walked passed her and patted her shoulder.

'No, child, he isn't,' she said and then turned to Jacob. 'Where is he?'

'He's in the village. He's gone mad. No one knows what to do. Please come, Anna,' Jacob begged.

'I will help,' she said. 'Go and tell Mr Danvers that it is time and that I will meet him and his men at the cemetery.'

'But they need your help in the village, Anna. You must come to the village,' Jacob persisted.

'There is nothing I can do in the village. Just tell Danvers to meet me in the cemetery.' Jacob nodded, turned and started to run back towards the village. Anna closed the door and leant against it, her eyes closed.

'Carla, take the baby into the other room and shut the door. Keep her quiet and do not come out until I come home. Do you understand?'

'Why? What's happening?' Carla asked.

'Just do as I ask, child. Now, go and don't come out until I come home for you.' Anna shooed Carla away and she turned to go.

'What about me, Mama?' Isabella asked from her bedroom doorway. Carla stopped and turned to hear Anna's reply, but Anna just looked at Isabella and then left the house.

'How dare she!' Isabella said and slammed her bedroom door, causing Rebecca to start crying again. Carla picked up the wailing child and took her into the bedroom, rocking and soothing her all the time.

She closed the door and laid the baby on the bed and then pushed a set of drawers across the doorway. She then climbed into bed and cuddled Rebecca to her. It was there she waited, just as Anna had told her to.

CHAPTER 44

Carla jolted awake at the sound of hammering on the front door.

'Who is it?' she heard Isabella ask, but Carla didn't hear the reply. She heard the door open and then she heard Isabella scream and then nothing. Carla snuggled further under the covers, with a now sleeping Rebecca, and squeezed her eyes shut, tears seeping down her cheeks. *What on earth was going on?* She rocked herself backwards and forwards, praying for Anna to return.

She had no idea how long she'd been there, but finally she heard the front door close. Several minutes passed, but no one came to the door. Carla heard shuffling in the other room and what sounded like weeping. She listened for a while and then, steadying Rebecca between the pillows on her bed, Carla crept over towards the bedroom door. As quietly as she could, she lifted the drawers and moved them just enough so she could open the door a crack and peered out.

The fire was dying in the hearth so the light wasn't very good, but Carla could make out the back of a figure hunched over in the chair. Suddenly, the figure sat back and let out a wrenching sob.

'Anna!' Carla called, alarmed at the sound emanating from the old woman. The sobbing stopped almost immediately and slowly Anna turned round to look at the partly open doorway.

'Oh, Anna,' Carla said as she saw her ravaged face. She yanked the drawers out of the way and ran out of the bedroom and into Anna's arms.

Anna squeezed Carla so tightly that she thought she would stop breathing.

She rocked Carla back and forth and cried. Carla had never heard Anna cry like this before and the sound, coming from the strongest woman she'd ever met, chilled her to the bone.

'Anna, don't cry,' Carla crooned. 'Please don't cry. What's happened?' But Anna didn't respond. She continued to wail and cling to Carla as if for dear life.

'Where's Isabella, Anna? Someone knocked at the door and I heard her scream and...' Anna pulled away from her at that point, holding her by her upper arms and stared at her. Carla had to stifle a scream as she looked into the watery blue eyes. The death and destruction she saw there told her more than any words ever could.

'Oh my God,' Carla whispered and in a voice so calm, a voice so quiet that it belied the agony of a few minutes earlier, Anna spoke.

'Isabella is dead. Antony is gone. There is more to come, child.'

'D-d-dead? W-w-what do you mean? Anna, what's happened? Where's Antony? Anna, talk to me,' Carla pleaded, but Anna shook her head and pushed herself to her feet. She leant both palms against the fireplace and stared into the dying embers.

'Please, Anna. I need to know,' Carla begged.

'NO!' Anna shouted. 'You don't need to know the details, child.'

'I'll find out,' Carla said, folding her arms in defiance across her chest. 'I'll go into the village tomorrow and I'll listen and then I'll know.'

'So be it,' Anna said, 'but you'll find a very different village than the one you're used to.'

'Why, Anna? Tell me what's happened? It would be better if I heard it from you,' Carla said and took the old woman's hands in her own.

'Oh, child, I never could refuse you anything. I just wish you didn't have to know...' Anna drifted off, pain evident in her eyes. She was silent for a few minutes and Carla was just about to prompt her, when she started to speak.

'Antony had returned, child, but it wasn't really him. Let me talk,' Anna said and held a hand up to silence Carla. Carla closed her mouth and sat back to listen.

'He was different. The devil was in him and there was no one who could reason with him. I don't know exactly what happened in the village. All I know is he killed many people.'

'But Antony wouldn't…'

'I've already told you, child, it wasn't Antony. Not the Antony we knew. Remember the boy who came to visit?' Carla nodded. 'Well, the letter he brought told me what had happened to Antony, so I knew what he'd done, I knew it was coming, I just didn't know when.' Anna considered Carla and sat down in her chair with a sigh.

'There is a very dangerous warlock who lives deep in the woods. He is responsible for the demon inside Antony. Isabella had damaged his pride, child, and like any man, he wanted revenge.' Anna fell silent again and stared into the smouldering hearth.

'He killed her in front of me, Carla. Snapped her neck as though it was a twig.' Tears filled her eyes again and Carla rested her head on Anna's lap, herself too stunned and shocked to respond.

'He had to be stopped and I stopped him.'

'Y-y-you killed Antony?'

'No, child, I didn't kill him. I did what had to be done. I stopped him. He'll not hurt anyone else and that's all I want to say about it.' Anna made to get up, but Carla stopped her.

'H-h-how did you stop him?'

'It doesn't matter, child, and I don't want to hear anymore about it. Now, where's the baby?'

'She's asleep. But…'

'No, Carla. It's over for now. We'll deal with the rest when it comes.'

227

'What do you mean, Anna?'

'I'm not sure, child,' she replied and averted her gaze from Carla. Carla knew she was hiding something, but she knew better than to ask.

'Come on, child. It's late. Off to bed. Tomorrow will be a big day.' Anna shooed Carla off towards the bedroom and then sat down in her chair. Carla turned to speak to the old woman, but then changed her mind and climbed into bed. She hugged the baby tight to her, some kind of instinct telling her that they were going to need each other.

CHAPTER 45

Carla woke early the next day and left both Anna and Rebecca asleep in the cottage. She had to find out the truth about the previous night and she knew that the only way to find out was to go to the village.

What she found when she approached the square stopped her in her tracks. Everywhere she looked, people were sitting in groups, some weeping, some staring blankly ahead of them. Aside from the sound of crying, there wasn't another sound in the village. It was eerie and Carla shivered and hugged herself.

All the doors to the houses were wide open and Carla glimpsed overturned tables and chairs and, as she picked her way up the main street, she saw blood spattered up the walls and doors. Tears filled her eyes and she started to shake as realisation dawned on her. *But Antony couldn't have done this*, she thought, not the Antony she knew.

Her path led straight to the only house where she knew she would find some answers. As she neared Father Tom's house she saw a gathering of people outside. She edged to the back of the group and listened to the heated voices. She couldn't believe what she was hearing. After everything Anna had done for this village and especially after she helped them last night, they still hated her. Carla couldn't keep quiet any longer.

'Just listen to you!' She shouted, her anger evident in her tone. 'If it wasn't for Anna, you'd all be dead. I don't know why she bothered!' The rabble turned to face her and she could feel her blood boiling as she stood there, fists clenched ready for battle. She was too busy looking from face to face, waiting for one of them to challenge her, to listen to much of what was said after. How could these people hate Anna so much? She switched back in to what was being said and thought her heart would stop beating as she listened to the farrier's words.

'Well, Father, as I see it, you have two choices. Either you get rid of her or we will.' With that she turned on her heel and ran. She had to get home. She had to warn Anna.

'Carla!' she heard Father Tom's anxious voice, but she ignored him and carried on. Fear gripped her heart. *Not Anna as well! Why would they do this to her? Anna had never harmed anyone in her life; it wasn't in her nature.* As she ran, Anna's words floated into her mind.

'Tomorrow will be a big day,' Anna had said the previous night. *Had she known? Just like she'd known Isabella would bring ruin on the family. Would all this have happened anyway, without the previous night?* Questions swam through her mind as she raced towards the cottage.

CHAPTER 46

'Anna! Anna!' Carla screamed as she burst in through the front door, out of breath from running.

'Quiet, child!' Anna scolded. 'I've just got the baby off to sleep.'

'But, Anna, they're coming! You have to hide!' Carla panted, her eyes wide with fear.

'I know, child, I know,' Anna said, rocking the baby back and forth.

'But you have to go. I'll get you some things.' Anna grabbed her as she rushed by.

'No, child, I'm not going...'

'But you have to,' Carla said, her voice high, her body shaking.

'Carla, look at me,' Anna said, strengthening her grip on the girl. 'You are to go now and take the baby. I have packed enough food and clothes for you both. Go through the woods to my sister's house. She will protect you,' she said, handing a sack to the girl and then passing her the sleeping baby. Carla stared at her in disbelief.

'Go now, child. Before they come.'

'But you have to come,' Carla said as tears slid down her cheeks.

'I can't, child. I have to stay to face them, to protect you both. Now go!' Anna shoved the girl out of the door and closed it.

Carla plunged into the woods, tears streaming down her cheeks, Rebecca clutched tightly to her chest and the bundle Anna had given her banging against her leg. *Why was this happening to her? What was going to happen to Anna?* Again, questions swam around in her young mind. She couldn't take it all in. Her safe, secure world had been blown apart in the last day and she was reeling from it.

She hadn't gone very far when she heard the sound of horses and she dropped to the ground. Slowly, she turned round to look back the way she'd come. She could just about make out the cottage and the men on horses drawing up outside it. Instinct told her to carry on towards Anna's sister's house, but she couldn't tear her eyes away from the scene in front of her.

She couldn't hear what was going on, but about five minutes after they arrived, she saw the men dragging Anna out of the cottage. A scream emanated from Carla before she could stop it and this set Rebecca off, crying. Panicked, Carla placed her hand over the baby's mouth and rocked her to try and quieten her. She held her breath. *Oh God, please don't let them have heard me*, she prayed. Her gaze remained fixed on Anna and her heart almost broke as she watched them force the old lady into the back of a cart.

Nobody appeared to have heard her and Carla relaxed a little. Tears coursed down her cheeks for the woman who'd taken her in. Deep down Carla knew what would happen to Anna. She'd listened to the talk in the village about the growing revolt against witches. She'd heard the villagers talk with glee about witnessing witches burnt at the stake. She knew this was where they were taking Anna, her help the previous night conveniently forgotten.

Carla wanted so badly to run back through the trees to Anna. She wanted to be with her, to hold her hand, to tell her that she didn't feel the same; that she would always love her, but she knew she couldn't. She also knew that Anna already knew all these things.

Carla studied the now sleeping face of Rebecca and a fierce protectiveness swelled her heart. She'd made a promise to Anna that she would protect the baby and that's exactly what she'd do; whatever it took.

She pushed herself to her feet and started walking again. She clutched the letter Anna had given her in her hand and she prayed that her sister really would take them in. She winced as the bundle banged against her leg again, the corner of something hard jabbing into her thigh.

She'd been walking for hours and the sun was dipping below the treetops, when Carla saw the outline of a cottage through the trees. *Thank God*, she thought. She was tired and hungry and Rebecca was in need of a feed. She quickened her step and dragged herself up the three steps onto the wooden porch. Taking a deep breath and steadying herself, she knocked on the door.

Carla was on her knees when Elizabeth Emerson opened the door. Emotionally and physically exhausted she was no longer able to stand. As the door opened, Carla glanced up and her heart felt like it had skipped a beat. She stared into the same watery blue eyes as Anna's.

'I-I..,' Carla stammered and thrust the letter forward before she passed out.

CHAPTER 47

Carla woke, warm and cosy, to the sound of birds singing and, as she opened her eyes, she saw the thin rays of early morning sunlight through the cracks in the curtains. She stared around the room at the unfamiliar furniture and panic began to rise within her, until her sleep clouded mind began to clear and scenes from the previous day replayed in her mind.

'Oh God, Rebecca!' she shouted and jumped out of bed and ran to the closed door. Slowly, she pulled it open, just a crack, and peered through. From the angle she was at, the cottage seemed to have the same layout as Anna's, only on a larger scale. She couldn't see anyone, although she could hear muffled voices coming from the room next door.

She heard a door open to her left and loud footsteps headed in her direction. She gasped, caught off guard, and stepped sideways out of sight, but walked into the chest of drawers, dislodging a jug from on top of it. The jug fell to the stone floor and shattered.

Carla was staring at the broken jug, mortified, when the footsteps came through her doorway.

'Ah, good morning, young lady. Glad you're awake,' a deep voice boomed and Carla looked up into the bearded face of a bear of a man. She simply stared at him, open mouthed, and then stared down at the mess at her feet.

'Ah, don't worry your pretty little head about that. Lizzie will clear that after she's fed the baby. Get yourself dressed and come and help me with the cows.' He started to leave, but then he stomped back into the room.

'I'm George, by the way, George Emerson. Lizzie's husband. You'll be safe here, Carla, you and Rebecca will, so don't worry. Now, get yourself dressed.' He stomped off then and she heard the front door slam.

A little dazed, Carla dressed, but before following Mr Emerson outside, she crept along to the bedroom door next to hers and pressed her ear to the door. Inside, she heard Mrs Emerson singing softly and she heard gurgling sounds coming from Rebecca. Carla smiled and her whole body relaxed for the first time since leaving Anna's the previous day. If Rebecca was happy then she was happy. She turned on her heel and followed Mr Emerson outside.

It was a couple of hours later when Carla and Mr Emerson returned to the cottage. As they came in through the front door, chatting and smiling, the smell of fresh bread and eggs cooking greeted them.

'You'll love Lizzie's cooking, lass. She's a great cook. She'll put some meat on your bones,' Mr Emerson said and stomped over and planted a kiss on his wife's cheek. Carla smiled and looked around the room.

'She's in our bedroom, dear, sound asleep. She's fine. You can see her later, after you've eaten and after we've had a talk. Now, go and wash your hands,' Mrs Emerson said and smiled at Carla.

Carla didn't say a word, but washed her hands and then sat down to eat with the Emersons. Mr and Mrs Emerson kept up a lively conversation throughout breakfast and Carla marvelled at how different the atmosphere was there compared to Anna's. There was just warmth and happiness whereas, at Anna's, there had always been an undercurrent, a presence, almost as if they had always been waiting for something to happen. Carla felt herself begin to relax in their company, something she'd never really been able to do at Anna's.

After breakfast, Mr Emerson went back outside to work on the farm and Mrs Emerson took Carla's hand and led her to a seat in front of the fire. They both sat down.

'I know you've been through a lot lately, Carla. It's all in the letter you gave me, but there are a few things that we need to talk about. Is that okay?' Mrs Emerson asked and Carla nodded.

'In her letter, Anna asked me to take you and Rebecca in and to raise you and make sure you are both well cared for. I just want to put your mind at rest and assure you that you and Rebecca are both welcome here and that George and I are now your family,' Elizabeth squeezed Carla's hand, but again, all Carla did was nod.

'We talked about maybe changing your names, just in case someone comes looking for you,' Elizabeth continued and Carla shook her head vehemently.

'No!' she said. 'Rebecca is named after my mother. Please don't change that and no one knows about me....except Father Tom and he won't ever say. He and Anna were friends,' Carla said and started to fidget.

'It's okay, Carla. We won't do anything you don't want. We thought it would be safer for you.'

'No one knows about us except Father Tom,' Carla said.

'How can no one know about you?'

'Anna took me in after my mother died and she taught me from home. She didn't want me getting picked on by the other children because of what she was. No one knew about this and no one ever asked about me,' Carla said and lowered her head at this point. Elizabeth hugged her close.

'Father Tom took Izzy in when she was with child and then brought her back home. People knew that she was pregnant, but no one knew what happened to the baby. Anna kept her hidden and Izzy never spoke of her.'

'That makes sense,' Elizabeth said and Carla looked at her quizzically.

'Anna left something for you, in the pack she gave you. It is more for Rebecca than for you, but there is a letter for you which explains it all.'

'You read the letter?'

'No, Carla, but Anna did explain certain things to me as well,' she said and patted Carla's hand.

'Can I see the letter?'

'Of course you can,' Elizabeth said and handed Carla a little wooden box and a letter.

'There's something carved on the lid.' Carla said. 'You will know when,' she read aloud. 'What does that mean?'

'I'm sure Anna has explained it all in the letter,' Elizabeth said. 'Before I leave you to read in peace, I wanted you to understand that George and I are going to give you and Rebecca our surname so, as far as anyone will be concerned, you are both a part of our family. Is that okay, Carla?' Carla nodded and Elizabeth patted her hand again before standing up and leaving her to read the letter in peace.

Carla sat and stared at the discoloured parchment in her hands for a long time. Tears pricked at her eyes as she traced her spidery name with her finger, following the swirls and the lines, her heart heavy. With a sigh, Carla unfolded the letter and started to read.

My Dearest Carla,

I am so sorry, child, that you are reading this, for I know for certain that my worst fears must have come true. Please know that I love you, child, and I will watch over you wherever you are. I have always thought of you as my own and can honestly say that I wish you were. We wouldn't be where we are now if you were, of that I am certain.

I am so sorry about Isabella. I never wanted for you to see who she really was and a part of me wishes I'd never seen it either. Believe me, child, when I say I did my best with her. I never treated her any differently than I did you, yet you are both so different. You are such a beautiful person, Carla, so kind and gentle and Isabella was so...well, as I said to you before, some people are just born bad. It breaks my heart to admit that she was one of them, but she was. I only hope that Rebecca grows up to be different.

I am so sorry to burden you with this when you are so young and should be enjoying yourself and not worrying yourself with such things, but I had no choice. I know you are mature enough to deal with it, you have shown me that so much over the last few months, and I know how much you love Rebecca. Please, Carla, always look after her and love her as your sister, for she is going to need you as she grows up, especially if times remain as troubled as they are now.

Rebecca has the gift, child. I knew it as soon as I laid eyes on her and I need you to help her develop it. She may need it, in the future, although I pray with all my heart that she never does. Elizabeth and George are good people, Carla, but they do not understand witchcraft, so you will have to take a great deal of care. They will not judge you, but they may discourage you. Rebecca is the protector and it will pass down the line to her granddaughter and so on, as I told you before.

There is a box in the bundle that I sent with you and with it, a key to open it. The box is for Rebecca. I pray she never has to open it. Inside the box are the two spells that I had to cast to stop Antony. Antony is a vampire of sorts, Carla. He traded his soul with a ruthless warlock for the chance to get revenge on Isabella and her consorts. The cruel trick the warlock played was to make it so the only way he could become human again would be to kill Isabella and all her descendants. Antony didn't know about Rebecca until it was too late and there is no other way to stop him or break the curse. Until Ebenezer, the warlock, can be found, there is no way to cure Antony or destroy him. That is why I had to restrain him and bury him within a sealed stone sarcophagus in holy ground. The spells will hold him for eternity providing the ground remains holy. Because there is a chance that it may not always be so, I have put the spells in the wooden box. When Rebecca is old enough, you must explain all this to her. The spells can only be cast by a true witch. Your role, until she is of age, is to protect the sanctity of the ground where he is buried.

None of this is Antony's fault, Carla, despite the horror he has caused. One day I hope a cure can be found and he gets the chance to live the life he deserves, but that is not possible now. The beast within him is too strong.

Please, Carla, don't think about what they have done to me because I know you are fully aware of what that is. They are afraid of what they don't understand. One day this will not be the case, but that day is many, many years from now. Please protect Rebecca from the hatred and prejudice. Please show her the true joys of the craft and help her understand the good it can bring. When it is safe to do so, return to the cottage, dear child, and look under the boards in the kitchen. The Grimoire is there. She will need this as she grows.

I must go now, child, for I know you will be returning soon to tell me of my fate and I still need to get things ready for you.

George and Elizabeth will take you in as their own. Take their name and grow up to be part of their family. Both of you.

You are such a good and strong girl, Carla, and I only wish I could live to see you grow. Know that I love you and I entrust Rebecca's life and wellbeing to your protection. Please look after her.

I love you, dear sweet Carla. Goodbye.

Anna

Carla couldn't hold in the sob. *How could she ever do this without Anna?*

Jakes sat back in the armchair and rubbed his eyes. *Jesus!* He glanced at the clock on the wall and saw it was almost two in the morning. *What a story*, he thought. *Christ! To have all that dumped on you at twelve years old. Poor kid.*

Refocusing, he turned over the page, but there was nothing more. Dammit! His gaze dropped to one of the pages he had discarded on the coffee table, where he noticed some names and dates:

Carla Emerson:	Born 1680	Died 1732
Rebecca Emerson:	Born 1692	Died 1757

He rifled through the rest of the papers that the librarian had given him, but could find nothing else to progress the story of Carla or Rebecca.

He stared at the birth and death dates for Carla and Rebecca, his thumb playing with the edge of the diary page. *That's odd*, he thought, *this page seems thicker than the others.* Sure enough, when he looked, a few of the pages had become stuck together. Jakes rummaged in a drawer for a letter opener and carefully slid it between the joined sheets and prised them apart.

As he was pulling apart the final sheets, he caught sight of some handwriting on the last page. The writing was different to that of the rest of the diary. It had obviously been written by someone else and as Jakes turned the diary horizontally to see what had been written, he realised it was a family tree.

He started at the top of the page and scanned the names until he found Anna's, Isabella's and Rebecca's. He then skipped to the bottom of the page and his breath caught in his throat as he read the final name on the tree:

REBECCA MARTIN

CHAPTER 48

Becca sipped her vente latte and stared out of the plate glass window into the darkness. Her fingers caressed the wooden box on the table in front of her. It was almost soothing. The motion of her finger across the etched words seemed to be slowing her pulse down for the first time in hours.

She watched people passing by on the street; couples laughing and holding hands; businessmen still working, with their mobile phones attached to their heads and teenagers strolling around in gangs, with no cares in the world. *I wonder what their biggest worry is tonight*, she thought, as she blew holes into the foam on her coffee.

'I bet it's nothing like mine,' she muttered to herself and sighed, dragging her gaze back to the box in front of her.

Becca took the key from around her neck and opened the box once again. She pulled out the pieces of parchment, unfolded them and spread them on the table in front of her. She then glanced back in the box and saw the edge of a piece of paper sticking out from underneath the base. She got up to get a knife from the counter and then returned to her table. She picked the box up and turned it upside down, sliding the knife into the gap between the base and the side. Not wanting to break the box, Becca gently levered the base, but she needn't have worried. The false bottom of the box relinquished its secret quite easily.

A third piece of parchment fell to the table in front of her. Becca gently unfolded what appeared to be a letter. She picked up her coffee and began to read. Her eyes filled with tears as she read the letter that Anna had written to Carla and a sob escaped from her throat, causing other customers to turn and look at her with concern, but Becca was oblivious. Her mind was spinning. Everything her mother had told her that afternoon had been confirmed by a four hundred year old letter.

She felt a weight on her chest as she finally understood the meaning of the box being in her possession. She, Becca Martin, was a direct descendent of Isabella Cardover, the woman whose reprehensible behaviour had wrecked the lives of so many people, sent her own family into exile and condemned the only man who'd truly loved her, to an eternity of purgatory.

The fact that she was in possession of the box meant that she was the one who had to stop this. The fact that she was a witch, in denial or not, added to this. She glanced at the drawings on the other piece of parchment and knew, without a shadow of a doubt, that they would be identical to the ones on the sarcophagus at the site. She didn't need to check that. Her period of wilful denial had ended.

Her gaze then fell on the final piece of parchment, the one containing the spells, and her heart sank.

'But I can't do this,' she said to herself.

'Yes, you can, Becca,' Rosalind's voice replied and Becca jumped at the sound. She looked up and her eyes filled with tears again as she stared into the warm friendly face of her grandmother.

'Grandma?'

'Hello, Becca, dear,' Rosalind said and smiled.

'What? I don't...'

'Rebecca,' her grandmother said and Becca closed her mouth and waited for her to continue. 'You are perfectly capable of performing those spells. You just need to have faith.'

'But I haven't touched this stuff since you died. I can't remember...'

'Nonsense! You never forget. It's in your blood, Rebecca Martin. You just have to believe in yourself.'

'But I can't, Grandma. I just can't,' Becca said as tears ran down her cheeks.

'Yes, you can,' Rosalind said and reached across the table and took hold of her. Becca felt a strange tickling sensation on her upper arms and shivered.

'You have to, don't you see that?' Rosalind continued in her no nonsense way. 'If you don't, he will destroy you and your mother. He has to, to be free. Is that what you want?' Becca shook her head.

'Why can't I just stake him or something, like they do in the films?' Becca's voice had taken on that of the petulant child she always used to be when talking about her heritage.

'Because it isn't that easy. The curse that was placed on him can only be broken one way and besides, even if he could be stopped like that, he doesn't deserve that. Just remember that, Rebecca. None of this is Antony's fault.'

'He's choosing to kill us and you're saying it isn't his fault!'

'It's not Antony that is doing this. It's the demon within him. The warlock who did this to him is still alive. Antony deserves to be free of this beast and to be at peace. You can help him, Becca. You can right the wrongs that Isabella did. But first you have to contain him again. Only you can do that.'

'Only you can do that, Rebecca,' Becca muttered.

'Are you all right, Miss?' Becca jumped and her eyes flew open. Her coffee cup fell from her hand, sending cold coffee flowing over the table and onto the floor.

'Shit, you scared me!' Becca said to the barista and snatched the pieces of parchment out of the way.

'You were scaring us, Miss,' the barista said as he attempted to capture the contents of a super size mug of coffee in his saturated cloth.

'What do you mean?' Becca snapped as she pushed the pages back into the box and locked it, fastening the chain around her neck afterwards.

'Well, you were muttering to yourself as if you were having a discussion with someone, but you appeared to be asleep. We were a bit concerned.'

'I'm fine. I'm sorry for the mess. I better be going,' Becca said and stood up abruptly, causing the barista to jump out of the way.

'Sorry,' Becca mumbled as she ran out of the café.

CHAPTER 49

Becca shut the door behind her, leaned against it and closed her eyes. Her mind still raced with everything she'd heard that day. She felt a wave of exhaustion sweep over her as she lowered her head and opened her eyes.

'Hey, baby,' she said as she saw Spook eyeing her from the kitchen doorway. She dropped her keys into a bowl on the hall table and shrugged out of her coat. As she walked over to the hall cupboard to hang it up, the angry flashing light of the answer-phone caught her eye. She pressed play and waited for the message to kick in as she hung her coat up.

'R.E.B.E.C.C.A!' screeched the voice out of the machine and Becca winced. Dick's voice continued to grate through the air.

'Where are you, Rebecca? I don't appreciate you not coming to work and not telling me why. I am your boss, you know and if this sort of behaviour continues…' Becca pressed delete and his threats disappeared into the ether. She didn't need his aggravation tonight.

She wandered through into the living room and automatically went over to the photograph. She plucked it off the wall, slumped down on the sofa with it and stared intently at her grandmother's face. Rosalind just stared back at her, happy and smiling.

'Talk to me, Grandma,' Becca said to the photo, 'tell me how I can do this…please.' Becca kept asking, over and over again, but there was no response. Tears filled her eyes and she laid her head against the cushions, the photograph resting on her knees.

'How the hell am I supposed to do this?' she said to the empty apartment and thumped her fists into the sofa. 'HOW?' she shouted and burst into tears. She cried like she hadn't done in years, her whole body wracked with the force of her anguish. *How on earth was she going to be able to stop him? She hadn't practised magic in years and she'd never been that good at it anyway.* These thoughts careered around in her head, bouncing off each other, when she heard the buzzer.

Becca stopped crying and froze. Who on earth was visiting her at this time of night? The buzzer sounded again and again and again. Becca's heart started to beat faster as adrenalin coursed through her body. She remained on the sofa, immobile. As abruptly as it had started, the buzzing stopped and Becca relaxed. Probably only kids messing about. Then someone banged on her front door and she screamed. The hammering continued and, heart thundering, Becca got off the sofa and crept towards the front door.

Tentatively, she looked through the peephole and saw her mother standing on her doorstep. Becca's heart calmed slightly and she opened the door.

'What are you doing here?' she asked.

'That's no way to welcome your mother is it, darling?' Ginnie purred as she strolled into Becca's apartment, her fingertips tracing Becca's jaw-line as she walked passed.

'What the hell happened to you?' Becca said as she stared at the woman before her. 'Have you been on a date or something?' She closed the door and turned round to stare at Ginnie.

'What makes you think I've been on a "date"?' Ginnie emphasised the word "date" with a click of her tongue and turned towards the living room. Becca followed.

'Well, look at you. Your hair, your make-up. You just look different. Glamorous. I've never seen you like this before,' Becca said and stopped as Ginnie spun round to face her.

'Let's face it, Becca, you've not exactly been around much over the last decade, so what do you really know about me anymore?' Ginnie smiled at Becca and Becca shivered as she stared into her mother's eyes. There was something different about her and it wasn't only her appearance. She did look amazing, Becca had to admit. Her hair was a beautiful shade of red and her curls were expertly tamed instead of the pale ginger frizzy affair they had always been. Her skin had lost its rosy cheeked outdoor look and, instead, her face appeared to be expertly made up to give a peaches and cream glowing complexion, if a little pale. It had to be make-up. It was too perfect to be natural. Her whole manner was different. She exuded style, confidence and sophistication. A total contrast to the outspoken, clumsy woman that Ginnie had been that afternoon. There was also something missing. Becca had seen it when she'd looked into her mother's eyes. There was no warmth there, no soul.

'Oh, what a beautiful cat,' Ginnie said and bent down to stroke Spook, who had tried to hide himself away in the corner. Spook hissed at her and lashed out with his claws, tearing the skin on her finger.

'Nasty beast!' Ginnie growled and put the cut finger into her mouth.

'He's been acting weird for a few days now,' Becca said, a little relieved that it wasn't only her that he seemed to have taken an aversion to.

'What do you want, Mum? It's late.' Becca said, standing in the doorway with her hands on her hips while Ginnie settled down on the sofa.

'Aren't you going to offer me some tea?'

'Mum?'

'Well, you ran away so quickly earlier, when you were supposed to be staying, that I was worried and thought I'd come and check on you.'

'You've never bothered before, so why now? Why didn't you just phone like you did the other day? And, besides, you didn't get all dressed up just for me, did you? So, what's going on?'

'Now, now, Becca, don't be like that. Come and sit down next to your mother and tell me what's bothering you,' Ginnie purred and patted the sofa next to her. Becca felt herself walking towards her mother and sitting down. She then found herself talking.

'You know what's wrong with me. What you told me this afternoon. I can't do that. I don't have the ability.' Becca felt her mother's fingertips caress her hair and then move onto her neck. Instead of trying to shrink away from it, she found herself relaxing against the sofa and enjoying it. The coolness of her fingers seemed to sooth the burning of the marks on her neck.

'About this afternoon,' Ginnie started.

'Mmmm,' Becca murmured, her eyes closed. Her mother's touch was like ice quelling a raging fever.

'You know I tend to over exaggerate and worry about nothing?'

'Yes,' Becca said, small alarm bells starting to go off in her head.

'Well, this afternoon was one of those times. I really don't think we have anything to worry about and I really think you have simply been having vivid nightmares, that's all.'

'What?' Becca's eyes flew open and she snapped out of her trance as she turned to face her mother. 'So, everything you told me this afternoon was a lie?'

'No, not exactly, but…'

'So, the story is true?'

'Well, yes, but…'

'So, the sarcophagus belongs to Antony Cardover?'

'Yes.'

'And he escaped and is intent on killing you and me to free himself from his curse?'

'Not exactly.'

'That's not what you said this afternoon.'

'I know. I was worried. I overreacted. I mean, think about it, Becca, how on earth would he be able to get out of the sarcophagus, anyway?' Ginnie said and began to rub her fingers across the marks on Becca's neck again.

'So, these marks are just a figment of my imagination, are they?' Becca snapped and stood up.

'They're just bites, darling, they'll heal. The summer has been hot and it's brought the mosquitoes out.'

'These are not insect bites,' Becca said and walked over to the mirror above the fireplace and studied them. Each one was red and open and she could see them pulsing as though acting like some kind of beacon.

'You think too much,' Ginnie whispered and Becca jumped as Ginnie's breath ruffled her hair. She whirled round. Her mother was standing right behind her.

'What the...?' Becca said and turned to face the mirror. Only her reflection stared back at her.

'You need to relax, darling, and forget about Antony Cardover and the curse.' Becca felt her mother's breath on her neck again and she turned and shoved her away with all her might. Ginnie howled with laughter as she fell back against the sofa. Becca grabbed the poker from the tools on the hearth and whirled round to face her mother again.

'What the hell happened to you?' she sobbed and brandished the poker in her mother's direction.

'I was given a new lease of life. You should try it sometime,' Ginnie said. She stood up and started walking towards her daughter. Becca stepped backwards, but found herself backed up against the fireplace.

'You won't beat him, you know,' Ginnie said, 'he'll get you, like he got me, only you won't be as lucky as me.' She threw her head back and laughed, a deep guttural laugh, which was so much in contrast with Ginnie Martin's gentle laughter.

'This isn't my mother. This isn't my mother,' Becca said over and over again as she stepped from foot to foot, the poker held in two hands, straight out in front of her.

'No, it's not,' Ginnie said and Becca screamed as she stared into the face of a demon. Without thinking, she raised the poker and lunged forward. Ginnie tried to move, but Becca had surprised her and she howled in pain as the sterling silver poker, an extravagance from an antique store, plunged through her heart.

Becca screamed again and let go of the poker as she watched her mother start to burn from the poker wound outwards. Wide eyed, tears streaming down her face, she collapsed to her knees and sobbed at the same time as the poker clattered to the floor on top of a pile of ash.

CHAPTER 50

'Nooooo!' Antony shouted, slamming his fists into the lid of his sarcophagus as he felt the poker piercing Ginnie's heart.

'No, no, no, no, no!' he continued to shout and punch the lid, the echoes sounding hollow and empty within the crypt.

Why did he think it would have worked? Maybe a couple of days ago, when the girl was just starting to find things out, but now? Especially after her mother had told her everything? How could he be so naïve? Still, he reasoned with himself, *it was her mother and if anyone could have thrown her off the scent...*

Antony let his mind wander. *Maybe if he'd not turned her? Maybe if he'd simply frightened her into doing it? It was probably her appearance that gave her away.* That's the problem with turning people – they change, become the person they always wished they were – glamorous, confident and irresistible.

Still, if nothing else, he'd unbalanced Becca. She couldn't possibly be at full strength, having just killed her mother.

'Tomorrow!' Antony growled. 'Tomorrow this ends!'

CHAPTER 51

Jakes woke with a jolt and found himself slumped on the table for the second time in as many days. He stretched and felt the now familiar twinge in his neck flair up. He shook his head to start to clear the morning fog and glanced at the papers in front of him.

He jumped out of the chair; the papers clutched in his hand, and went in search of his mobile phone. He found it on the kitchen counter, punched in some numbers and waited.

'Becca, DI Jakes here. I need to talk to you urgently, please call me as soon as you pick this message up.' Jakes left the message on Becca's home phone and then dialled her mobile, getting voicemail again. He was in the process of leaving another message when a sudden hammering on his front door caused Jakes to turn and frown. Bloody landlord! If that door was working properly, he'd be able to vet the intruder before they arrived.

The hammering on his front door started again.

'Okay, okay, for heaven's sake,' Jakes said as he walked down the hall and opened the door. He found Robinson on his doorstep, all spick and span and perfectly groomed. Jakes groaned.

'There have been two more murders. Same MO as the others and, yes, I have checked, before you ask,' Robinson said and then stopped abruptly as he finally glanced up from his notebook to Jakes.

'Are you all right, Sir?' Robinson said as he scrutinised Jakes.

'I'm fine, why?'

'You look terrible, you haven't been drink…' he didn't finish his sentence as Jakes glared at him. *How bad could it be*, Jakes wondered and looked down at the clothes he had worn the previous day. They were all crumpled from sleeping in them and there was a huge brownish stain down the front of his shirt, where he had spilt coke at some point the previous night – not that he remembered doing that. He brought his hand up to his chin and scratched the day's worth of growth that decorated it.

'Just need a shave and a shower, that's all,' Jakes muttered, 'why don't you wait?'

'No, it's okay, I'll see you at the station,' Robinson said and disappeared down the stairs.

Jakes closed the door and leant against it. His shoulders sagged and he sighed. Robinson had, having referred to his drinking, brought back painful memories of his family and of the mess he'd made of everything. He had cleaned himself up, eventually, but for what? He'd already lost the only people that were important to him. He wouldn't get them back, he knew that. That ship had most definitely sailed. The only thing he had left now was the job. Without that, Jakes knew, he'd be on the slippery slope back to the booze.

He pushed himself away from the door and ambled towards the bathroom. He turned the hot tap on and listened to the pipes clunk and groan in protest. He leant on the sink and studied himself in the mirror, while he waited for the water to warm up. Christ, he did look rough. As he began to fill the sink with water, for a long overdue shave, Jakes' mind drifted.

He had tried to clean himself up after Jean had left. He'd enrolled himself in both Alcoholics and Gamblers Anonymous. He had a sponsor for each and he'd attended every meeting that had been going on in the surrounding area. He'd been determined to sort himself out, to get his family back. Then a huge case had come in. Some psycho had been slashing the throats of homeless people and prostitutes, doing his bit to "clean up the streets" he'd said, when he was eventually caught, six months and ten bodies later.

The meetings had been constantly interrupted by phone calls and texts. He'd never figured out how to put his phone on silent and he would never have dreamed of switching it off. Real cops were available twenty four hours a day, seven days a week as far as he was concerned. The constant phone interruptions, despite the rule of having to switch all phones off, proved so disruptive to the meetings that Jakes was asked to leave and come back only when he felt he could dedicate his full attention to getting himself straight. Thank goodness his sponsors had hung around for a bit longer.

Without them I'd never have got clean, Jakes thought to himself, wincing as his blunt razor nicked his skin every time he took a stroke. *Jesus!* He'd look like he'd put his face through a plate glass window if he wasn't careful. He'd never gone back to those meetings after the case was solved.

"Addictive personality", the technical term was, or "obsessive" as his teachers used to say when they had his parents at school, which was on a regular basis.

'Frank doesn't have an interest in things, Mr and Mrs Jakes; he has an obsession with them,' Mr Ballantine, his primary school headmaster, had explained to his parents one day. Jakes had been hauled down to the office, broken hearted over the death of the school hamster, which he'd still had clutched in his hand. The door to the headmaster's room had been ajar and Jakes had been able to hear everything that had been said.

'Every morning he'd come into class and drag the poor creature out of its cage. He'd then carry it around all day, constantly worrying it. It's not surprising it's died and now we can't prise it out of his hand.'

'He's only a child.' Jakes had heard his father say. 'He just loves animals.'

'It's not only animals, Mr Jakes,' Ballantine had replied. 'He is the same with paints, games, books and the other children. Once he has found something he likes, he won't leave it alone. It's very worrying.'

'I'm sure he'll grow out of it. It's just curiosity,' his mother had said.

'Let's hope so,' Ballantine had replied, 'but I suggest that you take him to see a doctor. They might be able to help him.'

The meeting had finished at that point and when his parents had emerged from the headmaster's office, the hamster had been on the chair next to him, wrapped in tissues. His parents had never taken him to a doctor.

'Maybe they should have,' Jakes muttered to himself. *But then he probably wouldn't be as good at his job as he was, would he?* With that thought, he climbed into the shower to try and seal some of the wounds on his face.

CHAPTER 52

Becca lay staring at the ceiling. Her sea of tears had long since dried and she could feel the paths of salt in the tightness of her skin. She had nothing left.

The sound of the cat flap caught her attention and she dragged her gaze towards the window. A pair of huge orange eyes stared back at her. Becca sighed. She didn't even have anything left to care about his coldness. Still watching her, Spook settled himself down next to his escape route. Becca dragged her gaze back to the ceiling.

Her eyeballs were dry and starting to get sore, but she couldn't sleep. She doubted she ever would again after what she'd done the night before. She shuddered as the memory of piercing her mother's heart with the poker flooded her mind. Her silver poker. That had been one of her grandmother's superstitions. She had always believed in having useful silver objects in her house, "just in case", she used to say. Just in case of what? Becca had always wondered and now she knew.

Becca closed her eyes and buried her head under the duvet as her mother's face swam into her mind. The pain, the sadness, the disbelief, had all been etched on it, the monster having been banished. A sob shuddered through her body, but it was dry. She had nothing left.

She pushed the duvet back and stared, immobile, as the first rays of dawn broke through the voile draping the windows. Spook, sensing that he probably would have to feed himself that day, disappeared out of the cat flap. Becca remained cocooned, her eyes open and staring. She needed to fall asleep, to have a break from the horror that was now her life, but she doubted sleep would ever come.

The screeching of the phone jolted Becca out of *Inferno*. She rubbed her eyes and turned to look at the clock. It was noon. *Had she been asleep?* She honestly didn't know. She didn't feel like she had. Her mind was whirring. She felt physically and mentally drained and she still had to do "it". She still had to stop him. She didn't want that responsibility. She didn't want to face him.

As Jakes left his message for her to call him urgently, Becca hid under the duvet. 'Oh please, God, let it all go away; let everything be okay again,' she murmured. She closed her eyes again and willed herself to sleep. *Maybe if she stayed here for a while, he would give up and go away? After all, he couldn't get in here without being invited, could he? She was safe here.* That thought sent a warm glow through Becca's body and she started to relax. That was all it took and she felt sleep overtake her.

CHAPTER 53

Becca still wasn't answering her phone and there'd been no response at her apartment when he'd called round. *Where the hell was she?* Jakes shoved his chair away from his desk in frustration; he hated waiting.

He slammed his fist into the wall as a vent for his impatience and immediately regretted it. He massaged his throbbing hand and stared out of his office window at the couples strolling by in the balmy afternoon air, not a care in the world.

'Lucky beggars,' Jakes said and flexed his hand to try and get the feeling back in it. He couldn't just sit here.

He strode to his office door and flung it open, allowing it to crash back against the wall.

'Where's Robinson?' he asked no one in particular.

'No idea, Sir,' one officer replied.

'Just seen him with a suspect, Sir,' said another as he dropped into his chair. 'Heading for interview three,' he continued, anticipating Jakes' next question.

'Thanks,' Jakes muttered as he left the squad room.

'Robinson, can I have a word, please?' Jakes called, just before Robinson disappeared into the interview room.

'Yeah, sure. Can you get Mr Ramply settled, please,' Robinson said to the officer escorting Dick.

'What's up?' Robinson faced Jakes, his hands on his hips.

'What are you doing?' Jakes gestured towards the interview room.

'I'm not sure I follow.'

'Why is Ramply here?'

'To be interviewed. He's our prime suspect.'

'Really? And why, pray tell, is that then, Sherlock?'

'Well, it's obvious it's him, isn't it?'

'Is it?'

'Well, yeah, of course it is. Both men worked for him. They were found on his site and, you've got to admit, there's been some weird shit going on over there.' Jakes raised his eyebrows and waited for more, but Robinson appeared to have finished.

'So, that's all you've got to go on then?' Jakes finally asked.

'Well, yeah, what more do we need?'

'What about the other bodies?'

'What about them?'

'I thought they all had the same MO and so were obviously done by the same killer,' Jakes said.

'Well, they do.'

'But they didn't work for Ramply and their bodies weren't discovered on his site.'

'So?'

'So, doesn't that kind of throw your theory out of the window? Anyway, I thought Ramply had an alibi for the nights of the site murders.'

'He does, but...'

'Well, if his alibi checks out, it is unlikely to be him, is it? Do you have any other leads?'

'No,' Robinson said, his eyes downcast. 'Do you?'

'Yes, I do. A real suspect and real motive.'

'Really, who? The girl?'

'His name is Antony Cardover,' Jakes said, turning to face Robinson.

'Who's that then?'

Jakes was about to tell Robinson the whole story, but decided against it.

'You wouldn't believe me if I told you. Let's just say that you were right on one count. The murders are linked to the site, but to the occupant of the sarcophagus, not to Ramply.'

'What do you mean?'

'No time to explain. I need to speak to Ramply before you release him.'

'Release him? I...'

'Yes, release him. If his alibi checked out, he is not a suspect,' Jakes said and stared down the younger man before heading to the interview room.

CHAPTER 54

'Where is she?' Jakes demanded as the interview room door banged against the wall causing the occupants to jump, spilling coffee all over the stainless steel table.

'Good heavens, Inspector, you made me jump,' Dick Ramply said, his hand pressed to his chest.

'Where is she, Ramply?' Jakes said again.

'Jakes, calm down! You can't speak to Mr Ramply like that!' Robinson said, having followed Jakes into the room. Jakes ignored Robinson's plea and turned to face Dick Ramply, who was now slumped really low in his seat as though trying to hide.

'Now, Mr Ramply, where is Rebecca Martin?' Jakes leaned on both fists and rocked his body forwards over the table, so that his face was only inches from Ramply's.

'How should I know?' Dick said, crossing his arms over his chest and sitting himself back up again, trying to recover his dignity.

'I asked you a question and I expect an answer,' Jakes said through gritted teeth.

'Why should I know where she is, I'm only her employer. What would I need to know her whereabouts for?' Dick said, his nose in the air, his gaze averted, his arms tightening across his chest.

'Where is she?' Jakes snapped and slammed his right fist into the table, inches from Ramply. Dick let out a squeal and his hand went to his mouth as he paled. The room went silent. Jakes had crossed a line and he knew it, but he couldn't stop now. He stared at Ramply, who looked down at the table.

'I don't know where she is,' Dick finally sighed. 'That's the truth. She hasn't been to work for the last few days and when I've called, the phone has gone straight to answer-phone.'

'Have you been to check on her?' Jakes asked, his temper simmering away below the surface.

'No, I haven't.'

'Why not?'

'Because I…I don't know, I just haven't,' Dick said. Jakes shook his head and pushed himself up off the table and turned to Robinson.

'Were any of the bodies brought in identified as Rebecca Martin?'

'I'm not sure,' said Robinson.

'Didn't you look at the names on the coroner's report?'

'Of course I did, but there weren't any. I don't think they've been identified yet.' Robinson called after Jakes' departing back.

CHAPTER 55

'The bodies that came in last night are all in the fridges over there,' Jan Doust, the pathologist, indicated to the row on the opposite side of the room from where Jakes was standing. 'I hope you catch him soon, Frank, coz I'm running out of space in here,' she said. 'I'll have to contact the local hospital for the use of their morgue, if we get any more.'

Jakes felt himself flushing under Jan's chocolate brown gaze. He had always liked Jan. She had a no-nonsense straight talking approach to life, which he found appealing, but which had also kept her single. He turned to look at her as she went to grab the paperwork he'd asked for and couldn't help admiring her compact, curvy figure and her glossy chestnut hair.

'Haven't the bodies been claimed then?' he asked.

'The bodies haven't all been identified yet,' Jan replied and thrust some files into his hand.

'Do the names Virginia and Rebecca Martin mean anything to you?'

'Uh-uh,' Jan said. 'Should they?'

'I hope not,' he said, handing her back the files, knowing none of them would be useful. 'May I?' he asked, indicating the fridges.

'Be my guest,' Jan shrugged. 'Oh, before I forget, I've got the results of those bloods you asked me to run.'

'And?' Jakes said as he went to open the first of the fridges.

'You tell me,' Jan said.

'What?' Jakes turned to face her, his hand still on the handle of the fridge.

'Well, I'm not sure what you swabbed, but some of it wasn't blood.'

'Some of it?'

'Yes, some of it. Look, the swab you marked as *Counter 1*, well that came back as animal – bovine to be exact – probably what was in the meat packet you found. A couple of the others were the same, but the swab from the floor, well…'

'Well, what?' Jakes said, his interest in the bodies forgotten for the moment.

'Well, I don't know, Frank, maybe they got contaminated or something, it's the only explanation..,' Jan drifted off again.

'For goodness sake, Jan, what is it?'

'Well, the results weren't animal…and they weren't human either. I have never seen anything like it and can only think the sample must have come into contact with another substance, but the lab wasn't able to identify what that substance was. I'm sorry.' Jan handed him another file.

'It's fine, don't worry,' Jakes said and laid the file on Jan's desk. He hadn't needed the results to confirm something he already suspected, but it was good to know.

'I've got to go and see the chief, so will you make sure the door is locked on your way out?' She touched his arm as she passed and Jakes shivered.

'Of course,' he said. Jakes waited until she had left and then went over to the fridges and opened the first door. Taking a deep breath, he yanked the tray out. He unzipped the black body bag and stared into the grey face of a forty-something man. He felt a little of the tension, which had been building since he had left the interview room, ebb away.

Jakes repeated the exercise until he'd seen all of Antony's victims. Finding none of them resembling Becca Martin, he hoped none of them were her mother. Without a description, at this stage, he could do nothing more.

He sat down to collect his thoughts. The silence of the morgue helped calm his mind, yet chilled him to the core at the same time.

He had to find Becca Martin. He had to find Antony Cardover. He had to convince Becca that she had to stop Antony. *How the hell was he going to do that?* She'd probably laugh in his face when he told her.

He glanced at his watch. It was five thirty. The sun would be setting soon. Jakes left the morgue, an ominous feeling settling over him.

CHAPTER 56

Antony stood in the doorway of the basement and watched the sky turn fiery red as the sun sank towards the horizon. He hoped Becca was watching it too; it would be her last. He reached his hand out into the light, clenching his teeth against the pain as his flesh smouldered. He had to test the water every so often, just to make sure.

He withdrew into the dampness of the crypt and began to pace. He hated waiting. He had already waited too long. He deserved his life back and no one was going to stop him this time. No one! He slammed his fist onto the lid of his sarcophagus and the echo resounded around the room.

Antony closed his eyes and remembered the moment when he'd realised he had been tricked. The moment he'd known Isabella had borne a child. In that brief moment, all hope, all hate and all his power had left him. He'd felt empty and at a loss. That was the only reason the old woman had been able to trap him. He could have fought her otherwise, could have snapped those vines, but the fight had momentarily left him. He believed that. He had to.

This time would be different, though. This time he knew Becca had no children; the mother had given that information up. He had already taken care of the mother and now all he had left was the daughter. He was going to enjoy every moment of this. Becca Martin would pay dearly for the sins of Isabella Cardover.

As the sun disappeared below the horizon, Antony Cardover swept out of the churchyard.

CHAPTER 57

Becca sat on her haunches in the living room staring at the pile of ash in front of her, a dust pan and brush in her hand, a silver jewellery box next to her. She gagged and closed her eyes, willing her body to calm down. She couldn't take being sick anymore; her insides hurt. All that remained was bile.

Tears ran freely down her cheeks and plopped onto her thighs, soaking into the faded denim of her torn and battered jeans. She leant forward and swept up her mother's ashes and watched them glitter in the glow from the overhead light as she poured them into the silver box. With a sigh, she closed the lid and pushed herself to her feet, picking up the heavy box as she did so. She wandered over to the mantelpiece and set the box in the middle, flanked by two silver candlesticks, all of which her grandmother had bought for her.

Becca wandered back to the sofa and sank into its comforting depths. As she did so, her hand brushed against some paper and, opening her eyes, Becca studied the pieces of parchment which marked her destiny.

With a heavy heart she sat up and read through the spells again. *Why?* She had no idea. They were etched on her brain for eternity, but it was like waiting to sit an exam. She just kept rereading things, even though nothing else was going in.

Becca's stomach growled. She hadn't eaten in over twenty four hours.

'I need my strength,' she muttered, feeling her grandmother's words wash over her. She wandered into the kitchen and opened the fridge. There wasn't much there, but there was enough. She grabbed what she wanted and proceeded to make herself a cheese sandwich. She poured herself a glass of milk and went and sat at the table. Absently, she began to eat as she watched the sun slowly sinking. The sunset reminded her of glowing coals. It filled her with a moment of pleasure as she thought of the beautiful day it signified for tomorrow.

She remained, transfixed, watching the sunset as though somehow it might be her last. She shuddered and broke her reverie.

'Stop thinking like that,' she chastised herself. 'I have to do it. Tonight, before he finds me.' Her mind made up, she stood up from the table and screamed as the buzzer cut through the silence of the apartment.

CHAPTER 58

'Who is it?' a whispered voice sounded intermittently through the intercom system. *Poor kid*, Jakes thought, as he imagined her shaking finger holding in the "talk" button.

'Becca, it's DI Jakes. I have to talk to you. Can I…' The door buzzed open before he had finished his sentence and he entered the vestibule of the apartment block. He could see her front door open, waiting for him.

'You really shouldn't leave your front door open like that,' he said as he walked into the apartment and closed the door. 'Anyone could just…Jesus! What happened to you?' He followed her into the living room, where she sat down, and crouched down in front of her.

She seemed so frail, even more so than usual. Her skin was almost transparent and her luminous eyes were now dull and subdued. She sat in front of him in a pair of ripped jeans and a T-shirt, staring at some papers clutched in her hand. He reached out to her, to comfort her, he couldn't help himself. She resembled a lost child. Becca shrugged away from him and shivered.

'What happened?' Jakes asked again.

'Rough couple of days,' she said, almost defiantly, as she regarded him. The pain and sadness he saw there almost broke his heart.

'Becca…'

'Look, what did you *have* to tell me?' she asked, pushing passed him as she stood up and walked over to the mantelpiece.

Jakes watched her as she went. He watched as she reached out and touched a silver box. He saw her head drop and her shoulders slump as she did so. Her pain was palpable. He could feel it in the air.

'What's in the box…?'

'Detective, I have something I need to do tonight so, please, tell me why you're here,' she interrupted him and turned to face him, her left hand still resting on the box, her right hand still clutching the papers.

'I've found something out about Antony Cardover, some things that you need to be aware of.'

'Let me guess,' Becca said and came to sit down on the sofa next to where Jakes had finally sat, his knees not allowing him to crouch any longer.

'What?' Jakes started to say, but Becca held up her hand to silence him.

'In a nutshell,' Becca started and proceeded to give Jakes an abridged version of what her mother had told her the previous day. 'Eternity ended a couple of days ago.' Becca fell silent at this point and began smoothing out the pieces, of what looked to Jakes like parchment, on her knee. He was just about to speak when she continued.

'The problem is that the spells Anna cast were only a part of it. Without the consecrated ground, they are not strong enough to hold him. He is already out and gaining strength,' Becca said and Jakes followed her gaze to the mantelpiece.

'I'm sorry, Becca, but that's not all. That's not the most important bit.'

'I know,' she said and turned to face him. She looked exhausted as she passed the pieces of parchment to him. 'I am the sole surviving descendant and I am the only one who can stop him.' She shrugged then and flopped back on to the sofa and Jakes glanced from her to the papers, trying to multitask. He recognised the words on the paper, but wasn't sure where from, as his mind was also trying to process what she had just said.

'You mean, you and your mother are the sole surviving descendants,'

Jakes corrected, deciding to concentrate on one thing at a time. 'But, how did you know?'

'My mother's dead,' Becca said, her voice flat and hollow. 'I went to see her. She told me everything. I retrieved these papers and left. He killed her.' It was almost like she was reciting facts for a class project and her detachment made Jakes shiver.

'What, how, when?' he said. He forgot the papers in his hand for a moment and stared at her. 'Tell me what happened, Becca. All of it.'

Becca sighed and leaned forward and looked up at him. The tears rimming her eyes made his heart ache.

'I'm here to help you, Becca.'

'You can't help me,' she said. 'Only I can put an end to this.'

'Tell me what happened, and then we'll figure out what to do next. Together.' He patted her hand. This time she didn't pull away, so he left his hand on top of hers, his warmth hopefully passing over to her. Her hand was freezing.

'I've already told you. You can't help me.'

'Maybe not, but I'd like to try,' Jakes said, rubbing the back of her hand.

'I went to mum's yesterday. God, it was weird. I haven't seen her for over a decade, yet nothing seemed to have changed. Everything was as I remembered it, even mum,' her voice broke at this point and she went quiet. Jakes waited.

'She told me everything, the whole nine yards. It kind of made sense, in a way. I'd always wondered why my grandmother had taken her paganism and witchcraft so seriously. I never had. I didn't want to be a witch, didn't want to be any more different than I already was from everyone else. But, I guess I should have listened, should have taken it more seriously, because it's magic I've now got to do to stop him.'

'What happened to your mother, Becca?'

'I don't know. Once I'd found the spells in the wooden box...' She indicated the parchment in his hands and he realised where he knew the words from.

'You will know when,' he muttered absently.

'How did you know that?'

'Research,' he said. 'Go on.'

'Well, I was kind of freaked out. I'd just been told some fairy story and been expected to believe it was true. Yet, I kind of knew that it was. The dreams I'd been having, the visions, these marks.' She put her fingers up to her neck and Jakes saw the raw marks pulsing, as though alive. 'Well, it all kind of made sense in a weird way, even though I didn't want to believe it and gave mum a bit of a hard time.' Becca wiped her eyes and fell silent again.

'What happened next?' Jakes prompted her, conscious of the time and of the darkening evening.

'As I said, when I opened the box and found the spells and realised that mum had been telling the truth, I freaked. I ran out of the house and left her. I went to the coffee shop and sat and stared at the spells for hours. I know them word for word now. Which is probably a good thing,' she smiled then, a wry, resigned smile. 'Only trouble is, I don't think I can do them.'

'Of course you can.'

'That's what she said.'

'Who?'

'My grandmother.'

'I thought your grandmother was dead?'

'She is, but...and now you're really going to think I've lost the plot...I saw her, as plain as you're sitting there. While I was staring at these spells in the coffee shop, I saw her.'

'And she said you could do them?'

Becca nodded. 'She said it was in my blood; I just had to believe in myself.'

'Maybe she's right.'

'I'm sure we'll find out soon, unless this is all a big farce, like mum later tried to tell me it was.'

'When was this?'

'After I'd got home from the coffee shop. She came round, which was odd because mum never strayed far from home. And she looked different.'

'Different, how?'

'Alive, vibrant, young. Maybe like she used to be when she was my age. But she certainly didn't look like my mum, especially not the woman I'd seen a few hours earlier. She didn't sound like her either. She was loud, confident and bullish.' Becca went quiet again.

'I thought she was going on a date or something. Why else would she be all dressed up, right?' Becca looked at Jakes, her brows furrowed in question.

'Sounds reasonable,' he said.

'But then she tried to convince me that everything she'd said to me earlier was a lie and that Antony wasn't coming after me.'

'Did you believe her?'

'I wanted to, so much, but deep down I knew it was all true. She could see I wasn't convinced and as she started to get annoyed with me, she started to change...her face, it became...it was awful...and I just reacted...and then she was gone.' Becca burst into tears and this time Jakes put his arms around her.

'I-I-I k-k-killed my own mother,' Becca sobbed, as her body shook.

'You didn't kill her, Becca. Antony did. He must have got to her and turned her. That creature that came here last night wasn't your mother. You have to remember that. You have to believe that.'

'I-I can't. I saw her face as I stabbed her,' Becca said, pulling away and looking up at him. 'That was my mother and now all I have left is in that box.' She nodded towards the silver box on the mantelpiece.

Jakes held Becca while she cried, but he felt time ebbing away and they had to move soon.

'Becca, I understand you're upset, but we have to…'

'I know. That's what I was getting ready for when you came. I just don't know whether I can…'

'You have to believe in yourself,' Jakes said. 'I'll be there to help.'

'As I said, there's nothing you can do. This is something I have to do.'

'Becca, you're not alone…' His sentence was interrupted by a loud bang on the front door, which made them both jump.

'What the…?' he said.

'It's okay,' Becca said, surprisingly calm. 'It'll be Brandon again, with another excuse to borrow something just to see me. We'd have heard the buzzer otherwise.' She gave Jakes a weak smile as she went towards the door. 'Come in, it's open,' she called.

Jakes had a bad feeling about this and ran after her to try and stop her.

'Becca, don't!' he shouted, but it was too late.

CHAPTER 59

'Hello, Rebecca,' Antony said as he dropped Brandon's body at his feet and wiped his blood stained mouth. Becca screamed.

'Run, Becca! Now!' Jakes shouted and shoved her hard into the kitchen and planted himself between Becca and the front door as Antony strode into the apartment.

'You can't come in here,' Jakes challenged as he regarded the bigger man.

'I can do anything I like, I'm family,' Antony replied and grabbed Jakes around the neck, lifting him off the floor as though he weighed nothing. 'You're lucky I've only just eaten,' he said as he hurled Jakes across the hallway into the wall. The wall splintered on impact and Jakes slumped to the floor, unconscious.

'Now, stay out of my way,' Antony said as he marched passed Jakes into the kitchen and out of the French doors, where Becca had exited a few moments earlier.

Becca rammed the Fiesta into first gear and slammed her foot down on the accelerator, lifting her foot carefully off the clutch, willing the little car not to stall. It lurched forward with a screech of rubber and propelled Becca away from the curb so fast that she almost lost control.

Her heart thundering in her chest, she took a right and headed towards the site. A loud thud on the roof made the car swerve and Becca screamed. She looked in her rear-view mirror, but couldn't see anything. She glanced out of all her side windows, but saw nothing either. She turned back to the windscreen and screamed again as she stared directly into the black pools that were Antony's eyes.

Becca slammed the brakes on and Antony went careering off the roof into the deserted road. She rammed the car into reverse and stamped on the accelerator again, sending the car speeding backwards before she flung the steering wheel to the right and spun the car back round again. She glanced in her mirror. Antony still lay in the road. She put the car in first gear, but let the clutch out too quickly. The Fiesta stalled. Becca cursed.

Impatiently she turned the key. The engine continued to whir, but it didn't catch.

'C'mon, c'mon,' she willed the little car as she glanced in her rear-view mirror. Antony was stirring. She could feel her heart start to constrict as she watched him stand up and turn round. She had to get to the site. She couldn't do this otherwise.

'Please, car, please,' she pleaded as she pumped the accelerator and turned the key at the same time. The car fired to life and Becca sped off, glancing quickly in her mirror. Antony still stood in the road behind her.

As she turned onto the main road she narrowly missed a silver Audi coming in the opposite direction.

'Idiot!' Robinson shouted as a beat up old Fiesta skimmed his front wing. 'Some people shouldn't be allowed to drive,' he muttered as he turned into the road where Becca's apartment was. He pulled up behind Jakes' Mondeo and looked around. There wasn't a soul to be seen, anywhere.

Robinson got out of the car and ambled up to the front door of the building. Surprised to see it ajar, he pushed the door open and strode in.

He stopped short as he saw the door to number three, Becca's apartment, wide open and a body slumped on the floor in front of it.

Robinson heard a loud groan and assumed it had come from the body in front of him.

'Jakes?' he called and rushed forward, rolling the body towards him and gagging as he saw the neck of the stranger, torn open. Robinson stood up and turned away, closing his eyes.

The groaning sounded again and Robinson turned towards the open door and rushed inside.

'Jakes!' he shouted as he saw his partner slumped on the floor below a badly damaged wall. 'Jesus, are you okay? What happened to you?' he asked as he helped Jakes up into a sitting position.

'What are you doing here?' Jakes said as he massaged the back of his head, which felt damp and sticky.

'Well, Ramply's alibi checked out, so I thought I'd come and give you a hand apprehending your suspect,' the younger man said, standing up and brushing debris off his designer suit.

'Did you now?' Jakes said, trying to stand up. A rush of dizziness sent him straight back to the ground with a thud.

'Help me up,' Jakes said and almost dragged Robinson to the floor, as the younger man struggled to manage Jakes' weight. As soon as he was on his feet, Jakes headed out of the front door.

'Where are you going?' Robinson asked, chasing after Jakes.

'To catch up with my suspect, where do you think?' said Jakes and slammed the car door after him.

'Can I come?' Jakes looked at him and pulled away from the curb, narrowly missing Robinson's toes.

Thank goodness the crime scene had been released, thought Becca, as she ducked under the blue and white tape. She'd have had a nightmare trying to explain to the officer on duty why she needed to get into the crypt.

Not looking where she was going, Becca lost her footing as she rushed down the damp stairs into the basement. She screamed as her ankle twisted painfully under her and she fell forwards on her hands and knees, bumping down the remaining steps.

She pulled herself into a ball at the bottom and blinked back the tears that were threatening to spill. She didn't have time for them now. Using the wall as a support, she pushed herself up and put her weight on her injured ankle.

'Shit,' she muttered as a sharp pain shot up her leg and tears pricked at her eyes again. She gritted her teeth and put all her weight on the leg. It held. It hurt, but it held.

She fumbled in her bag for the Maglite she always carried and switched it on. Nothing.

'Dammit!' She slapped the torch on her hand, something she had seen her father do when she was a child. The torch flickered for a moment and then came on. She shone it around the walls of the basement, to make sure she was alone, and then she pointed it in the direction of the sarcophagus.

The huge stone casket rested before her, its dark void almost drawing her in. She walked towards it, tracing the edges of the open lid with the beam of the torch. As she reached the casket she gingerly stretched out her hand to touch it, aware of what might happen to her again. The coolness of the stone was like a balm on her skin and she sighed with relief.

'That's because I am no longer in it.' His voice resonated around the empty basement and Becca screamed, spinning round, her torchlight picking up no other presence in the cold damp basement.

'Where are you?' Becca said, her voice not at all confident.

'Surely, you can feel me, Becca,' he whispered and she felt the warmth of his breath on her neck. She jumped and whirled round, her torchlight illuminating the empty basement behind her. Becca could hear her breath, short and staccato, matching the rhythm of her heartbeat.

'Feel me, Becca.' His voice echoed again and Becca felt the marks on her neck start to pulsate. She began to feel hot as her neck throbbed and she pulled at the neck of her T-shirt to try and cool herself, but it did no good.

'Feel me.' His voice whispered again and the basement started to spin in the torchlight. Becca's vision began to blur as the marks on her neck pulsed. Then she did feel him and her skin started to tingle.

She closed her eyes and inhaled the raw muskiness of him. The scent of him made her feel dizzy, drunk even; overpowered. Becca shivered as his warm breath rippled across her neck, her breath catching as she felt his fingertips tracing the contours of her body, through her T-shirt. Her whole body seemed to respond to his touch.

She felt his body press against hers as he pulled her close. She leant her head against his shoulder, her wounds exposed to him; begging for him.

'My Becca,' he whispered as his lips brushed her neck, touching the edges of the bite marks he'd left before. 'You look so much like her, so much like my beautiful Isabella.' His voice was like a lullaby to Becca and she felt all her resolve and all her control ebbing away from her. He kissed her neck again and Becca giggled.

She turned herself round to face him and stared into the disarmingly handsome face of her nemesis. She felt as though she'd been drugged and the events of the past few days played like a staccato tune in her head. Becca tried to push away from him, but he held her firm. She struggled against his grip, but Antony held her fast. All the while he was whispering to her, words she could not properly hear, words which seemed to make her more and more sleepy.

'I have to stop you,' she mumbled as his lips kissed her forehead, her cheeks and then her lips.

'I have to stop you, before you kill me,' Becca murmured again and then felt her body fall against him, as though she was a rag doll.

'And how do you plan on doing that, my dearest Becca,' Antony whispered and she felt his tongue caress the marks on her neck.

'I have two spells to cast on you,' she said as she nuzzled her lips to his and kissed him, long withheld passion bubbling to the surface.

'And do you think it will work?' he murmured, as he kissed her back.

'No..,' she said and let her head fall on his shoulder again. His tongue once again found the marks on her neck and she could feel her body aching for his touch.

'No, my love, it won't,' he said and Becca giggled, her willpower gone, her body his.

She could feel herself drifting. Her mind was battling with her body to gain control, but her body was winning. She flinched ever so slightly as she felt Antony's teeth sink into the wounds on her neck. She tried to push him away. The drag on her neck, gentle at first and then more insistent, sending alarm signals through her body. Signals that sparked her fight for survival.

'No!' Becca managed to scream and pushed against him, but her strength was leaving her. He was going to win. He was going to get what he wanted and she'd been weak enough to let him.

Becca started to mutter, 'By my Goddess and by my God, I call upon the power of the four elements. Of earth, of air, of fire, of water. I call upon you to aid me and to protect me.' She felt Antony pull away from her and start to laugh.

'You really believe you can stop me?' he asked, as he gripped her by the jaw. 'You don't have the strength!' He hurled her across the room and she hit the wall hard, collapsing in a heap on the floor.

She continued to murmur the lines from the spell, but she was beginning to see it as a futile gesture. Antony was overpowering her, little by little. She heard his footsteps approach her and didn't resist as he picked her up by the throat and pinned her high up against the wall.

'You honestly think you will win after all this time?' Antony spat in her face. 'There is no way I will get caught twice. You will pay for what that deceitful bitch did to me, just like your mother did. Only yours will be a slow and painful demise and I will be there to watch and enjoy it.'

Antony dragged her towards him again and with all the strength she could muster, Becca went to ram her thumbs into his eyes, but he was too quick for her sedate movements and he threw her to the floor again. Becca shook her head to try and clear her blurred vision so that she could focus on the man striding towards her, but the image became more clouded and finally went black.

'Leave her alone, Cardover!' Jakes shouted as he descended the stairs, a wooden stake in one hand and a crucifix in the other.

'What do you think you are going to do with those?' Antony asked, advancing on Jakes and snatching the stake out of his hand; closing his other hand over the crucifix and Jakes' hand. Jakes could feel an acute burning sensation and howled in pain. His hand felt as though it was on fire. Antony let go and Jakes stared down at the melted lump of metal which had burnt a hole into the palm of his hand. He looked up just in time to see the stake coming towards him. The impact caught him on the side of the head and knocked him into the stone wall. He fell to the ground, immobile.

Antony stood over Becca's inert form and stared at her. He had waited a long time for this moment and he was going to enjoy every minute of it.

He crouched down and rolled her onto her back. The likeness between the two of them was uncanny and it certainly helped. He laughed to himself as he traced a line from Becca's chin to her pubic bone with his finger nail, slicing through her T-shirt and her flesh as he did so. He watched as her blood flooded the wound and fanned across the material surrounding it.

There was still enough left, enough to keep her alive while he tortured her.

He felt the anger bubble within him as he remembered the past again and he dragged Becca across the basement by her hair.

Grabbing some rope off the floor, he bound her wrists and then lifted her off the floor and looped the rope over a hook he had driven into the wall. She hung there, her arms over her head, her head lolling forward onto her chest, her feet three feet off the floor, blood running from the wound on her torso and starting to drip onto the floor.

Antony started to slap her face. He wanted her conscious for this, but her head just kept rolling from one side to the other.

'Jakes, are you down there?' a voice echoed down into the basement and Antony snorted in annoyance.

'Jakes? Is that you?' Antony heard footsteps and a tall well dressed man came into view. He had had enough interruptions for one day and before the man knew what had hit him, Antony sliced his open hand across the man's throat and watched in amusement as shock registered on the man's face. Antony stood back and observed, as the man's hands flew up to his throat to try and stop the bleeding. A gurgle erupted from the man as he tried to speak and then he slumped to the ground, dead.

Jakes watched, unable to help, as Antony's nails sliced through Robinson's neck, and closed his eyes as the younger man dropped to the floor. He pulled himself up to a sitting position and tried to calm his mind. With Becca unconscious, he had to try the spells, he had to. He doubted they would work, but he had to try. He focused his mind and the image of the parchment floated into it. The words began to appear in his mind and Jakes started to recite them, quietly at first, but then his voice got stronger.

'You are joking aren't you?' Antony's voice sounded above him and Jakes opened his eyes to see the bigger man standing before him.

From across the room, Becca heard the sound of voices through the thick haze that surrounded her mind. Her arms ached like hell; she felt so weak and so tired. She tried to open her eyes, but the sheer effort exhausted her. All she could do was listen. As the fog of her mind cleared, she heard the words of Anna's spell and she began to repeat them. Her voice was a mere whisper, but as she got into the rhythm of the words, she felt a surge of energy course through her, and her grandmother's voice echoed in her head.

Antony laughed at the crumpled delusional heap in front of him.

'You can't cast the spell,' he said, his arrogance evident in his words and he leaned down and picked Jakes up by the throat. Jakes carried on with the chants, though stilted now, due to restriction in his air flow.

'What makes you think you can stop me?' Antony asked, his face inches from Jakes'.

'I'm not trying to stop you,' Jakes said. 'She is!'

'What?' Antony said and dropped Jakes to the floor. He whirled round to face Becca and realised, all too late, that he had been tuned into the wrong person's chanting.

'No!' he shouted and lunged for Becca, but he was too late. He was almost upon her when she raised her head and stared straight at him.

'Through my actions, though our power, we commit him to his tomb!' she shouted at him and then her head slumped forward again and she fell silent.

The vines shot out of the basement floor and wrapped themselves around Antony's legs. He lost his balance and fell forward, hitting the ground hard. He fought to keep them off him, but they were too strong. Within minutes he was covered and he lay still.

Jakes dragged himself across the floor to the inert form and prodded it. Nothing. He jumped as he heard thunder crash overhead and then berated himself for being so soft. He jumped again as he heard footsteps on the stairs and he turned round only to be blinded by torchlight.

'Detective? Are you all right? What on earth is going on down here?' Jakes winced as Dick's whiney voice grated through his aching head.

'Mr Ramply, what are you doing here?' Jakes said, shielding his eyes from the harsh light.

'For goodness sake, Ramply, you're going to blind the man.' Jakes heard Father Michael's voice and then the torchlight was redirected.

'Goodness me!' Father Michael said and Jakes followed the glare to see Robinson's body slumped on the floor.

'What...?' Jakes started.

'I came because of the gathering storm just above this church. I know the story. I came to help,' Father Michael said and directed his own torch around the basement, lighting up Antony's form on the floor and then resting on Becca, who groaned as the harsh light hit her face.

'Help me get her down. We need to finish this,' Jakes said to Father Michael and eased himself to his feet.

'Ramply, phone an ambulance and then get back down here and help us move him,' Jakes indicated the vine covered body in front of him.

'Ramply?' Jakes prompted the slight man who stood motionless on the steps. 'Ramply, hurry, we don't have much time,' Jakes shouted, causing Dick's eyes to flick away from the scene before him.

'W-w-what's happened?' he said.

'Never mind now, I'll explain later. We need an ambulance, now, or she'll die,' Jakes shouted again, shifting to allow Dick a view of Becca's bloodied and inert form.

'Oh my God, Rebecca!' he screeched and started to move towards her.

'No!' Jakes said. He gripped Dick by the shoulders and shook him until the smaller man looked up at him, his eyes wide. 'Look, I know this is a lot to take in and I promise I'll explain it all to you, but, right now, Becca doesn't have much time. Hell, we don't have much time and I need your help. Do you understand?'

Dick nodded, his gaze flicking from Becca to the mass, wrapped in vines, lying ten feet away from him.

'Go, Ramply, now. Phone for an ambulance and then get back down here as we need your help to move him.' Jakes nodded towards Antony's shrouded form.

'Who?'

'The killer.'

'But why don't you just arrest…'

'Go, Ramply, now!' Jakes said, shoving him back up the steps. 'Quickly,' he shouted and Dick's steps picked up pace and Jakes heard the beeping of his mobile phone as he dialled. Jakes shuffled over to where Father Michael was trying to untie Becca. As the priest took her weight, Jakes untied her and they lowered her to the floor.

'Becca?' Jakes said, tapping her face to try and bring her round. 'Becca, wake up.' She groaned and her eyelids fluttered. Her brow creased as though she was in pain, but she forced her eyes open and stared at them.

'What's happening?' she whispered.

'It's almost over, Becca. The first spell is done. Just one more to cast.'

'I can't,' she muttered. 'No strength…' She closed her eyes again and her head fell backwards.

'Her pulse is weak. She really needs to get to a hospital,' Father Michael said as Becca groaned again.

'We will, but she needs to finish this first,' Jakes said and studied the shape close by, which was now twisting and turning in an attempt to get free.

'Ambulance is on its way,' Dick said as he positioned himself at the bottom of the steps, keeping his distance.

'Help us lift him into the sarcophagus and then I need you to round up your men as we need to move it to consecrated ground immediately.'

'W-w-what, I don't understand,' Dick said and looked at the two men.

'Mr Ramply, everything will be all right once this casket is buried once again in hallowed ground. Please, we need your help,' Father Michael said, as he walked over and placed his hand on Dick's shoulder.

Dick looked at Father Michael and nodded, then allowed himself to be guided towards Antony's writhing form. Each of them positioned themselves along Antony's body and crouched down, Jakes wincing with the effort.

'After three,' he said. 'One, two, three, lift.' He gritted his teeth against the pain. The three men heaved Antony's heavy form over the side of the sarcophagus and let it fall to the bottom. They then put all their weight behind the lid and, inch by inch, eased it back into place.

Thunder still crashed overhead and Jakes could hear the faint sound of sirens in the distance.

'C'mon, we haven't much time,' he said and went back over to Becca. 'Father, help me bring her to the sarcophagus. Ramply, call your men and then try to hold off the ambulance men until we've finished.'

Dick left the crypt while Jakes and Father Michael carried Becca over to the casket and sat her up.

'Becca,' Jakes said, gently slapping her face again. 'Becca, it's time. Let's finish this, hey?' He held her chin in his hand and slowly she opened her eyes and looked at him.

'I can't,' she mumbled and he saw tears forming in the corners of her eyes.

'Yes, you can,' he urged. 'The hard part is over with. All you have to do is seal the tomb.' They all jumped as a crash emanated from inside the sarcophagus. 'We need to hurry, Becca, and then you can rest,' Jakes said, worried that Antony might have broken out of his bindings.

Becca nodded her head and Jakes smiled at her. He took her hand and pressed her fingers against the gap between the lid and the base. He then started chanting the Spell O' Internment. 'You who are bound within this tomb, will reside encased for none to see.'

Becca's lips moved with his words, but no sound left her body. Jakes started to panic as he heard Antony crashing around inside the sarcophagus.

Suddenly, as though jolted back to reality, Becca lifted her head up and stared at him. Her voice grew stronger as she took over the chanting. Jakes fell silent as he listened to her.

Becca shouted the spell at the top of her lungs and, as she finished, a bolt of lightning shot through the basement ceiling and through her body, sending both men flying backwards. Jakes watched in horror as Becca's frail body shuddered as the light pulsed through it and out of her fingertips, sending a thin sliver of light around the join of the lid and the base. Once the circuit was complete, the light pulsed twice and then faded.

'By my Goddess and by my God, my humble thanks for supporting me. I bid you take the intention behind my actions and see it executed for all time. As I do will, so mote it be,' Becca whispered before she slumped against the sarcophagus. No sound came from within it and no sound came from outside. The storm had died.

CHAPTER 60

Becca's inert form was rushed straight to hospital, while Jakes insisted on being treated at the scene. He had to see the sarcophagus buried. Then he could relax.

Robinson's body had been removed by the coroner and was on its way to the morgue, while a plain clothes officer was despatched to inform his wife.

'Do you want to travel with me to the church?' Father Michael asked and Jakes nodded, waving away any further treatment from the medics.

The wind howled around the cemetery as the men struggled to manoeuvre the sarcophagus along the narrow walkways. Jakes waited with Father Michael, next to a hastily dug grave, in a deserted part of the cemetery. He stared up at the angry sky, which was illuminated periodically by the isolated storm. No rain fell and the two men were sheltered from the wind by the imposing oak tree, residing at the head of the grave.

The stone casket was lowered into the ground, the mechanism of the hoist protesting at the unusual weight. Father Michael prayed. Jakes relaxed.

At the hospital, the machines tracked Becca's heart rate and blood pressure, while a drip fed her the nutrients her body so desperately needed, but she remained locked away inside herself, leaving the doctors bewildered as to why. As the final load of earth was emptied onto Antony's grave, her eyes fluttered open and she gulped in a deep lungful of air.

EPILOGUE

Becca sat on the bench, her eyes closed, her face turned towards the sun, allowing its warmth to penetrate her skin and the light to fill her body.

She tugged gently at the scarf around her neck, alleviating the sensation she still felt from time to time. Her scars were still raw, but her wounds were healing. Her memories of that time and that night would always remain fresh. She shivered as she thought of how close she had come to death.

Becca leant against the wooden slats of the bench and let the unseasonable warmth be absorbed by her clothing. She reached out her hand and felt along the bench until she touched something cold. It was still there.

She smiled to herself as her mind wandered onto thoughts of her boss. Dick Ramply was in his element right about now, the shock of what had happened having worn off. He'd been none too pleased at her taking the day off, but when she'd explained to him the reason, he'd ushered her away.

Since the "incident at the site", as Dick liked to refer to the murders and her attempted murder, interest in the apartments had been phenomenal. Ramply Homes could have sold each one ten times over. The story of Antony and Isabella had been revived and Dick, in true Ramply style, was milking it for everything he could. His "themed apartment" had sold for three times the original price and it wasn't even finished yet. Dick had decided to give all the apartments a gothic theme and it seemed to be paying off; all of them had been sold.

'At least he gave me a pay rise,' Becca muttered and laughed to herself.

'Sorry, Becca, did you say something?' a voice came from behind her and Becca turned to see Frank Jakes walking the last few feet towards her, still not in tune with his walking stick; his constant companion now.

'Oh, hi, Frank. I was just talking to myself, I'm afraid,' she said and patted the bench beside her.

'Not the side effects from those painkillers, I hope,' he said, easing himself down and letting his right leg rest straight out in front of him.

'No, just thinking about Dick counting his money.'

'Yep, this little "incident" has certainly benefitted him,' Jakes said, rubbing his right knee.

'How's the physio going, Frank?' Becca asked, remembering what he had gone through to help her.

'Oh, it'll heal, just not as quickly at my age,' he said and Becca laughed.

'And retirement?'

'Now, that's another story. That's not good.'

'Why? Because they keep calling on you?'

'No, because I keep calling on them.'

'Well, as long as they pay you a decent rate,' Becca said and laughed again, giving Frank a hug.

Jakes had faced disciplinary action after he'd allowed the sarcophagus to be moved; it was, after all, a crime scene. He had explained to the Disciplinary Committee the history of what had happened in the town and the reason why Antony had come back. Father Michael had stood as a witness to the story, which had helped Jakes' case. The Committee, however, weren't convinced, but as he was held in such high regard by his superiors, it was decided that he should "retire" and be called upon as a consultant on particularly difficult cases.

'Any news on how they are handling the murders Antony committed?'

'Not really. As expected, they are struggling with the whole vampire thing and the fact that we entombed Antony again rather than arrest him hasn't helped. It's the usual story; people don't believe what they haven't seen with their own eyes.'

'Yeah, but surely they'll have to believe it now that bodies have stopped appearing, won't they?'

'I doubt it, to be honest, Becca. More likely it will end up as an unsolved cold case, ready for some hotshot to pick it up again in ten years.'

'Blimey, you sound cynical.'

'No, just realistic.' Jakes patted her knee and they both fell silent.

'Look, thanks again for everything you did that night. I couldn't have done it without you,' Becca said, breaking the silence between them.

'Stop thanking me. There's no need. You've not stopped since you left the hospital.'

'Yeah, well, I had long enough in there, didn't I?'

'I suppose, but three months rest would appeal to a lot of people,' Frank joked and tweaked her leg.

'I don't think they'd want to go through what we did to get it though, do you?' she said and they both frowned.

'No, I suppose not. How are you, Becca? How are the scars healing?'

'Slowly,' she said and smiled at him. 'They feel worse than they look. Sometimes I think I feel them twitch, like they did when he was here. It's weird, but I guess they'll stop over time.'

'Have you decided yet what you're going to do?'

'Yeah, Dick's been fine with it, although he was a bit annoyed at first because he wanted me to manage the new site for him.'

'How long has he given you?'

'As long as I need and Christ knows how long that will be.' They both fell silent then and studied the gnarled old oak tree in front of them, each lost in their own thoughts.

'Frank? They're ready to start,' a husky voice sounded.

'I'll be there in a minute, love,' Jakes replied, turning to smile at Jan. 'Well, I suppose we should go now,' Jakes said turning back to Becca. 'Everyone's waiting and Father Michael did send me to find you.'

'I won't be long,' Becca said and watched as Jakes pushed himself up, balancing his weight awkwardly on his walking stick. Just before he turned, she reached out and took his hand. 'I'm really pleased for you, you know, for both of you. You deserve to be happy, Frank.'

'So do you, Becca,' Jakes replied and watched as a cloud passed across her face. 'Promise me you won't let this take over your life? You may never find him, you know, this Ebenezer guy.'

'I know,' she said and watched as he hobbled away to join Jan. She linked his arm and leant her head on his shoulder as they walked away.

Becca smiled and returned her gaze to the old oak tree and then to the blackened ground beneath it. Her gaze finally rested on the simple wooden cross she had made.

She stood up and walked forward. She knelt at the graveside and placed a single red rose at the base of the cross and rested her hand on the grass.

'I will find peace for you, Antony. I promise you that,' she whispered and stood up and went back to the bench.

As she picked up the silver box, Becca felt a gentle breeze caress her and she closed her eyes.

'B...E...C...C...A..,' it whispered into her ear and she shivered. With a final look at his grave, Becca turned and made her way to the other side of the churchyard, where she planned to say goodbye to her mother.

THE END

ABOUT THE AUTHOR

In February 2005, Marie Anne Cope had her first short story - Three Silver Bullets - published in *Thirteen* magazine. Her second publishing credit relates to a competition she entered in *Climb* magazine. She did not win, but her story - Sheer Hell - was published on their website in November 2007.

In addition to being a writer, Marie is also a Chartered Accountant and a yoga teacher. She lives in an old stone cottage in North Wales with her two cats.

BONDS is her debut novel and got through to the quarter finals of the Amazon Breakthrough Novel Award 2012 (under the original working title of FAMILY TIES). Marie is currently working on her second novel.

Why not follow Marie at the addresses below:

scaryramblings.blogspot.co.uk
www.facebook.com/BondsByMarieAnneCope
www.scarygirl.co.uk

3074574R00161

Printed in Great Britain
by Amazon.co.uk, Ltd.,
Marston Gate.